THE RED CHAIRS
MYSTERY

HOLLY ANGEL
INVESTIGATES

———

THE

RED CHAIRS
MYSTERY

———

L. D. CULLIFORD

Matador
9 Priory Business Park,
Wistow Road, Kibworth Beauchamp,
Leicestershire, LE8 0RX
Tel: 0116 279 2299
Email: books@troubador.co.uk
Web: www.troubador.co.uk/matador
Twitter: @matadorbooks

ISBN 978 1789016 482

British Library Cataloguing in Publication Data.
A catalogue record for this book is available from the British Library.

Printed and bound in Great Britain by 4edge Limited

Typeset in 11pt Adobe Garamond Pro by Troubador Publishing Ltd, Leicester, UK

Matador is an imprint of Troubador Publishing Ltd

Dedicated to the memory of Alex King, professional golfer
(1926 – 2006) and Sylvia King (1928 – 2014)

"When the going gets tough, the tough go golfing!"

PROLOGUE

Summoned to his elderly father's study, a small boy stands trembling before his protector. Expecting rebuke for another unwitting and unintended domestic misdemeanour, he feels only relief when the judge, looking stern, remains silent and simply holds out a letter.

The boy's name on the envelope is written in an uncharacteristically shaky hand, but the elaborately cursive script is nevertheless without doubt his mother's. The note is short; a few lines that, despite already reading quite capably, he still cannot understand. He has no difficulty, age six, making out the words, but what do they convey? He knows only that his dear mother had been thin, pale and withdrawn for several weeks, and then disappeared from home.

The youngster had been at school when the ambulance called. As he searched room by room on his return to the house, the judge's resonant voice intoned firmly, 'Your mother has been taken to the hospital'. Nothing more. 'When will she return?' he wanted to ask, but felt too exposed. As if he were somehow in the dock, but disallowed from defending himself, speech seemed completely forbidden.

Twelve interminable days have passed since she vanished. The household routine continues as before; and now the letter. Dimly, the boy begins to grasp the portent of the situation. Perhaps he will never see his mother again. Why else would the words, 'I want you to be brave', and, 'Have courage', be inscribed before him in a rush of unsteady lettering on that fateful notepaper, which still smells faintly of lavender? What the letter does not say is that, although only thirty-six, the unfortunate woman has a cancer of the stomach, and will be dead within forty-eight hours. She and her son are indeed destined never to meet again. Omitted too from the note is any indication whatsoever of esteem, affection or love.

Later, despite remaining forever averse to the aroma of lavender, the boy barely remembered his mother. He was excused attending the funeral; or succumbed rather to a conspiracy that ensured his absence; his aunt and uncles keen to avoid any risk of emotion erupting to the surface during that most solemn of occasions. His father became increasingly distant.

The boy was lonely and unhappy at first; but began to realise that, without close supervision, he could behave in whatever way he liked. By the time he went to the boarding school, two years later, he had grown crafty, clever at getting his way. By charm or threat, he wheedled people and manipulated situations for both personal advantage and the seductive amusement of mischief. He had a cruel streak but, strangely enough, people tended to like him. He excelled, when necessary, at eliciting absolution for his lapses.

On the other hand, some people would never forgive...

THE 1ST CHAPTER

Archie had been roused by the insistent loud yapping of a dog. Ella was quiet, and for this reason the old man realised that the sudden sound in his ears must have come in a dream, or a hallucination. Soon after, at the usual time, six-fifteen, because the dog in the warm kitchen hadn't stirred from her basket, he knew for sure that it had not been the Labrador barking. Shaking his head, Archie raised a hand to his deaf right ear. 'I must be going soft', he thought.

The grizzled widower lived in one of a short row of cottages, their gardens backing onto the third fairway. With consent from golf club officials, he had put in a garden gate, giving him access. Man and dog were through onto the course before seven o'clock. This was their ritual. Ella chased about here and there, sometimes finding golf balls. Archie carried an old seven iron with a worn grip. Play was not officially permitted before eight, but he only used the club for fossicking around in the undergrowth, and for hitting the occasional shot. Still able to make the ball travel a respectable distance with that club, he had had it a long time.

A lean, stooping figure, Archie set off across the mown grass walking north-west, skirting the great pond that was one of two filled-in gravel pits making the course so distinctive and tricky to play, with Ella out front scampering left and right, following the morning smells. It had rained sharply during the night, long-awaited September rain after a dry summer, but the sky was already clearing. Past the fourth green they went, the pair, rounding great bushy thickets towards the long fifth hole.

Archie took an old ball from his jacket pocket and let it fall there, beside the tee, manoeuvring it onto a convenient tuft with the head of his club, setting it up before taking a swing. As the favoured weapon reached shoulder height, bright sunshine broke through distant clouds. The sudden shaft of brilliant light upset his concentration a touch. Hurrying the shot, he mistimed it, launching the ball away, fading it to the right where there was heather. 'Bother,' he said quietly; and then, aloud to the dog, always on the alert, 'Come on Ella! Let's go and look for the blasted thing'.

Heather is unfriendly to golfers, burying balls without trace. Archie decided not to spend long searching, particularly as the ground was wet, but Ella had already lost interest and was bounding on ahead. He heard her barking, loud and insistent, before he had given up ferreting around. This time he was definitely not dreaming. Normally placid, the friendly black Labrador was excited now. 'What is it, Girl?' called Archie, lifting his rheumy eyes to look down the fairway. Then, softly to himself, 'What the dickens is that?'

Ella stood almost two hundred yards away and continued barking fitfully while he covered the ground. At first, in front of her, he could only see something large, red and rectangular, more or less blocking the fairway where it narrowed with bunkers on either side, a decent nine-iron shot forward of the green.

Coming up, he put a reassuring hand softly on the dog's velvet neck. 'Ssshh,' he whispered. 'Be quiet Girl!'

Silence enveloped them. Nothing moved. Archie looked down at the two, large, bright red leather armchairs in front of him. They had been placed carefully, touching, side by side, facing north-east back up the fairway towards the tee. Slumped carelessly in the left-hand of the pair was a tiny, thin, pale, damp figure, a girl or young woman. Her curled-up body, clad loosely in only a threadbare, dusky blue man's dressing gown, seemed terribly thin, wasted to the point of emaciation. 'Like something out of Belsen', Archie would say later. He could see no obvious blemish on her, but she was definitely dead.

The scene instantly brought the old golfer back to another sorry event, four years earlier. He had taken her favourite summer drink, a cold lime-soda, to his wife Marjorie, sitting in the back garden one fine evening; but she too was gone. There had been no warning. Apparently healthy, she had departed nevertheless in an instant. The ambulance people did their best to revive her, but age, they said, made resuscitation unlikely. The Coroner's report had confirmed it: "A massive pulmonary embolism", it said, meaning that a silent blood clot, formed in her legs, had suddenly travelled up through the heart, giving it a fatal shock and blocking both of the arteries to her lungs, choking her body of oxygen from the inside. He had stood and cried then for a few long moments before finally going back into the house to ring for help. Now too, with the dog beside him, he found himself crying again.

It seemed odd to Archie how inertia gripped and prevented him going faster to call for an ambulance the first time, although he knew later that those tearful seconds would have made no difference. And when he thought about it afterwards, it seemed odd this time too that he had just stood there over the corpse, grieving in a way – and growing angry – before he could think; and having thought, before he could act. He felt a sense of urgency, but he needed time to get to grips with the matter; to get to grips with himself.

Eventually, it was Ella who moved first, letting out a soft yelp of sympathy. 'Come on then, Girl', said Archie. 'It's no use standing around here. We'd better go and fetch someone.' He decided to cut across to the clubhouse, and muttered aloud, 'There'll be somebody there by now.' The dog appeared to agree and they moved off. After a few paces, however, Archie turned back. He had remembered the phone in his pocket. There was no signal. He could not call anyone; but something prompted him to take photographs. 'I know I'm going soft', he thought, 'But I don't want anyone suggesting I made all of this up'.

On that same Thursday morning, September 27th 2012, Holly Angel was, unusually for her, still in bed after nine o'clock. When the phone started buzzing, she was propped up on pillows, sipping a cup of jasmine tea. The call annoyed her because she had taken the day off to visit her father on his birthday and treat him to lunch at his favourite pub. A conscientious detective, however, she could not reasonably ignore a direct communication from her section chief.

'I'm sorry, Holly', the conversation began. 'I do know you have plans for today but… I don't think this will take long. I need a female officer to go and have a look at the scene. And you're the only one available right now. The possible victim is a woman or young girl.'

'Yes, Ma'a', she said, leaving out the final 'm', deliberately making herself sound like a lamb bleating for it's mother. 'And what about you, Detective Inspector Laura Garbutt? You're a female officer too.' The question formed, but was never spoken as Holly put the phone on 'speaker' and continued to listen.

'We are not treating it as particularly suspicious'; the deep-throated voice continued after explaining the matter. 'This is a prestigious club and it could be delicate. I've decided to keep everything low-key for now; but if it turns out that she was murdered, we'll obviously have to step it up. Take a quick look around. Speak to a couple of people on the ground and you can follow it up when you're back at work tomorrow… You probably won't even need to cancel your lunch… Also, before you mention it, I know you've still got the missing-person case to finish tidying up'.

Holly paused a moment after switching the phone off to glance at the icon of the Virgin and Child on her bedroom wall. It came from the shop at Westminster Abbey where she had bought it on impulse during a visit a couple of years earlier. Her then companion, Michael, had somehow talked her into taking part in the annual national pilgrimage to the shrine of Edward the Confessor along with hundreds of others. Unfortunately, she had felt no particular inspiration during the visit until the end, in the shop, gazing into that most serene of maternal faces. Even the briefest moment of contemplation before its timeless image still brought her a satisfyingly deep inner sense of serenity.

Feeling calmer, she decided to call the pub and cancel her booking, and then telephone her father. A former soldier turned school-teacher, he understood at once. 'I know you don't think much of Laura *Garbage*', he said cheekily, 'She is your superior officer, though, and we can always go for lunch another time.' 'But I don't know anything about golf!' his daughter replied, laughter in her voice. 'I can teach you', he said. 'You know it's never too late.'

There were three good things about Tony Angel: his name (Holly loved being an Angel); the fact that after the divorce, several years earlier, he had gone to live and work in America, leaving her in peace; and the settlement, big enough for a deposit that allowed her to buy her own property. Although the Sussex Police Headquarters are in Lewes, Holly's unit was based in Sussex House, an extensive, modern, somewhat airless and decidedly soulless, purpose-built facility in Hollingbury, not far from the main Brighton by-pass. Her work was usually focused on the stretch along the coast from Brighton and Hove to Littlehampton, so she had chosen a small house in Shoreham Beach, very close to the sea, where she could take her daily run up and down the shoreline in all weathers, keeping fit.

The journey to SRGC – the Sussex Royale Golf Club – took about fifty minutes, leading her through pleasant scenery, with broad fields and the South Downs tracking down her left side as she went. Turning southwards, shortly before reaching Petworth, Holly found herself on a tranquil, winding country road amid leafy woodland, with fields of sheep and horses interspersed on either side.

It was a little after ten-thirty when she arrived at her destination, the black Nissan Micra, covered in measles spots of Saharan rain-dust, looking slightly out of place beside a deep green, open-topped Porsche on one side and pristine lilac Jaguar on the other as she parked up. Both cars, she noticed, had personalised number plates: 'SUS 1E' on the Jag and 'RIP 1T' on the Porsche. She also noted, near the rear entrance to the clubhouse, a green delivery van bearing the elegant gold script of a respected local wine merchant. Filing information like this in her memory-banks helped considerably with her work. You never knew what might be important.

Having telephoned ahead from the hands-free device in her car, the club secretary was waiting for Holly in the vestibule, once the hallway of a magnificent Sussex farmhouse that now formed the centrepiece of a well-appointed clubhouse. Peter Harding was also ex-army, known to members as 'the Colonel'; and it was his pride that the club ran smoothly for all concerned. His methods were based on what he called 'friendly efficiency', but which others saw as a combination of ruthless attention to detail and not suffering fools gladly. The present situation was, of course, entirely unwelcome, but he was not one to create a fuss and perfectly capable of making day to day decisions independently, confident of the support of the Club Captain and members of the Committee. In post for three years, he was generally regarded as sound.

'I've closed the course', he said after the introductions, 'And called in the head green-keeper, John Tranter. He'll have brought all his people in too. We don't want anyone disturbing anything, do we? And I've also sent a round-robin email to members, telling them about some "unusual course conditions" making play impossible – without giving the game away, naturally. But the phones have been buzzing, and members want to know what's going on. Despite the downpour, there wasn't enough rain in the night to account for preventing play. Most of the course is on gravel and greensand, and the drainage is generally good. I've told Valerie, my assistant, to leave an answer-phone message that we'll be reviewing the situation at 2.00 pm.'

The Colonel paused to look Holly in the eye. She returned his gaze but said nothing. 'It's tricky', he continued. 'I realise you won't want the area disturbed at all, but I'm still hoping you'll let me open at least the back nine holes this afternoon.'

'We'd better go and have a look at the scene, then.'

Holly, recognizing her host as a man of action, was already turning for the door.

Impressed, he guided her outside towards the professional's shop where three golf buggies stood in a line. With Holly aboard the nearest, he took control, only too aware of his attractive passenger, despite her prim navy outfit and somewhat severe haircut. Passing behind the first tee and second green, he headed the buggy down over the rough grass beside the third fairway. 'It's been quite a summer, hasn't it?' he said to break the silence, trying to make conversation. 'Has it?' Holly replied. 'Yes. You know... Bradley Wiggins' superb win in the Tour de France, great success for Team GB at the Olympics, and then Murray' beating Djokovic in the U.S. Open the other day.' 'I suppose so.' Holly's response was vague. She was clearly preoccupied, looking intently around, familiarising herself with the undulating heathland scenery.

Once past the water on the right, they turned and followed Archie and Ella's route uphill beyond the fourth green, cutting back then down the fifth after rounding an extensive patch of gorse shrubbery. They soon reached a white van parked off the fairway, emblazoned with the words 'Technical Medical Unit' and the emblem of Sussex Police. Beside it, a uniformed police officer stood on guard, carrying a clip-board to record the names and details of all who entered the cordoned off area. Holly made the Colonel stop the golf-cart, gave their names, and noted that a Police Surgeon had already attended and declared life extinct. They were still a few yards short of the taped-off scene. Holly insisted on going ahead on her own. 'I've been close enough to those chairs already', replied the former soldier. 'I've seen things in my time, but this is still rather grim... I don't need to go ringside again, thanks'.

A photographer in white coveralls was taking shots from different angles as Holly approached the crime site. Another, similarly attired forensic officer from the Chichester branch stood by ready to erect a tent over the corpse and out-of-place furniture before the pair continued their meticulous work.

Holly suited up and went forward, stepping onto the duck-boards around the scene. She bent over, looking carefully at the red armchairs and their contents. She could see the chairs were worn and scuffed in places, and the deceased woman was probably not as young as Archie Hunter had reported to the first officer on the scene. She looked closely at the dressing gown, noticing how the corpse's right arm alone was correctly inserted into the sleeve, and how the rest of the garment had been pulled loosely around, over the left shoulder, to cover the torso and tops of the legs. Its edges were frayed, and the clenched fingers of the left hand held tightly to the chest were clearly visible. Had the wind disturbed the cloth, she wondered, or had whoever placed it there done so hurriedly, without due care for the poor woman's modesty?

Holly took photos for storage on her phone, useful for showing to people who might possibly identify the sorry, almost skeletal corpse; and she asked the photographer to follow the body to the hospital in Chichester, where it would be examined later, to get better shots of the face and any other identifying features.

Extracting a notebook and pen from the dark brown leather bag carried over her shoulder, she began writing down the key questions:

Who is this woman?

When did she die? Where and how did she die?

Had she been starved or tortured?

Was she murdered?

How did she get here?

Who moved her?

The chairs... How were they brought and placed here?

Why?

Circling the last question with a firm stroke of the biro, Holly looked up again to survey the wider scene. The golf course boundary to the south was marked by low mesh rabbit fencing that appeared intact. There were medium-size birch trees and tall conifers forming a loose barrier inside the fence, beneath them an irregular landscape of bare earth, gorse bushes and general scrubland. Beyond, there was further woodland and a sunlit clearing where movement suddenly caught Holly's eye. Two or three small deer and a larger buck with antlers stood alert, then quickly disappeared into the shadows beneath the trees.

'I must get out into nature more often', she thought, taking a deep breath as a green woodpecker flew east to west in long low swooping arcs across her gaze. The bird's movement carried her eyes further to the right, along the line of the fence. A large bracken-covered bank obscured her view of the green and whatever lay beyond. Advancing past the near bunker into the long grass of the rough, she beckoned to Peter Harding and climbed aboard the buggy as it approached.

'Let's take a look', she said, pointing. 'Could there be a way in and out of the course over there?' 'There used to be, I believe', the Colonel replied. 'Before my time... When everything was new and only the first nine holes were open, some members used to drive out here along Stave Lane and start play at the sixth. That way, you can get more people onto the course first thing. They would get held up again, of course, when they got back to the clubhouse and had to start again at the first; but that's golfers for you, always a little impatient. Some members still use it when we play shotgun-start competitions.'

'What does that mean?' Holly was intrigued. 'I hope you've got a licence', she said, only half-joking. 'And that no-one gets hurt.'

'Oh, no... Not at all.' The secretary was quick to reassure her. 'A shotgun start is when teams of four golfers are stationed on each of the eighteen holes and start play simultaneously. It doesn't happen at this club very often. It's not popular… Takes a long time to get everybody round and then there's an almighty crush in the changing-room and the showers when play finishes… The signal used to be a shot from a shotgun into the air, but these days we just use a siren… And we don't need a licence for that.'

'So there is a gate and car park somewhere near here', Holly answered. 'Yes', said the Colonel. 'Over there.'

They manoeuvred around the bunker, keeping to the long grass. When the buggy drew level with the bracken-covered mound, Holly could see a gap in the trees framing a broad footpath. 'Stop here', she said and alighted. 'Wait for me.'

There was little wind. The silence was broken only by the repetitive high-pitched call of a chiffchaff high in one of the birches. A cloud drifted in front of the sun, darkening the scene as Holly advanced carefully, eyes fixed on the terrain, looking for clues of vehicular access. The path widened beneath the trees, and then opened out into a small clearing, beyond which a narrow lane could be seen. The exit was marked by a sturdy, white-painted gate stained with algae, but this was open, pulled right back against the boundary fence. She could just make out the initials 'GGC' on the top bar, over-painted in white. Near the gate was a neatly-stacked pile of birch logs, and nearby a smaller pile of green-keeper's waste, tining plugs and grass cuttings, partially rotted down. There were a few small puddles in the clearing, and there were many tyre tracks visible, especially near the lane; but Holly was disappointed. If the vehicle carrying the two chairs and the dead woman had left distinctive marks here, it seemed unlikely that they would stand out from all the other indentations. Across Stave Lane a low bank led to a stone wall edging a large field in which sheep were grazing. There was no sign of traffic.

Retracing her steps slowly, Holly made a detour behind the green, scouring the area, including the nearby sixth tee, for clues.

Returning to the duck-boards from the northern side, she spent a few minutes talking to the senior of the two forensics men, asking him to tape off the gate and car-parking area, add to their search remit and keep her informed of any findings.

Making her way across to the golf-cart again, she said to the Colonel, 'The guys say the turf beneath those two chairs is completely dry. That means our corpse arrived before the rain, which is a pity.' 'You mean there won't be any tracks, because the ground was hard and dry before it rained?' he asked. 'Yes. And if there were, they could have been washed out anyway.' 'Let's go!' Holly added. 'I need to get back to the clubhouse, or somewhere there's a phone signal.' 'Yes Ma'am!' Peter Harding replied. He said the word deferentially, rhyming with 'Sam'.

'Did you recognize the woman, by any chance?' Holly asked the Colonel a little later as they trundled back up the fairway.

'No… She wasn't a member', he replied.

'Are there many women in the club?'

'Quite a few… We've about a hundred and fifty on the books, but regular players? I should say only about a third of those. The average age, for both men and lady members, is quite high. We reserve the course for ladies games and competitions on Tuesday mornings and some Thursdays, but not thankfully today.'

Approaching the clubhouse, Holly said she was going to make some calls in her car. The Colonel offered her his office, but she said she preferred the privacy and familiarity of her own regular workplace. 'It may look like a car to you', she explained, looking him firmly in the eye, defying him to make fun of her, 'But it's where I spend most of my time.'

He had a call to make himself, he was thinking, but it was too early in the day. The club's founder and Life President, Jamie Royle, who normally kept himself apart from the club's day-to-day affairs, needed to know what was happening, but it would have to wait a couple of hours.

The sun was shining again as, crossing the car park deep in thought, Holly was spotted by one of the less ancient club members. Mark Berger got out of his silver-grey Hyundai Coupe, hoisted a set of care-worn golf clubs over a lean shoulder and strolled over to the Nissan, just as the detective was winding her window down to let in the breeze. She looked up as his shadow fell across her face. 'Hi! I'm Mark', he said. 'I haven't seen you here before. Are you new?'

Holly was taken off-guard, finding it hard to feel particularly affronted by such a friendly, tall, handsome man with curly ginger hair and very steady blue eyes. 'No', she said. 'I'm only visiting.'

'That's a pity', he replied, thinking how well short, dark hair framed her perfectly-formed face. 'What's your name?'

'Detective Sergeant Holly Angel... Sussex Police', she said.

'Cripes!' Mark replied, laughing. 'I wasn't expecting that.'

They looked at each other for a few more seconds. 'Please go away', said Holly finally. 'I'm busy'.

'Alright, Detective Sergeant!' said Mark, backing away with a little bow of mock-humility, still smiling. 'But I may want to talk to you later', Holly called out as he retreated. She knew that, together with her colleagues in uniform, she would be talking to as many club members as possible over the ensuing days, but wondered still why she had said anything. The impulse had surprised her, but she quickly put it out of her mind.

Mark, an estate agent running his own successful, small company, having under-performed in the monthly medal competition the previous weekend, was taking time off work to try and restore his usually reliable golf game. A few minutes after his brief encounter with Holly, he was standing on the practice mat adjusting his grip on the five-iron in his hands at the start of a lesson from his friend, the club's assistant professional, Kyle Strong.

'Show me what you're doing.' Born in Trinidad, at school in Sussex since the age of twelve, Kyle retained a marked Caribbean accent. The men were in the three-sided hut on the practice ground east of the clubhouse with a plastic bucket full of golf balls between them. Kyle placed one of the neatly dimpled orbs down carefully as Mark took his stance, swung the club rhythmically and propelled the ball in a fine arc over towards the left side of the practice range. The next one went further left still, as did the third; and the next went high, away to the right. Mark was irritated.

'You see!' He exclaimed. 'I'm inconsistent. I'm mostly drawing it to the left, but sometimes it's a full-blown hook, and then I'll cut one way out to the right. It's hopeless!'

'It's not hopeless, Mark!' Kyle sounded patient and confident. 'It's just your grip has got a little strong. Your hands are working against each other. When you put the ball back in your stance, it goes one way. When you have it in front a touch, you overcompensate: the clubface turns open as you swing through and forward, and the ball goes off in the other direction. That's all it is; and we shall soon have it fixed. Open your hands and re-grip them again, like this...

Kyle demonstrated, placing his left hand down carefully first, then covering it in an overlapping fashion with his right. Then he gently corrected Mark as he tried to copy him.

'Soft hands, remember!' said Kyle. 'Always keep your hands soft.'

Twenty minutes later, after learning to relax his grip and place the ball more centrally in his stance, Mark was hitting the ball straighter, not only with the five-iron but with all his clubs, even the driver. As a result, he was happy.

'You're a genius', he said to Kyle. 'Do you want to play a few holes now? I can't wait to get on the course and try this out.'

'Haven't you heard, Man', said his friend. 'The course is closed. They found a dead woman out there this morning. Look!' He took out his phone and showed Mark Archie's photo.

'Wow!' said his friend. 'That's weird! How did you get that picture?'

'I was alone in the Pro's shop this morning when old man Hunter came in real upset. He showed it to me', explained Kyle. 'He had found the body and taken this photo. While he was phoning the police from the shop land-line, I sent myself a copy from his mobile. I don't think he knows.'

'Well, at least that explains the visiting policewoman', said Mark. 'Did you meet her?' His eyebrows were raised, Kyle noticed, and his eyes were widening. 'Holly, her name is... And very cute she is, too.'

———————

Despite the slight breeze, it was too hot in the car. Holly soon got out and stood near the vehicle as she phoned the duty pathologist. 'Dr Narayan, I want you to come out to inspect the woman's remains *in situ* as soon as possible', she said in a firm tone. 'That's not going to happen. I'm sorry', came the abrupt reply. 'I'm doing a post-mortem for a Coroner's hearing at two o'clock, so there's no time. Get the body transferred to the exam room at the mortuary and I'll take a look later.'

Holly was unhappy. The pathologist, she had always been taught, simply must attend the scene and view the body in situ before organising its removal. However, Dr Peter Narayan was a serious man, and had always previously been reliably thorough, so Holly had to be satisfied that his excuse was genuine. Any complaint she made would likely fall on deaf ears anyway, so she decided to let it go this time, and was soon on the phone to D. I. Garbutt with a preliminary report, asking for the required personnel to help with interviews. Then, glad she had cancelled the lunch with her father, she went back into the clubhouse, passing through the hallway and up the stairs to the Secretary's office along the corridor. Inside, Holly found Colonel Harding at his desk, telephone in hand, also a short, buxom, neatly-dressed woman, who came straight up to her, hand outstretched in greeting.

'I'm Valerie Parton, Detective Sergeant', the woman said primly. 'Please let me know how I can help. This is just such a terrible thing.'

Holly made an immediate mental note to herself to the effect that, however much the Secretary's secretary may resemble the singer (with a mane of blonde hair, over-sized bra and such), never to call this woman 'Dolly'. That would be a cheap and unnecessary mistake. At the same moment, out of the corner of her eye, she noticed the Colonel put the phone down quickly, but said nothing. Forcing herself to say, 'Thank you, Mrs Parton', she asked for a list of the club's staff and members, which, it turned out, had already been carefully prepared for her. 'Is there somewhere private, where I can interview people?' she asked.

'The Committee Room would be best', said the Colonel, rising from his chair. 'I'll take you, shall I?'

———

Back along the corridor, past the head of the staircase on the left, was a large room with an oversized, dark walnut boardroom table occupying the centre. Along the north wall was a magnificent trophy cabinet, full of silverware. 'We've had to put all this in here after a break-in downstairs a couple of years ago', the Colonel explained. 'The insurance company now insists the trophies are stored away from public view in a room that's normally locked.'

'Were the culprits ever caught?' Holly asked, wondering if the earlier crime might in some way be connected to the present one. 'No, they were not', was the reply.

'And is that when you installed CCTV?' Holly continued. 'I noticed the cameras in the car park and around the clubhouse on my way in... We'll need the tapes from last night, of course', she added. 'I don't suppose they cover the road approaching the club?'

'No. They don't, I'm afraid', said Peter Harding. 'I did take a quick look at the tapes before you came, but couldn't see anything unusual or suspicious after about 8.00 pm yesterday until this morning when the first staff members arrived.'

Holly turned her attention back to the Committee Room. The windows to the west looked out on the practice putting-green and further, across the first tee and the second green, towards the third fairway, partially obscured by an enormous, old but still vibrant oak tree.

Sitting down in the chair at the head of the table, Holly found herself facing a large photographic double-portrait on the wall in front of her. She seemed to recognise one of the two smiling men, standing side-by-side in the sunshine, arms around each others shoulders. They were typically dressed in bright colours with the golf course as a backdrop. The older of the two men had a colourful open umbrella logo on his primrose yellow sports shirt. 'That's the famous Arnold Palmer', Peter Harding was pointing at him and saying, 'Probably the greatest living golfer... And that's our President with him: Jamie Royle.'

'Tell me about him', said Holly, 'and about the photo.'

'It was taken in the autumn of 1983, I think. Jamie had bought the club a couple of years earlier, when the original owners ran into financial difficulties, together with a chunk of the neighbouring farmland. That's when he had the course enlarged and redesigned by Palmer's company. The gravel beds were made watertight and filled, for example, and brought into play more. Palmer's people did all the design work and supervised the construction. Mr Palmer himself only agreed the plans and signed off the contract. He was sent reports and photographs to keep an eye on progress, but had never actually visited the site.

In 1983, though, he came over to London for the annual World Golf Match Play event at Wentworth. He was knocked out of the competition by Seve Ballesteros in a quarter-final match and was going to fly home to the States the following morning, but somehow Jamie contacted him and persuaded him to stop off here. I believe he flew his own jet from Heathrow into Dunsfold aerodrome and Jamie met him there. They played nine holes, together with the pro and the club champion, stopped for photographs, had a snack lunch, completed the round and Arnie was off again. The local press were full of it. I've copies somewhere of the some of the articles. Jamie wanted the publicity for the newly branded club, of course. And for himself, I suppose.'

'So that's when it became Sussex Royale?' enquired Holly.

'Yes', the Colonel replied. 'It's not such a big step from Royle to Royale, and Jamie is a real James Bond fan. I think Ian Fleming's early book, 'Casino Royale', influenced him. There's our sister club, too: the Hampshire Royale, not far from Liss. Jamie rebuilt the clubhouse over there when he bought it, incorporating a stylish 'Goldfinger' bar, a 'Thunderball' restaurant and a 'Moonraker' patio.'

'Don't tell me they've got an 'Octopussy' swimming pool', interjected Holly. 'That would not be a good thing.'

'Ha!' The Colonel's laugh was surprisingly high-pitched. 'I'm glad we've been spared all that glitz, to be honest. This place used to be plain Graffham Golf Club, once upon a time, and it's still mainly about the golf. When Jamie took over, it was just a rough track, used mainly by a few of the local farm-workers and people like that.'

'That explains the GGC I saw painted over on the gate by the fifth green earlier', Holly interrupted. 'I'd better speak to Mr Royle as soon as possible. Where does he live?'

'His wife lives here in Sussex; but he's usually in London, or travelling. At the moment he's in America. I was trying to get hold of him earlier', said the Colonel. 'He's in Chicago this weekend. Then he's going to Oregon, to play at the famous Bandon Dunes resort for a few days before flying across the Pacific to Hong Kong and Bangkok. He's not due back for a while.'

Holly needed explaining that this was going to be a big weekend in the world of golf. The Ryder Cup match, pitting a twelve man European team against twelve Americans, would be played at the Medinah Country Club a few miles north-west of Chicago. Jamie Royle was there as the guest of a business associate, one of the Medinah Club's vice-presidents, Charlie 'Chuck' Flanagan.

'It's the final practice day today, and then the Opening Ceremony', the Colonel was saying. 'The three-day match starts tomorrow. Jamie won't like his trip interrupted by what's happening here.'

'I don't suppose he will', replied Holly without a trace of sympathy. 'But we can't help that, can we? You'd better give me his number.'

THE 2ND CHAPTER

Holly began her series of interviews with John Tranter. The head green-keeper, a giant of a man in his forties, had spade-like hands in constant movement while the rest of him sat square, upright and motionless. Splayed out on the table one second, these great paddles clenched themselves into fists the next, then clasped together, thumbs twiddling a moment later. There was grime in the creases and under the nails, Holly noticed as she tried not to fall under their swirling, mesmeric spell, forcing herself to look into the man's open, almost blank face as he pondered her questions. His answers were monosyllabic.

Tranter had brought with him a plan of the golf course, manipulating his colossal fingers with surprising dexterity to unfold and spread it out on the table, and then indicate the cluster of sheds and machinery buildings where he and his staff were based, over on the newer, second half of the course, well away to the east of the fifth fairway and green. He had noticed nothing untoward in the previous days, he said, or that morning, and had no explanation for the arrival of the incongruous red chairs and their gruesome contents. Some birch trees had been felled, he said, and the logs stacked by the Stave Lane gate during the previous autumn and winter seasons, and the grass cuttings there had been added to periodically, most recently about two weeks earlier.

This was as much as he could recollect. Holly stared silently at him for a full minute while he cast his eyes down, as if trying to pin his restless hands to the table by the force of his gaze; but they went on drumming softly and persistently anyway. She had never known anyone so obviously anxious during a police interview, but did not think he had anything in particular to hide. He was just that kind of person, someone who preferred a simple outdoors life and his own company. 'You're not in any trouble, you know', she said eventually. 'Thank you, Miss', he replied, shambling to his feet, upsetting the chair and getting his legs in a tangle as he turned and tried, failing, to prevent it from clattering down. 'I'm sorry', he mumbled, picking the chair up again. 'Off you go', Holly waved him out of the room, 'And send in someone from your team. I want to interview them all, one by one.'

An hour later, Holly was none the wiser, having spoken to the three other men and one young woman on the green-keeping team. She went in search of the Secretary, a list of the bar and kitchen staff in her hand. He took the opportunity of asking again whether she would permit him to open holes ten to eighteen. Checking the course plan, she agreed, if reluctantly, then returned to the Committee Room to continue her interviews.

First up was one of the two chefs, Liam, a cheery fellow who had nothing of interest to tell her, but who returned soon after his interview with a turkey sandwich on a plate, garnished with some crisps and a small dressed salad, accompanied by a knife and fork, neatly rolled in a napkin. There was also a cup of coffee in a porcelain cup and saucer. The napkin and all the items of cutlery and crockery were distinguished by the SRGC crest: a turquoise golf club at an angle, wearing a lop-sided golden crown. Holly was delighted. 'I thought you were looking a little peaky', said Liam. 'If you don't like turkey, I can do beef or smoked salmon or prawns. Just you say!' 'This is perfect', she replied with a grin.

It took another hour to interview the remaining club staff and the few members who remained in the building, but Holly learned nothing more to help her work out what had happened during the night. She said as much to Peter Harding before collecting the previous 24-hour CCTV tapes and asking for a key to one of the club's golf buggies. It was time to revisit the scene.

Dark clouds had gathered, but it was not yet raining as Holly returned to the car park with the tapes, putting them securely in the boot of the Micra. The Porsche and Jaguar were no longer there, only Mark's Hyundai, a smart black Range Rover, a white VW Passat, and a few less swanky vehicles that she presumed belonged to house staff. The Colonel's smart metallic-blue Audi A4 estate was in the reserved space marked 'Secretary', with Mrs Parton's tiny red Toyota Aygo in the spot next to it.

Holly took one of the buggies and headed off again towards the mysterious red chairs where, this time, she found a black undertaker's van close by the duck boards. Two men in dark suits were manoeuvring an awkward package into the back. The dead woman's torso could not fully be straightened, hence the use of a body bag rather than a temporary coffin. The men were soon securing this onto a trolley in the back of the van using foam cushioning, the idea being to prevent as far as possible any risk of further damage while the body was in transit. Holly worried that they would not get her to Chichester in time for Dr Narayan to carry out his inspection. She had little time to be concerned, however, before one of the forensic men called her over. They had uncovered something: writing on the leather seat underneath the body. The marks had been made by a felt-tip pen, and she could make out just the one word, written in inch-high capitals: MURDERERS.

Holly shuddered involuntarily, took out her phone to photograph the accusation. 'Who wrote it?' she thought, 'And who was the message for?'

The men, starting to pack up their kit, told her that a police removals van was on its way to collect the chairs for storage and for further inspection as evidence. They had also retrieved a curiosity, part of the wrapper of a chocolate bar inserted down the right side of the left hand chair. 'It could yield fingerprints', the senior man said, 'As might the chairs themselves'. 'What kind of wrapper is it?' Holly asked. 'Yellow writing on a blue background, with the letters 'R' and 'L' visible in lower case script... I'd say it was probably the one called a *'Twirl'*.

'Okay', said Holly. 'Thanks.' She refused permission for the removals van to use the Stave Lane entrance, still hoping for clues from that quarter. 'Too bad', she thought. 'It will just have to bump its way across from the clubhouse.' Then she decided to continue her tour of the golf course. Having studied John Tranter's large-scale map, and having a retentive memory, she was confident of finding her way, making use only of the little map on the back of one of the course scorecards that she found pinned to the buggy's steering wheel.

The sixth hole running north, uphill, to a plateau green, was a mid-length par 4; and from the elevation, Holly had a beautiful view back southward over the course towards the clubhouse across the big pond to the south-east. The elegant rolling chalk uplands of the South Downs formed the perfect backdrop in the distance. As she watched, a shaft of sunlight broke through the clouds. A glorious rainbow appeared briefly. One end of it seemed to emerge magically from the earth about two hundred yards in front of her, rising apparently out of the dead centre of the seventh green, an exquisite sward like a smooth and tranquil emerald island set in an expansive ocean of heather, still a vista of beautiful pink, purple and white, despite patchily in places turning autumnal brown. A large birch tree stood shining to one side, silver bark shining, and softly yellowing leaves shimmering in the breeze. Opposite, a curling sentinel bunker guarded the right part of the pristine putting surface. The gravel pit behind threatened a watery end to wayward shots hit either beyond or to the left. Holly couldn't help wondering why golfers seemed bent on always making things so difficult for themselves.

The sun went in and droplets began falling on the Perspex windscreen of the buggy. Anxious to complete her tour before the rain grew heavy, she set off downhill, her foot a touch firm on the accelerator, until uneven ground threw the machine sharply up and sideways, the two right-hand wheels momentarily losing contact with the earth. Mastering the unsteady vehicle again, she trundled on more slowly, pulling up next beside the eighth tee on the edge of the water, pausing deliberately to take in the view and the atmosphere. As the rain eased, it all became strikingly quiet and peaceful.

The sun reappeared and Holly noticed a couple of moorhens, readily identifiable with red and yellow beaks, and white stripes against the bluish-black of their flanks, paddling backwards and forwards. A grey heron stood motionless nearby, poised to strike. A pair of damselflies darted here and there among the fronds of water plants near the edge. Holly was reminded of a magazine article she had seen, describing a new phenomenon being flagged up in America: 'Nature Deficit Disorder'. Children who were paying little attention to anything other than what could be displayed on their smart-screen devices, were said to be missing out, putting themselves at risk of failing to develop important social skills, spending so much time and energy on establishing and maintaining 'virtual' relationships on-line, but very little in face to face communication, even with their family members. The remedy, according to several authorities, was for families, especially including the grandparents, to get out into nature together more often.

Alone there for a moment, taking it all in, Holly recognised that she had been paying little attention in recent years either to nature or to personal relationships, except of course with her dad.

The sun vanished again. A blustery chill wind caught her, so she decided to cut short the expedition and head back to the clubhouse. From the eighth tee, she had to loop back around a wide tongue of the pond that the golfers were meant to hit across. Regaining the fairway, looking ahead, she saw a lone golfer moving in her direction. Mark Berger had already played the back nine holes with Kyle, who had then left to resume his duties in the professional's shop. With nothing else better to do, Mark had decided to go round the loop once more, and was now playing the sixteenth for the second time, a hole which shared a large double-green with the eighth. Holly watched him play a high shot, the ball landing three or four paces from the flagstick, stopping dead where it pitched. She caught up with him after he putted out and was making his way to the seventeenth tee box, right beside that of the ninth, the two holes facing off at right angles to each other.

'Hello again', he said, smiling, as she drew up nearby in her buggy. 'How's the investigation going?'

'It's early days!' She replied to avoid revealing her lack of progress.

There was a silence. Unsure what to say or do next, but spotting an opportunity, Holly decided to ask about golf. 'What's so wonderful about it?'

'I wouldn't know where to begin', Mark answered, giving a little frown. 'It's physical… You know, it is a healthy form of exercise… Walking. You are out in the open… There's beautiful scenery! It takes skill to play well… And it's character-building. You need patience, not letting your emotions get the better of you… Also it's sociable, being part of a club, meeting new people, playing with friends. And, you can travel anywhere in the world and get a game, because – due to the handicap system – anyone can play with anyone on more or less equal terms… And no two courses, no two holes even, are alike. There's constant variation. If nothing else, the weather makes sure of that.'

Some of these ideas were new to Holly. Hitting a small, hard, white ball that wasn't moving couldn't be that difficult, she thought, and not very exciting either. 'Was it Winston Churchill or Mark Twain who called golf, "A long walk spoiled"?' she said, 'Somebody like that'.

'I don't think it was Churchill. He used to play golf when he was younger. My father told me he was once a member at Walton Heath, one of the famous Surrey clubs', said Mark. 'Anyway, golf is golf and going for a walk is something else. A person can enjoy both, you know.'

'Alright, then', Holly enquired, 'What are the negatives?'

'Let's see', said Mark. 'It's expensive, and a little bit exclusive; except in Scotland where there are more public courses and lots of folk learn to play when they are still at school… It takes time to play: at least three hours, often more than four… And it is a difficult set of skills to acquire. You need lessons and lots of practice… Also, to be honest, it can be very frustrating. On the other hand, when you're hitting the ball sweetly and your short game is on song, there's hardly a better feeling in the world. You only have to hit one great shot in a round, or sink a long, curling, downhill putt, say, and you're always going to be eager to come back for more the next day.'

'It sounds like a sorry form of addiction to me', Holly broke in, half-serious.

'Some addictions are better than others, though. Don't you agree? Golf is not so bad… Let me show you.' Mark took a nine iron from his bag and dropped a ball on the turf. 'Come and stand over here, please.'

Wary, unsure what to expect, Holly realized she had been asking for trouble, but could not immediately think of a way to back down.

'Now, take hold of this club, swing it and hit the ball.'

Mark watched closely as Holly gripped tightly, right hand an inch below the left, swung her arms up and outwards, bending both elbows, then made a bit of a lunge downward towards the ball, missing it, hitting the grass a couple of inches behind it. The ball itself did not move even a fraction, despite getting heavily spattered with mud.

Holly expected him to laugh, but when she looked up, Mark's face simply showed kindly concentration. 'That's what we all do as beginners', he said. 'We swing our arms a bit wildly and lose control of the club. Actually, you did well to bring it down so close to the ball… But now, let me ask you, did you ever play baseball or rounders?'

When Holly admitted to playing rounders at school, Mark asked her to show him with the club in her hands how she would hit a rounders ball, whereupon she re-gripped it with her hands closer together, overlapping slightly, lifted it to waist height, took it back by rotating her shoulders clockwise, rather than by moving her arms, and then reversed the process to strike an imaginary ball back at waist height in front of her again.

'That was great', said Mark. 'Did you notice what you did with your hands? Approaching the point of impact, your left hand was on top, and at impact you suddenly switched, bringing your right hand over. That's where extra power comes from. Try again!'

Holly repeated her earlier effort, hearing a satisfying swish of wind as she did so.

'That's perfect', said Mark. 'You kept your head completely still... Well done! That whole performance is exactly the same for a golf swing, except you bend forward from the waist so that the clubhead points down at the ground where the ball is. I'll show you. Stand up straight.'

Mark walked behind Holly. Turning her head, she was looking slightly alarmed, prompting him to reassure her. 'Don't worry', he said. 'I'm just going to show you something.' Moving close, he put his arms around her and covered her hands, still holding the golf club, enfolding them in his own. 'Bend forwards a little', he said. 'Now turn with me.'

It felt odd, but Holly relaxed as Mark rotated the pair of them gently to the right, paused, and then rapidly brought the club-head back and through its original starting point. 'Like that, see!' he said.

Holly was suddenly breathless, whether from the effort or from Mark's physical proximity, she wasn't sure. Mark immediately released her and stood back. 'Try it without a ball to start with,' he said.

Holly, a junior champion tennis player in her day, understood immediately about rotating her body. She repeated the baseball swing slowly first, to imprint it in her mind; then she leaned forward, allowing the clubhead to touch the turf, and replicated the movement as nearly as she could to the way Mark had done it. At the third attempt, the club, on the return, brushed neatly through the grass at the exact point between her feet where she was concentrating her gaze.

'That's wonderful!' said Mark. 'Keeping your head still ensures that you turn, rather than sway sideways. Did you also notice that, as your shoulders and hands return to the starting point, the point of impact, your hips are turning too? They have only half-rotated on the backswing, as you coil yourself up like a spring, but now they are free to be unleashed, and at the end of the swing your hips have turned anti-clockwise so as to be facing the target.'

Less afraid of looking ridiculous, Holly wanted to try hitting an actual golf ball again, confident that she would not make such a mess of it this time. She no longer played tennis, or any other sport except going for a jog along the beach, but she had been attending a mixed yoga and Pilates class for three years, as a result of which her balance, core stability, body-awareness and muscle control were well developed. The next time then, following Mark's instructions, she made good club-head contact with the ball, which consequently flew up in a perfect arc, landing almost a hundred yards away, more or less in the direction she was aiming.

'Wow!' said Holly. 'That's fantastic! Let me try it again.'

Mark couldn't help smiling. He wanted to give her a big hug, but instead took three more balls from his bag and threw them down. Two of them successfully followed the first, but the third went sharply to the right, across the ninth fairway, into the pond. 'Oh golly!' said Holly.

'That's okay', Mark assured her. 'It's what we call a "shank". You swung the club a little bit too quickly and it came back out of alignment. Shanking happens when the round shaft at the bottom end of the club hits the ball, rather than the club-face... We all do it once in a while.'

A sharp gust of wind hit them suddenly at that moment. 'I've got police work to do', Holly realised. 'I'd better go', she said.

'I'll go and pick up the balls', said Mark. 'Would you mind waiting a second and giving me a lift? I haven't got a waterproof with me, and it looks like I'm in for a soaking.'

Holly dropped Mark off by the entrance to the men's changing room, left the buggy by the pro's shop and took the key inside. 'Miss Marple, I presume', said Kyle Scott as she entered. 'What are you doing with my friend Mark? I saw you ferrying him around out there.'

Holly, outwardly unembarrassed, re-adopted a professional demeanour. 'I need to ask you some questions', she told Kyle matter-of-factly. 'Tell me where you were last night.'

A few minutes later, Holly returned to the office to tell Peter Harding she was leaving and would be in contact again the following day. The Colonel, meanwhile, had tried again to get through to Jamie Royle by phone but had been unsuccessful. Instead, he had simply left a brief text about a visit from the police and a polite request to call back.

As she was leaving the building, Holly caught sight of Mark and Kyle together at the bar, but decided she had no pretext for approaching them and hurried on. Sitting in the car for a moment, she pondered the day's events and findings, or lack of them; then her phone bleeped and it was a message from her father. He was getting a meal ready and wanted her to join him. Finally, she put a call through to an unhappy Dr Narayan. There had been a lengthy delay at the Coroner's Court. The dead person's family had retained a lawyer to ask difficult questions of witnesses at the inquest, which had consequently overrun. He had barely commenced examining the corpse from the golf club, he said. She should call the following day.

THE 3RD CHAPTER

Leaving the club, making her way westward, Holly found herself stuck behind a slow-moving tractor pulling a trailer piled high with hay bales. Eventually it pulled into a narrower lane, heading towards a barn, and she was able to speed up again, turning south soon after onto the main road south. Continuing on through Cocking and Singleton, she drove up over the steep sweep of the Downs, past the majestic stands of Goodwood racecourse and down gentler, rolling countryside towards the Chichester by-pass, the cathedral spire clearly visible to her right, poking provocatively skyward. From the edge of the city, it was only a short skip eastward to her father's place in the ancient village of Oving. She came to a stop outside the house, parked carefully next to his ancient maroon Ford Cortina, then stood for a moment admiring his garden of late-blooming hydrangeas.

'There you are!' Sam Driver's warm voice greeted her from the open doorway. 'Come on in!'

Holly's father was medium: medium height, medium build, a Caucasian male with a medium complexion; neither dark, nor light. He gave her a quick hug and a broad smile. Because of what had happened when she was eleven, this was the only parent Holly trusted. She never saw her mother, who had abandoned them both for a new life with her so-called 'Uncle Bob'. Thereafter, the bond with her father was absolute. 'Perhaps', she sometimes thought, 'this was what got between me and Tony'. The two men used the same expressions and even sounded similar at times, father and husband; but she admitted to herself that, even if things had gone better between them, she could never have loved the younger man as much as the older. 'It was good between us', she admitted, 'but it wasn't like being on the same wavelength all the time, like I am with Dad'.

'What's cooking?' she said, once inside, dumping her jacket and big brown bag on a chair in the sitting room, donning an old, favoured, pea-green cardigan hanging there… 'The usual repast, I presume?'

'Well, Madam! Since you ask… I've prepared slow-cooked, stewed onky-bonkles to start, and some twice-turned-over fried flapdoodles to follow. Also, for your delight, there is some lovely late-picked stinging-nettle wine.' Her father was always a big tease.

Going in, Holly found that a small table had been laid in the conservatory, which overlooked the lawn and farm fields to the east. A bottle of red stood open, and a kind of cheesy pasta smell emanated from the kitchen. 'As always… It's your famous Granny's lasagne, Dad!' said Holly with a laugh, turning to face him. 'I wouldn't want anything else.' Then, changing tone, 'I'm so sorry our lunch plans didn't work out.'

'No matter!' Her father gestured with his left hand, as if to wave all disappointment away. 'Try this wine! It's from South Africa and, would you believe, it's a blend of five different grapes? There's Cabernet Sauvignon, Merlot, Petit Verdot, Cabernet Franc and Malbec. I memorized them.'

'I never know when you're telling the truth,' his daughter exclaimed.

'You're the detective!'

'You're so devious sometimes, Dad! I think that's why I *became* a detective.'

'Try it anyway! I think you'll like it... Especially with the flapdoodles!'

Holly couldn't help laughing again. The wine was good; and the pasta dish too. When Sam brought in the coffee afterwards, there was a sponge cake with icing and a small lit birthday candle to go with it.

'Who baked you a cake?' said Holly in surprise.

'Mrs Rivers.'

'Oh Dad!' This was a running joke between them. Mrs Rivers had been their housekeeper for a time, and it was she alone who baked Holly's birthday cakes after her mother left. Sam was always acting envious, begging the recalcitrant cook to bake him one too. 'You finally got your wish, did you? I'll bet you had to bake it yourself.'

'Well, I had nothing better to do today than a little baking', he replied. 'It should be alright. I've been practicing.'

'Well, I won't tell your mates at the bowling club! But, do you mind if I give it a miss this time, Dad. I'm feeling rather full.'

They sat comfortably side-by-side for a few minutes as the sun went down, watching a bunch of rabbits chasing around the edges of the field. Later, Sam went inside to do the dishes while Holly continued to sit. As it grew darker, she too went inside, closed the conservatory door and turned on a light just as her father came in with a tray of cheese and some crackers, and another open bottle of the excellent red wine. He put the things on the table in front of the couch and motioned Holly to relax.

'You don't have to drink any more', he said, 'But you can always stay in the spare room if you do.'

'Well, I've no wish to get caught by a traffic cop tonight, if that's what you mean.' She had often stayed with her Dad in the bungalow. It was handy if she needed to be in Chichester early, for example. 'I've got to go and see the pathologist first thing, anyway', she said. 'So, I think I will join you in another small glass.'

But her father, having eventually found the remote under a cushion, had another surprise in store. Switching on the television, he suggested she might like to watch.

'What is it?' Holly asked.

'Golf!' he replied. 'From Medinah, in America… It's the Ryder Cup opening ceremony.'

The screen suddenly showed a large, colourful crowd of people in front of a stage on which the two twelve-man teams and their captains were paraded. Spot lit, on a plinth at the front, was the famous golden trophy, about two-feet in height, topped by a figurine modelled on the leading golfer of his day, Abe Mitchell.

Sam wanted to show off his knowledge, 'Mitchell lived in Sussex, you know! He had a house or cottage right next to the fourteenth tee of the golf course in Ashdown Forest. He was a close friend and the golf coach of Sam Ryder, the businessman who donated this very cup for the first official match between professional golfers of America and Great Britain, back in 1927'.

As they watched the screen, the US captain, Davis Love, was introducing his vice-captains and team members one by one. As his name was called out, each – all in matching blazers – stood up and took a bow.

'Did I hear that right?' said Holly. 'Bubba! Is one of the Americans called Bubba? He looks perfectly normal.'

'He looks normal, but he has a truly wild and idiosyncratic golf swing, hits the ball prodigious distances… with a pink-headed driver, no less… and is totally unmistakeable when he's playing, because he is also left-handed.' Sam was only too happy to inform his golf-wise ignorant daughter.

'Now Davis is introducing his "wild cards": Dustin Johnson, Steve Stricker, Jim Furyk and Brandt Snedeker… These are players he has picked personally, based on their experience in previous Ryder Cups and their current form; although Stricker has not been particularly successful this year. The other eight are chosen strictly on their standing in terms of "Ryder Cup" points, "World Rankings" and such like.'

'That's Tiger Woods, isn't it?' Holly pointed at the screen. 'He's about the only one I recognize.' They watched in silence for a few more minutes until it became clear that they had already missed the presentation of the European Team by its captain, Jose Maria Olazabal. As the speeches and commentary continued, Sam switched the sound off.

'This is a big year for Europe', he explained. 'The match is played every two years, and alternates between the USA and Europe. We won last time, at the Celtic Manor in Wales, but it was very close: 14½ to 13½. Some say we were lucky, mainly with the weather. The US team didn't have adequate rain gear at the start of the contest. Because it rained such a lot, the three-day match had to be extended into the Monday. On that fateful final day, the twenty-one year old Ricky Fowler showed extraordinary calm and maturity, fighting back to win the last three holes to tie his match against one of the Italian Molinari brothers… Edoardo. That left everything, the entire Ryder Cup, hanging on the last of the twelve matches, the one between Graeme McDowell and Hunter Mahan. McDowell made a birdie at the sixteenth to go two up, and Mahan eventually conceded after making a poor attempt at seventeen, so it was over and the European team had the victory.'

'I know there are eighteen holes in golf', said Holly, cutting in 'But what exactly is a "birdie"?'

'Good question! Let me explain...You've heard the expression "par for the course"? Well, a par for each hole is determined by its length. If a good golfer can hit a ball in one shot from the tee to the green, where the flag is, with an allowance of two putts, that makes it a "par-3". If it takes two shots to reach the green, it's a "par-4"; and if it takes three shots, that makes it a "par-5".You add up all eighteen and you get the "par for the course". In other words, it is all done by measurement. There are no par-6's, by the way. For a championship course, the total is 71 or 72, usually made up of four par-3's, four par-5's and the remainder par-4's. The course where I play is shorter. There is only one par-5 and five par-3's, so that makes the total par score 68, and that's how our handicaps are worked out.'

'Oh, yes', said Holly. 'You explained that to me once... If a good golfer completes the course in a par score of 68 shots and you regularly average 78, you are given a handicap of ten. Is that it?'

'Something like that. Anyway, as I was saying, it's always harder for the away team in the Ryder Cup, and we lost heavily at Valhalla, a golf club in Kentucky, in 2008. The last time we won in the States was in 2004. What a match! I still remember the fantastic 45 yard putt Sergio Garcia holed to halve the fourball match he was playing with Lee Westwood against Jay Haas and Chris DiMarco. It was enormous, and pretty much sideways, right across the rolling final green. Sergio won his three other matches that year too, beating the other great left-hander, Phil Mickelson, on the final day to round it off.'

'You talk about them by their first names as if you know them personally', Holly remarked.

'It's true. I guess we pick that up from the commentators.' Sam was balancing a piece of cheese on a water biscuit, before putting it in his mouth and washing it down with a big gulp of the 'Constantia' red, as they continued watching the screen. 'The

Spaniards are special when it comes to match play', he began again on the same theme. 'Garcia, Olazabal, Jimenez... They are all fantastic, but the greatest was undoubtedly Seve... Severiano Ballesteros.'

'I have heard of him', Holly interrupted, keen to show off her recently acquired knowledge to Sam. 'He was the golfer who beat Arnold Palmer in the World Match Play event at Wentworth in 1983. Didn't he get cancer or something?'

Sam was impressed. 'He had a brain tumour of some kind. It was only about four years ago that he had to stop playing, the most fabulous golfer ever... So imaginative, so passionate! It was such a tragedy when he became ill; and now he is dead. He died in May last year, only fifty-four.'

Holly had not often heard her father express such strong feeling about a sportsman, or anyone, before; awe, admiration, joy and grief mingled together.

'He must have been really something', she said sympathetically.

'Seve always used to shine in the Ryder Cup', Sam continued. 'I think he was in it eight times, often teamed with Olazabal. They were hard to beat. Now his legacy is going to act as a kind of mascot, spurring on the European team. They are going to try their hardest to win it for him, I imagine... And I'll bet Olazabal even said as much in his opening speech.'

'So what happens now?' said Holly.

'The Medinah Club is near Chicago. That's about six hours behind us. It's a very tough golf course. Tomorrow morning, each team will field four pairs who play match-play – hole-by-hole – against each other in a 'fourball' format; which means all four players complete each hole and the team's lowest score counts. In the afternoon, four more pairs play a similar match, but this time it's called 'foursomes' and only two balls are in play. The players on the same side take alternate shots until the ball drops into the hole, and the team with the lower score wins each hole until they run out of holes and the match is decided. Then on Saturday they go through the whole thing again, just the same.

The captains decide on the teams each day so, for instance, it is possible for a player to be left out of play altogether. Usually though, to give everyone a chance to experience the atmosphere and prepare for Sunday, everyone plays at least once during the first two days. Similarly, to avoid anyone getting too weary, the twelve players on each team usually get rested at least once. Then on Sunday everybody plays in the twelve 'singles' matches, one-on-one. That's when the match gets really exciting... the Ryder Cup at its best!'

The following morning, Holly awoke to the pleasing aroma of coffee. She took a quick shower, put on a clean blouse and underwear, and was looking tidy, fresh and smart when she joined Sam for breakfast. 'Eggs and bacon?' he called. 'You bet!' she replied.

A few minutes later, as they sat at the table together, Holly said, 'I've got a question, Dad'. Sam put down his coffee cup and looked up. 'Okay!'

'You remember you told me the Ryder Cup was played every two years?'

'Yes.'

'And it was first played for in 1927?'

'Yes.'

'So, how come it's being played this year? 2012 is an even year.'

'Very clever, Mrs Detective! Have you been thinking about that all night?'

'No, I haven't. It just came to me in the shower.'

'Okay. The match jumped an extra year between 2001 and 2002. See if you can work out why!'

'Really... The 9/11 terrorists managed to put the Ryder Cup off track for a year?'

'Yes, that's it... Well done! Play would have started at The Belfry less than three weeks after the twin towers attacks, at the end of that same September, so the two captains and the officials agreed to wait a year; but they did also agree to play with the same two teams already chosen in 2001, so maybe not all of them were on such good form when it came to it twelve months later.'

'What happened?'

'It was a good match. The teams were tied after day two, but Europe won the singles convincingly on the Sunday, resulting in an overall win of 15½ to 12½.'

'It sounds exciting!'

'It always is... That's the terrific thing about the Ryder Cup. The players are not paid a penny to represent their countries, but they give everything to win if they can. That seems to make it more special each time. You wait and see... Why not come over on Sunday evening and we'll watch the climax together?'

Holly said that she might.

Soon after nine o'clock, the Micra turned into the staff car-park behind the hospital in Chichester. Looking at the combined mortuary and pathology building in front of her, Holly could not help but vividly recall the embarrassment of the first post-mortem she had seen there years earlier during police training. Eight probationers were supposed to go that day, but Holly arrived first. Two or three other spectators, student nurses from elsewhere in the hospital, went into the building, so she followed them. Once inside, unsure what to expect, she hung back against the wall where the light was dim. At the front, a demonstration table under bright lights held a body covered by a green linen sheet. Everything was still and silent, then a small, dapper man in a fully buttoned-up black suit appeared through a side door, followed by an attendant. The demonstrator slowly took off his jacket and passed it absent-mindedly behind him with his right hand while stroking his fussy little toothbrush moustache in a nervous gesture with his left. The attendant passed him a starched white laboratory coat, which he donned swiftly and moved to the table, tugging mercilessly at the covering, leaving his minion to gather the green billows and fold up the sheet.

Holly had been mesmerized. It was as if a conjuring trick had magnificently gone wrong. The pale, mottled naked female body lay there still, when according to expectation it should have vanished, or maybe come alive. Suddenly, confronted by the finality of death for the first time in her life, and by thoughts of its inevitability, she felt dizzy and slightly nauseous. Afraid she might actually be sick, and anxious not to disgrace herself, she made her way along the wall and back into the fresh air, where she quickly began to revive. She then noticed that the other seven recruits in her group had arrived and were mustered there like docile cattle. While remaining outdoors herself, she motioned the other cadets forward into the building. Five or so minutes later, when she was sure the risk of humiliation was over, she decided to go back inside. Her earlier departure had not been spotted so, on re-entry, people naturally assumed she was late.

Catching sight of her, the demonstrator abruptly stopped showing off the cadaver's internal organs. Appalled at her apparent tardiness, he fixed Holly with a withering stare and shouted loudly, 'Go! Go! Get out! You're late.' He clearly felt personally insulted. Holly was utterly shocked. Nevertheless, to her credit, she stood her ground and stared back at her irate accuser until, with a slight shrug, he resumed his macabre task, ignoring her totally after that, but paying special attention to Lizzie, the other female recruit.

'What was I supposed to do, caught in the headlights between a rock and a hard place?' Holly thought to herself as she remembered that unhappy encounter. 'He should have let me explain.' But there were no qualms or dizziness this time as she entered the building. There was a different, more scrupulous atmosphere. For a start, everyone wore full protective clothing, including Wellington boots, partly to negate the risk of cross-contamination. The old professor in his street clothes would immediately have been asked to leave. Holly was even smiling to herself as she changed in an anteroom. Peter Narayan, though serious as ever, seemed in a friendly mood when she stepped into the examination room. 'Have you got something to show me?' she asked, approaching a clean, modern table, rather different from the simple slab of former times. And this time, of course, the corpse upon it was one she had already met.

'I think I have', the handsome pathologist replied affably. 'But first… Tell me what you see here.'

Holly studied the body again. 'She's exceptionally thin', she began, 'Even thinner than I realized when I saw her yesterday. I wondered if she'd been deliberately starved by someone.'

'You might find it better just to observe for now, and only speculate about causes when you've finished the full inventory of your observations', Narayan said quietly. 'That's what I teach my students.'

'Okay', said Holly before continuing. 'Her hair is very soft, like babies' hair. And she's older, isn't she? She's not a teenager just reaching puberty, as I first thought.'

Narayan nodded in agreement. 'Anything else?'

'Well, I can't see any signs of trauma or any other obvious cause of death.'

'So what does what you have seen so far suggest to you?'

'That she may have had a serious eating disorder. Anorexia, I imagine.'

'And where would you want to look now?'

Holly had a hunch. 'In her mouth?' she asked. 'I think I'd want to take a look at her teeth.'

'Yes. Here you are.' The pathologist leaned across and arranged the head a little to one side. Then he adjusted an angle light to shine directly into the mouth, which he then held open. Holly, peering in, made a mental note of the marked wearing away of the enamel of the blackened back teeth on either side.

'That's classical in cases of bulimia, Holly. You know that, don't you?' Narayan was explaining. 'Anorexia nervosa affects mostly women. It is a kind of extreme form of slimming addiction, so that sufferers also make themselves vomit after ingesting food or drink. That's the 'bulimia' part; and they do this especially if they've been on a high-calorie binge. In severe cases, though, they just get into a habit of making themselves sick after eating anything at all. The teeth get worn down by acid from the stomach, which is normally there to help digest the food we eat. In this case, some acid is refluxed into the back of the mouth whenever a person makes themselves sick; and it affects the teeth particularly when there's only a little food to regurgitate.'

'That's not very nice, is it?' Holly was determined not to let herself feel sick again in that miserable, sterile room.

'No. It is not nice at all', the pathologist sounded sympathetic. 'And you can only wonder what damages a person's self-esteem to such an extent that they want to make themselves so small as to disappear entirely from the face of the planet.'

'Yes. It is sad', Holly responded. 'Do you think that's what it was like for her?'

'Who knows? I don't think anybody properly understands what makes people do this kind of thing to themselves, but it must be pretty awful to overrule the basic human instinct to survive, don't you think?'

Silence held sway in the room momentarily. Holly had begun to notice a chill in the air when the doctor turned from the body, facing her with a serious look on his face. She sensed he had something important in mind.

'I am a Hindu, you know', he spoke quietly in a confidential tone. 'I would not say I am religious, but my people are, my grandparents especially. I don't go to the temple, but we do have a small shrine to one of the many gods, the elephant-headed Ganesh, in the house, and my wife does *'puja'*, says prayers, every morning and night. We've two girls, and we try and teach them to respect the truth at the heart of all religions. I always tell them that they are indivisibly linked by a powerful energetic life-force to a magnificent universal whole. We all are. So I suppose it means I do believe in something... something truly great... Some kind of order in the universe, the order we understand, partly anyway, through science. And, you know what? This idea sustains us. It speaks of some kind of seamless bond between people as individuals, and also between people and nature. This, I call it a 'spiritual' bond, is what gives us a comforting feeling of belonging, a sense of responsibility, and thereby too a sense of purpose. This, anyway, is what helps me get through all the hardships and bad days.'

Realizing that Holly was growing embarrassed by his earnest tone, the pathologist quickly apologized. 'I'm sorry', he said. 'I shouldn't go on like that... But what I mean is that people, religious or not, need to take some kind of account of life's sacredness, of its spiritual dimension. This is the only way to properly make sense of things; and it makes it so much easier to cope with life's challenges. Otherwise you risk ending up here, on one of my dissecting tables, dead from anorexia, alcoholism, drug abuse, from a cancer caused by smoking, obesity or some other destructive form of behaviour. If only people could all see how they end up!'

'I think, perhaps, you need a holiday', said Holly, trying to be helpful. 'Your job seems to be getting to you.' She was certainly not yet prepared to think of herself, or even her father – already in his late sixties – as ending up on one of these slabs.

'And my job', she said then, bringing her mind back to attention, 'Is finding out who this person was and what happened to her. What set of circumstances brought her here to your gloomy little fiefdom? And, for that reason, I must ask, do you think self-starvation is the main cause of death?'

'I am sorry.' Peter Narayan had relaxed and was cheerful again. 'It's just a hobby-horse of mine, despite my background in science, that people need to look deeper than the common superficialities of everyday life, shopping, social media, what's on television and whatnot, for their own good… But this woman? Yes. She certainly had advanced and severe anorexia nervosa with secondary bulimia. In addition to the signs you've seen, we've checked her bone density and she has advanced osteo-malacia. That's thin, brittle bones caused by a prolonged inadequate diet, lacking especially in protein. That's why her body is rounded over. Some of her spinal vertebrae have become squashed or have even collapsed completely. I was just going to take some X-rays when you arrived. The condition must have been very painful while she was alive… And, before you ask, I reckon she was about forty, plus or minus five years when she died.'

Involuntarily, Holly began reaching out to smooth back a wayward strand of wispy hair from the pallid, lifeless face, then caught herself and withdrew her hand. She knew the rules: 'Do not touch anything'. But she had felt and acknowledged a wave of tenderness towards this hapless individual that was going to feed her commitment to uncovering what had happened.

'So, yes,' the doctor was continuing blithely, 'She had anorexia, but did she die of it? She may have. It's possible. But equally, she may not have. Frankly, I don't know… Not yet. Not until we get the toxicology results back, to see if she was drugged or poisoned. So far, I have seen no bruises or other signs of foul play, but you will have to wait until I have completed the examination. I'll let you know if I find anything. Also, I have one more thing to tell you at this stage… She was frozen.'

This was unexpected. 'What do you mean?'

'I mean that, after she died, someone put her body into a deep freezer, and only took her out again to transport her to her resting place on the golf course.'

'Can you be sure?'

'Well, I've already looked at her heart muscle under the microscope and found cell damage characteristic of the type we see in animal hearts that have been frozen and thawed out again. There were no ice crystals as such, and I may be wrong, but it seems likely… The problem, of course, is that now I won't be able to give you an approximate time of death. In fact, I could not reliably tell you even in which month she perished!'

Holly was disappointed. There were now almost too many questions. She decided she needed to concentrate only on one for the time being: Who was this unfortunate woman? Before leaving, she called her boss, who told her to return to headquarters for a briefing with the Superintendent later in the day. Decisions about the investigation were going to have to be made.

THE 4TH CHAPTER

Holly's next appointment that Friday involved a longstanding missing person case that she and a colleague from Brighton had been working on together. Jack was an old friend. They had first met years earlier when, as a newly-appointed detective-constable, Holly had been sent to an address in the Brighton suburb of Moulsecoomb. It was a hot summer's morning and she had to park at the foot of a steep hill, more than a hundred yards from the terraced house in question. A raid by the Drug Squad was in progress on the premises, and the roadway was blocked by a number of their vehicles.

Grabbing her satchel, the novice detective made her way up towards the target building. She was still on the street, showing her warrant card to a uniformed constable at the foot of the steps, when plain clothes officers filed past leading three men wearing handcuffs. They could have been brothers, swarthy, scowling, unshaven, thickset men in heavy gold necklaces, dirty singlets and billowing black trousers, with only thongs on their dusty feet.

As this group made its way towards three separate police cars, another prisoner emerged from the house, a tall West-Indian woman of about fifty, thick, tangled hair pulled back, her angry face like thunder, wearing a tight black top, matching skirt and a strong pair of sandals, her arms pinned behind her, escorted by a uniformed policewoman on either side. Suddenly, coming alongside Holly, raising her head, this woman, like a cornered wild animal, spat vigorously in her direction. Fortunately, Holly moved quickly enough to avoid the arc of saliva hitting her face.

'Charming!' she said, as the bland-faced women officers simply tightened their grip on the prisoner.

'Are you alright, Love?' In contrast, the deep voice from above sounded genuinely sympathetic.

Holly looked up, squinting in the sunlight. A tall man in sunglasses and a dark suit stood by the open door, his hand held up in greeting.

'I'm fine', she said, getting a wipe from her shoulder-bag to clear a few splatters of spit off her lapel. 'It will take more than a few gobs of that Madam's phlegm to get me upset.'

'That's the spirit!' said the detective admiringly. 'I'm Jack, by the way... Jack Sylvester. You must be the Angel they've sent me... And not a moment too soon, thank goodness! Wait till you see what's inside!'

It was hard to see anything at first. The windows were covered by thick blankets, firmly tacked around their frames. Firearms and forensic officers were already combing the place for weapons, drugs and other evidence as Jack Sylvester ushered Holly into one of the front rooms, where a standard lamp showed four pale thin ghosts huddling together on a large couch under a couple of filthy duvets. As Jack pulled blankets back away from the windows to let in light, Holly watched as the ghosts turned into pale young women, dressed only in skimpy underwear. She spotted needle tracks on all their arms. Those who were awake, or not narcotized in some way, seemed utterly terrified. None of them, however, made a sound.

Jack explained that the drug squad people had broken in an hour or so earlier, without realizing that the pushers were also people smugglers, slave traders and prostitution-ring managers. The girls were from Eastern Europe and the Middle East. None of them spoke any English. He and Holly were to interrogate them, but realized that they now had to wait for three separate interpreters. With a stoic, 'all-in-the-line-of-duty' look, Jack added that it could be a long wait. One of language specialists would be coming from London.

So they had spent the day together, baby-sitting these terrified hapless girls, one of whom appeared no older than sixteen. Even the oldest was only about twenty, and when this one came out of her daze, she railed at them persistently in what seemed like Arabic for half-an-hour, before finally lapsing back into silence when she could not make herself understood. Eventually, when she was allowed to go into the kitchen, Holly made a pot of tea and brought in some biscuits she found there, but none of the girls touched a drop or a morsel. Later, one by one, she escorted them to the bathroom and tried to get them to shower, but all they wanted was make-up, to try and look pretty again. She found clothes for them, and later she and Jack were forced to shepherd the little flock into the other front room, dirtier and less comfortable, the men's room, while the forensic work continued where they had been.

Finally, a social worker turned up, but soon left again when she realized the extent of the communication problem, leaving a number for Holly to call when the interpreters arrived. Time passed and, as it did so, the girls grew increasingly restless and distressed. Jack soon realized that the effects of the drugs were beginning to wear off.

'They're going to go cold turkey soon if we don't do

something', he said. 'I'm going to call the Super and see if we can get a psychiatric nurse over here.'

It did the trick. The nurse arrived at almost the same time as the first two interpreters, and swiftly decided that all four girls needed methadone and had to go to A & E. This meant two ambulances, with Holly and Jack in one each.

Once at the hospital, there were more hours of waiting around. Jack kept checking that Holly was feeling alright, and she kept reassuring him that she was. Eventually, the original social worker turned up and said she'd found temporary accommodation for the girls in a hostel in Hove, and she would arrange transport for them when the doctors said they could leave. The third interpreter arrived and, by late afternoon, Holly and Jack had the brief statements they needed. The oldest of the girls wanted asylum. The other three wanted repatriation home. Finally, the detectives were free, but their vehicles were stranded in Moulsecoomb so they decided to share a cab back.

Jack had the taxi drop them off by a grassy park area at the foot of the hill near their cars. It was a fine, warm evening. Some teenagers were throwing a Frisbee about, and a mother was trying with little success to interest her toddler in flying a small kite in the light breeze.

'How about an ice-cream?' Her companion asked.

Holly agreed readily. 'What could be nicer?' she said.

They were still both officially on duty until end-of-shift at six-thirty. 'My other half won't be home until eight this evening, anyway', Jack explained. 'There's nothing for me to rush home for'.

They were soon sitting together on a bench near the parked-up ice-cream van. Holly realized that she didn't feel like hurrying back home to Shoreham Beach just then either; also that she would enjoy spending some more time with Jack, getting to know him better. His obvious concern for her throughout the day was a pleasant change. The men in her life so far had been rather less caring. Having spent so many hours in each other's company and shared a quick snack in the hospital cafeteria, she already knew Jack to be thirty-six, a Brighton and Hove Albion FC supporter whose father had also been a Brighton copper, and whose widowed mother had died earlier that year. She was impressed at how easily he felt able to share this kind of personal information, so it was of limited surprise to her when, without a trace of self-consciousness, as he was finishing the last of his cone, Jack said, 'Did you know I'm gay, by the way?'

She did not. 'I would never have guessed', she replied truthfully. Except for his evident compassion, nothing in his speech, manner or appearance had given her that impression at all.

'I thought you might have heard my nickname at the Station. They usually call me "Sylvie"... Sylvie Sylvester, get it?' With an inquisitive sideways look, Jack added earnestly, 'I don't like it, Angel; and I hope you won't ever call me by that name.'

'I won't', she said. And she never did; and on that first day working together they had become firm friends. It was also in the relaxed and happy company of Jack and his partner, Brian, in the well-tended garden of their pretty home in Portslade a few weeks later that Holly felt safe enough to mention something she was feeling ashamed about, a problem she could not resolve by herself.

After the divorce from Tony, Holly tried keeping to herself. In the early days, their lovemaking had been passionate and inventive so, naturally, while increasingly enjoying solitude and independence, she missed the physical side of a relationship. She had a brief fling with another probationer on her course, but broke it off quickly when he told her once that he loved her. She wasn't ready for that. She met someone at a friend's wedding and slept with him a few times, but he lived in north London and neither of them wanted to travel. Her friend Brenda was always trying to fix her up with a partner, and she occasionally went along with it, but realized eventually that she didn't truly have the stomach for casual sex. It could be fun, but often left her feeling somehow tainted.

She decided to take a vow of celibacy to herself, and kept it faithfully for many months until, one November evening, still in uniform before transferring to the detective squad, she was called to the seafront between Brighton and Hove, not far from where the burned-out shell of the old West Pier jutted up out of the sea. A fully-clothed woman had been seen running into the cold sea in the dark and was still out there, floundering desperately in the waist-high shallows, when Holly and PC Winter arrived.

The scene was illuminated by lights from the shore and, with Holly hesitating for a second, her colleague plunged right into the waves. The woman tried swimming away, but with waterlogged clothing weighing her down, she was making little headway. When he reached her, she tried to hit him, but her blows were feeble. Holly could hear her shouting for him to get away, but John Winter was a judo expert, and soon had her under control, dragging her back to the beach.

Someone appeared with a blanket, which Holly grabbed gratefully, and threw it over the woman, who seemed terrified and continued to resist. The back-up van had arrived, and with it Sergeant Drew, who took command. His men quickly bundled the would-be suicide up the beach, into the back seat of a squad car. Holly was told to get in. PC Winter, nearly hypothermic, was simply told to go home, dry off and get warm.

On the drive to the custody block at Hollingbury, Drew said they had had a missing person call from a psychiatric hostel somewhere near Davigdor Road. This woman fitted the description of Ruby Hawkins, a fifty-eight year old who suffered from paranoid schizophrenia.

'That's when they hear voices in their head, isn't it?' Holly enquired.

'Well, I'm no expert', Drew replied, 'But basically... Yes. They have voices that say bad things about them, that people are out to get them, that they are worthless and should kill themselves... Things like that!'

'It must be horrible, terrifying', Holly said.

'Apparently Ruby has been having episodes like this since she was seventeen and first went into St Francis's, the big asylum up at Haywards Heath. The hostel people say she's been living peacefully in the community since it closed in the late 80's, completely free of symptoms until recently. She was on some medication that was working well, but it began to kill off her white blood cells for some reason, putting her at risk of death from even a mild infection. They had to switch her to something else, and it hasn't been working as well. Even after all this time, the voices have come back. She's going to need to be sectioned, so you're going to have to speak to the doctor and the social worker on duty.'

'Why the custody block?' Holly asked.

'Because we've used the Mental Health Act to put her on a Section 136, an emergency Police section, and it only allows us to transfer her to a so-called 'Place of Safety' for assessment. For some reason I don't understand, we're not allowed to take her either to A & E, or to Mill View, the psychiatric hospital in Hangleton. They are not deemed to be safe enough.'

'Well they should be!' Holly was astonished. 'Freezing wet as she is, it can't be right to bang Ruby up in a cell for the night, can it?'

'You tell me', said the Sergeant.

In the event, the patient was treated very gently. She seemed to realize she was safe and had calmed down, although still responding in a whisper to her voices. Once she was dry and had warmed up, she was given a cup of tea and a slice of pizza, before being placed in one of the bare and functional cells. Holly spoke to the social worker and the 'Forensic Medical Officer', as the Police Surgeon was now called, but still had to wait until the duty psychiatrist arrived.

It was late now, and the canteen was closed, so she got a cup of coffee from the machine and found a seat against the wall in the busy custody suite. A woman from the hostel was there too, saying how normal Ruby was between episodes, always thinking of others, even donating regularly to charity from her meagre benefits allowance. 'She always says there's someone worse off than she is', the hostel-worker explained. 'It's such a shame the clozapine had to be stopped.'

She had brought Ruby some dry clothes, and was called away, leaving Holly alone for an instant when one of the custody officers, taking a break, sat himself down beside her.

'You're looking a bit weary', he said. 'Is there anything I can get you? Something to eat, maybe?'

'I'm fine, thanks', she replied. Something about this solid figure of a man was appealing. 'I'm Holly, by the way', she added.

'Hello Holly… I'm Dave!' He said, testing his wit. 'Do you come here often?'

She liked his silly attempts at humour. Even though not looking her best that night, he could still tell she was a looker. 'I've got to go', he said ten minutes later. 'What's your number?' She gave it to him and he called the next evening. 'Want to go to the pictures?' he asked. 'What's on?' she said. 'Does it matter?' he replied. 'I'll let you choose if you like.'

Dave Antrobus was also divorced. He seemed uncomplicated to Holly, living for the moment, not driven to worldly success

as Tony had been, and she found that refreshing. They went to
see a movie starring Matt Damon as a CIA hit-man who had
lost his memory. It was good; and later, after a beer and a burger,
they returned to his flat and made love. A month later when,
by chance, his lease was up, Holly let him move in with her.
She told herself she did not love him, or he her, but she liked
having him around. They were both working shifts, which did
not necessarily coincide, so she also had a reasonable amount of
time on her own.

They bought a kitten, a beautiful English Blue, and called
him Horatio. Dave installed a cat-flap in the kitchen door. Holly
took charge of feeding and cleaning the litter tray. It was an
affectionate creature, but one day – only six months old – he
went missing. Holly made laminated signs, 'Missing Cat', with
a photo of their pet, but he was never found. Dave made the
mistake of telling her that Horatio had probably been eaten by a
fox. It may have been true, but she did not want to hear it, and
she began to notice more evidence of a callous streak in him
after that.

One Sunday, a few weeks later, as he was driving them to
Hayling Island, she opened the passenger glove box to look for
the packet of strong mints he kept there. Dave was a smoker.
He had been on a late shift the night before. He had slept in
until past 10 am, and they were already overdue at his sister's.
It was her birthday, and they were invited over for a big roast
lunch with her husband and two teenage children. Dave had
not been looking forward to it. 'They're a couple of smart-arses,
those kids', he said. 'No respect… Always taking the mickey!'
He was in a bad mood, driving too fast, and had just lit another
cigarette.

Holly thought a mint might take the edge off the foul smell
of his Gauloise; but there in the glove-box was a half-empty
packet of Silk Cut. 'Dave would never smoke those', she thought,

her instincts alerted and suspicions aroused. 'But this is definitely not the time to say anything. He's already about to explode.'

This was the problem she confided to Jack and Brian that sunny afternoon, a few weeks later. Like most good listeners, they knew the right questions to ask. It was a relief to Holly to relate her doubts about the relationship. When she said she suspected Tony of being unfaithful, Jack simply asked if she wanted him to find out. When she agreed, he asked her for her duty rota and Dave's, so he could work out when she would be at work and he would be free.

Two weeks later, Jack met Holly in a café and passed over a note and a computer disc. Alone later, she inserted the disc in her laptop. It showed several photographs of Dave with a pretty blonde woman, younger than Holly. There appeared to be a sequence, the impression confirmed by date and time markings in the corner of each frame. First, they were sitting outside a pub, smoking and having drinks. On the table in front of them were packets of both Gauloise and Silk Cut. Next, they were shown getting into a car together. Then they were disappearing inside the front door of an apartment building, hugging each other closely, the location identified in the following picture as being a street in Kemptown, not far from the Royal Sussex County Hospital. An hour and a half later, Dave is seen emerging, smiling, lighting up a cigarette and hailing a blue and white Brighton cab.

Jack's note simply said, 'She's a student nurse called Sandra Webb. I had them followed. There's more graphic stuff if you need it.'

The following Saturday, after Dave went off to work an early shift, Holly let the locksmith in, as arranged earlier in the week, to change the front door lock. At about midday, she went out for an hour, taking a hold-all with her. When Dave returned, she was ready. Having let herself out through the kitchen door, making her way quietly through the back gate, she came up behind him as he was out of the car, fumbling with his keys.

'They won't do you any good, Dave', she said. 'The locks have been changed.'

'What's this about, Holly?' he asked, genuinely surprised and perplexed.

'I know about you and Sandra', she said. 'And you are leaving my house today.' She was holding out to him a six-inch long piece of driftwood. Dave looked at it. He could see a key dangling from it on a loop of string that was hanging from a small hole drilled in one end. He took it. The word 'Esplanade' and the number '5' had been burned artfully into the smooth, pale surface. 'What's this?' he said.

'It's the key to your hotel room at The Esplanade in Lancing. You know it, don't you?' Holly's voice was steady. Dave could tell she was angry, and that she meant business. He wasn't going to be able to argue with her.

'I've paid for two nights', Holly continued. 'After that, you're on your own. You'll find a bag with some clothes and your wash things in the room already. Let me know when you've found another place to rent and I'll send the rest of your things along then.'

'Holly!' Dave's strained voice contained both a groan and a plea. 'The thing with Sandra... It doesn't mean anything to me.'

'It does to me', she replied, turning away. 'Goodbye, Dave.'

That was it, but it took a long time for her anger to subside, and her mistrust of men lingered longer. She dated seldom after that episode. Michael, the man who took her to Westminster Abbey, had been an exception; but, because he was so mild-mannered, although admittedly safe and reliable, there was never any thrill or excitement. The relationship quite soon fizzled out.

She had continued to see Jack and Brian from time to time over the following years. She and Jack occasionally worked together, as well as the three meeting up socially. Now, almost a decade later, they were on a job together again.

THE 5ᵀᴴ
CHAPTER

After the awkwardness that morning, Holly spent the time driving east pondering that strangely intense conversation with Peter Narayan. The road took her through the Southwick Hill Tunnel, cleverly mined through ninety million year old chalk, up past the new golf course at West Hove, towards the Devil's Dyke turn-off. She always thought Hindus worshipped hundreds of gods with animal heads and such like, but the Anglo-Indian said they only ultimately believed in a single Godhead, one Absolute that was called 'Brahman'.

'Every Hindu is taught', he had told her in a friendlier, less preachy tone than before, walking her out to the car, 'That we are all one with this Universal Being, which is a kind of Divine Spirit pervading everyone and everything. As such, seamlessly connected, every soul is equally part of your soul and my soul; which inevitably means that in hurting anyone at all, we are likewise hurting ourselves. Similarly, in loving and being kind to anyone, we are loving and being kind to ourselves… Is that not similar to what Christians are taught?'

Holly thought it was Native Americans who worshipped a universal Great Spirit, not Hindus but, uncertain, she decided against revealing her ignorance and stayed silent. She realized now, driving along, that although her mother had made sure she was baptized, she did not know much about what Christians were taught beyond what her father had called 'The Golden Rule': to "do as you would be done by". He had first told her this when she was little. It was his basic creed, and it had always been good enough for her. She thought about the Virgin and Child image on her wall. 'How come that always settles whatever's bothering me?' she wondered... 'It's a mystery!'

Putting an end to her ruminations, turning off Woodland Drive near her destination, Holly soon spotted Jack's patrol car outside the luxury home they were about to visit. His lanky figure emerged from the vehicle as she was parking up. 'I've just had a sermon from a Hindu pathologist', she said, making a joke of it after they had shaken hands. 'I hope he's left you in a good mood', replied Jack. 'Are you ready for this? I'm not sure how they are going to take this news.'

Fifteen months earlier, Jack had called Holly's boss and asked permission for her specifically to help with an unusual missing person case. A rich property developer, Wayne McInnes, had recently gone to the John Street Police Station with his daughter, Hazel, to report his wife missing. Rita McInnes had disappeared six weeks earlier. When asked why he had not come in sooner, he said that she had gone off before, but had returned after about a month when she had run out of money. He had been sure she would do the same this time.

The desk officer had asked him why, then, he had picked that particular day to come in. To which he replied that the day before had been Hazel's fifteenth birthday, but Rita still hadn't made contact, so Hazel had persuaded him to do something about it.

'Apparently, he didn't seem at all concerned', Jack had said as they went together, late on the same day, to this beautiful mansion overlooking Hove Park. First, they had spent time with Wayne in his study, looking through a selection of photographs. The one they chose, kept and had copied for use throughout the enquiry, showed the missing wife to be an attractive natural blonde with luxuriant, beautifully coiffed hair and a smiling freckled face, a woman in her prime, wearing a simple, cornflower-blue summer frock.

Sitting across from the self-assured businessman at his desk, Jack began leading the questions. Rita McInnes, according to her husband, had no friends and seldom left the house. She had been working part-time as a lettings agent since Hazel first went to school, but had given up the job almost a year earlier. When asked the name of the estate agents, McInnes, prompting himself, surprised them by saying, 'Think tennis!' After a slight pause, he gave a little chuckle and continued, 'That's how I remember things sometimes. Yes, tennis… Andy Murray! You see, it was called Murry Associates. Andrew Murry was her boss… but no 'A' in Murry for him.'

When Holly asked why Rita stopped working, McInnes simply said, bluntly, 'Because I told her to pack it up'. When pressed, he explained that they didn't need the money, and he had wanted his wife to spend more time on the housework, cooking and gardening, and on being a mother to Hazel.

'You could have hired some help for her', Holly remarked.

'Oh I did', said Wayne. 'We have a cook-housekeeper and a gardener. That's what I meant, really. I wanted Rita at home to keep an eye on them, give them instructions and so on; but she was a bit lenient, not very assertive. She did prefer staying at home, though. She even did most of her shopping on the internet.'

Jack took down the details of the hired help. After a few more questions, which McInnes answered somewhat nonchalantly, he thought, they took a tour of the house and garden. When they came upon Rita's Mercedes saloon, parked in the garage next to Wayne's Lamborghini, her husband also mentioned that she had left behind her mobile phone and house keys, which seemed odd. The couple had a joint bank account, he added helpfully, but since her disappearance his wife had not withdrawn funds or made any use of her credit or debit cards.

Jack asked if his wife had any other savings or sources of income.

'No', said McInnes. 'Her father died some years ago... Heart attack playing squash! He was only fifty-three. I took over the business, and he left everything else to Dora, Rita's mother. She's had Alzheimer's for years... Lives in a home in Partridge Green at fifteen hundred quid a week. That's where that money has all been going.'

'How is she?' Holly asked.

'Completely gaga!' was the reply. 'Away with the fairies... Nothing she says makes any sense. The last time Rita went, more than six months ago now, Dora didn't recognize her or Hazel. Rita said she wasn't going back there again.'

After the tour, Holly put a few questions to Hazel in the sitting-room as Jack and her father stood by. She was very aware that here was a young woman in a situation similar to the one she had found herself in when her mother disappeared with Uncle Bob, her seducer; but Hazel seemed much less distressed than she had been at the time.

There was not much to go on. Neither Wayne nor Hazel could say if any of Rita's clothes were missing, for example; so many remained in the wardrobes of the master bedroom and in the principal guest room. They both denied that Rita might have been particularly unhappy. Hazel confirmed that her mother was a shy person who had few friends and kept to herself. The detectives were given the strong impression that she had been living to keep the house and garden spotless and orderly. To have the child of a successful man, to supervise and keep house for him, was all she had ever wanted.

Hazel went back to her room. When invited to explain his wife's earlier disappearance, McInnes gave a shrug, holding his arms up, palms open, as if to question whether anyone could truly explain a woman's mysterious impulses. When pressed on the matter by Holly, he glanced at her with a sullen, contemptuous look, then smiled quickly at Jack and admitted that at the time he had briefly been seeing another woman. 'We got over it', was his way of dismissing the episode now.

This time it was Jack who tried pinning him down. 'Have you been seeing any other women recently, Mr McInnes?' He asked. The reply was a curt and emphatic denial. 'No, I most certainly have not.'

Jack was unfazed. 'Just so we know', he replied.

The two detectives left, filed a report together, and set in train the usual missing person's enquiry, circulating the photo and description, alerting the media and other regional police forces. The bank confirmed that there had been no activity initiated by Mrs McInnes on the joint account for several weeks. The house and her mobile phone records showed nothing unusual, only a few calls, mainly to service providers of one kind or another. Holly made a note of Rita's hairdresser's number, her GP surgery details, and contact information for one or two other people who might have been able to shed light on the missing woman's whereabouts.

Holly and Jack spoke separately to the cook and the gardener over the following days. Both gave a different, brighter picture of Rita as a relatively chatty and sociable person, house-proud and proud too of her daughter's achievements. She had never discussed the relationship with her husband with either of them. As far as they knew, she was content with her life. Neither had been present on the day she disappeared. Mrs Sampson had two weekdays off each week, and Jim, the gardener, only came to the house on Tuesdays and Thursdays. When she disappeared, Mr McInnes had simply told them that his wife had gone away for a couple of weeks, and neither had thought much more about it.

Without a body, there was little Jack's boss would allow them to do to extend the investigation, but when nothing transpired after six weeks, they did go back to the house. On this occasion, a warm Friday afternoon, they had not arranged an appointment. McInnes, a tanned, well-built, clean-shaven figure, came to the door in swimming shorts with a bath towel over his shoulder. Showing no surprise, alarm or irritation, he led them casually to his study, from where, through the window, they could see Hazel on a lounger by the swimming pool with another, slightly more mature young woman on a water-float nearby.

'Who is that?' Holly asked pointedly.

'That's Susan,' McInnes replied. 'Susan Bettany. She's moved in to help me look after Hazel.'

'Did she come from an agency?'

'No. As a matter of fact, she works in my office. She needed somewhere to live, so I invited her here... It seemed like a good idea to kill two birds with the one stone, so to speak.' His voice, she noticed, remained calm. There were no immediate grounds for suspicion. Nevertheless, Jack made a point of asking to be introduced.

'She's a flirty little minx, that one!' He said to Holly when they were back on the pavement outside later. 'Even I felt the sex oozing out of her, and that's saying something!' Adding, as a cautionary afterthought, 'You'd better not tell Brian I said that.' Holly noticed the sudden pink glow, his cheeks briefly on fire.

'Do you think she's his mistress?'

'There could very well be more here than meets the eye'.

Jack, quickly regaining composure, gave a non-committal response. 'Let's have a chat with the Chief.'

It became a murder enquiry. The suspicion fell on Wayne McInnes that he had fallen for young Susan Bettany at work and started an affair. Rita had either found out and confronted him, or he had possibly decided to forestall her and do away with her before she noticed anything. But it was all circumstantial. There was no direct evidence. Wayne did later admit to being in love with Susan, and she with him, but both insisted that this had only happened after she moved into the house, at least two months after Rita disappeared.

'He's got a sailing-boat moored in the marina', said Holly one day, 'He could have murdered her and disposed of the body at sea in the dark, couldn't he?'

'Well, he could have', said Jack, 'But it's all supposition. Unless he confesses, or the body turns up somewhere, we've got nothing. I think we should dig a little deeper.'

They discovered from his business records that McInnes had often used his wife as a sleeping partner, listing her as a board member of some of his companies and therefore owner, or joint-owner, of several properties. He was already wealthy in his own right, but would stand to gain a lot more if Rita were dead. According to the family solicitor, Donald Barkham, her Will left everything to Wayne, apart from a portfolio of shares invested in trust for Hazel when she reached eighteen.

They arrested and held Wayne McInnes in custody for forty-eight hours on suspicion of murder, interrogating him relentlessly during office hours in the official presence of Barkham. Throughout, he maintained his innocence. They went to search the house, and then the garden, using specialists with archaeological radar equipment to try and find buried remains; but all this searching was fruitless too, apart from a single tiny bloodstain on the master-bedroom carpet that matched Rita

McInnes's DNA, taken from one of her hair-brushes. They had to let him go. Susan, who turned out to be twenty-two, exactly half Wayne's age, was interviewed as well, but gave away nothing. The detective duo had to admit to a stalemate. For many months, that's how it stayed.

Jack and Holly either met or spoke on the phone about the case every week. They gleaned nothing significant from the hairdresser, staff at the GP practice or from anyone else, until they visited Andy Murry at his Hove office in Church Road. He was a kindly man in his late sixties who had been running his independent estate agents for more than thirty years. His 'associates' were his wife and three children, none of whom actually worked in the business.

He remembered Rita McInnes very well, he told them. He had taken her on about nine years earlier. It transpired that after leaving school she had worked for a chain of estate agents, so she knew quite a lot about the business, even though she had not been employed since her daughter was born. She had come into the shop one day enquiring about a job, just when he had needed someone to help with the lettings. Her duties involved viewing properties and assessing their suitability, and later showing these flats and houses to potential rental clients. She was hard-working, competent, reliable and friendly, he said. Her clients spoke well of her, and she seemed to like engaging with them. She also got on well with her colleagues on the sales side, but he didn't think she had made any particular friends. He had been sorry to lose her when McInnes telephoned one day to say she would not be coming in again. He had wanted to speak to her himself, but Wayne wouldn't allow it. He had not heard that she had disappeared and was clearly worried for her.

'My wife and I give a garden party in the summer each year for my staff', he told the detectives. 'The McInnes's only came once, and I did notice that Rita seemed a different person in her husband's company, very wary and inhibited. He, in contrast, was extremely outgoing, charming all the lady employees and such like. He drank quite a bit, too, I noticed. I got the impression that he felt he could do what he liked, and that he really dominated Rita. She was the one who had to stay dry, for example, so she could drive them both home. I felt sorry for her, and I often tried to give her the opportunity to talk about it afterwards, but she was definitely the loyal type and never spoke up.'

Mr. Murry then asked a couple of women from the sales section to step into his office, so that Jack and Holly could quiz them too. Both confirmed, in the main, what he had already told them. Rita was friendly but highly discreet. She never gossiped about anyone, and she never spoke about personal matters. The only person they thought she might have confided in was another Rita, Rita Punnett from Australia, who had been taken on a year or more earlier on a temporary basis to help with lettings when a new block of luxury apartments was opened and Murry's had twenty-five of them on the books all at once. The Aussie Rita was such an extrovert, you couldn't help but like her, they said. But Rita Punnett had returned to New South Wales after she left the job a few weeks earlier, when almost all the new flats had been let or sold. It wasn't much of a lead.

Before dismissing the two women, Jack asked if they had ever met Wayne McInnes and what they thought of him. They both remembered him from Mr Murry's garden party and had been flattered by him at first for his cheeky comments; but they both soon saw through this empty repartee. 'It was all flannel, you could tell', one of them said. 'I wouldn't let him sell me a house'. 'I wouldn't let him sell me a doormat', rejoined the other.

It was clear that, ultimately, they had not found him trustworthy or likeable at all.

Hopes rose briefly, about six further weeks into the enquiry, when a woman's body, comparable to Rita's, was found washed up on a beach in Cornwall, but the DNA tests did not match. At first, Holly suspected the possibility that Wayne had rigged the hairbrush they had collected from among Rita's possessions, so they asked for a blood sample from Hazel, as her DNA would be measurably close to her mother's. The detectives had to admit they had nothing new, though, when Hazel's DNA proved more of a match for the hairbrush than for the Cornish corpse.

It was a frustrating time. More months went by without any progress. Occasional reports of sightings, in Sussex and further afield, turned out to be false alarms. After a year, Jack's chief suggested closing the enquiry, which would have meant Jack and Holly no longer having an excuse to meet to discuss the case; but finally he agreed to a three-month extension before they would have to relegate the matter to the 'Cold Case' file. Fortuitously, only days before that time limit expired, and just ten days before Holly began investigating her golf course mystery, there was a dramatic development.

It came from the Norfolk Constabulary in Norwich. A routine message reached Jack's computer stating that a woman had visited the Police Station in Sheringham claiming to be Rita McInnes. The woman said that she had left her home and her husband deliberately, and that she was perfectly alright. She was planning to divorce Wayne, and did not want him knowing her whereabouts. Attached to the report was a message, 'Can we take her name off the missing-person's register now?' Jack's immediate instinct was 'No'.

When he contacted Holly that same morning, they discussed the possibilities, including the idea that Wayne had arranged for someone to impersonate his wife, travel to Norfolk and make the reported claim. They asked the Norfolk Police to ask the woman to return, or visit her at the address she had given, to obtain fingerprint and DNA samples. It was a shock then, a few days later, when the results appeared to confirm the woman's identity as the missing Rita. Jack, his boss, Holly and Laura Garbutt then held a conference by telephone, the upshot of which was that, as this was still officially a murder enquiry, the two detectives would go to Norfolk and interview Mrs. McInnes, assuming she would co-operate.

Jack said he would make the call, not entirely trusting Holly to stay neutral and keep calm on the phone. 'How could she just leave her daughter like that?' Holly had been incandescent when first hearing the news.

'You haven't completely forgiven your mother yet, have you, Angel?' Jack had said gently. 'You know we can't afford to let that affect your judgement in this case.'

'It won't... I won't let it.' Holly was irritated. 'I do know how to be professional, Jack. I'm not going to judge Mrs McInnes. I'm sure she had perfectly good reasons, leaving so suddenly without letting anyone know; but I do really want to know what they were.'

Jack had been sympathetic but firm. 'If you can't get control of yourself and your feelings, Angel', he said, 'I will not be asking you to come with me'. So she assured him again that she would remain perfectly calm.

THE 6TH CHAPTER

It was two hundred miles to Sheringham by car, or a five-hour train ride involving changes in London and Norwich. After discussion, they decided to go by road and take turns driving the unmarked police vehicle. It was going to be a long day; but Jack still felt the need to restrain Holly from speeding as the needle tended to rocket above seventy on the motorways when she was at the wheel. 'Do you always drive this fast?' he asked her one time. Eyes focused intently on the road ahead, Holly slowed down just a little, but she did not reply.

They switched over after stopping for petrol. Holly noticed immediately how cautiously and correctly Jack handled the car. 'I did the advanced driving course once', he explained. 'And I was a traffic cop for a couple of years, remember. I saw many hideous accidents, most of them preventable; most caused by people speeding. I just make it a rule to go quietly, always stay back from the car in front and leave plenty of room to stop. I won't let anyone get too close behind me either. I draw away or let them pass. It doesn't do any harm.'

Holly was chastened, and as they went along admitted to feeling rather tense. 'I had a dream about my mother last night', she said. 'It wasn't horrible. She was just there, at the end of a passageway of some kind, as if she was waiting for me.'

'Maybe you're right', she added. 'This case has got to me more than I realized.'

'You'll be fine, Angel', Jack replied, giving her a reassuring glance. 'You are a true professional, no doubt about that at all.'

They took another break later for coffee, but Jack volunteered to carry on driving. 'I want you rested, not wound up like a Dinky Toy', he said.

Holly did not resist. They were motoring on in silence through the landscape, flat Norfolk farming country, when Jack switched on the radio. Holly said she preferred news and current affairs programmes, but Jack insisted on tuning in to a classical music station. 'It's soothing', he said, as they listened first to a Vivaldi concerto and then a gentle piece by Ravel.

'It was Brian who got me interested in classical music', Jack mentioned, switching the radio off again when the programme reached a commercial break that was going on too long. 'He's much more knowledgeable and educated about such things than me.'

'How did you two meet?' Holly enquired, 'If you don't mind me asking'.

'I nicked him', said Jack.

'You arrested him?' Holly could hardly believe this. 'What for?'

Jack recounted how Brian, having finished university in London, had come to Brighton after being appointed to a job in local government. Having to repay his student loan, he had been forced to stay in cheap, poor quality lodgings. He didn't know anybody in Sussex. On his twenty-second birthday, he had decided to go out and treat himself. In a fashionable downtown bistro, he had ordered a meal of crab-filled ravioli, then Mediterranean rabbit stew, together with a bottle of Côtes du Rhone that he must have drunk rather quickly. After that, he had gone, for the first time in his life, to a gay bar. This was in The Lanes; and there he had started drinking Brandy Alexanders. Soon, a truck-driver type with a paunch and bad breath came over to where he was sitting and tried chatting him up. Brian was either too polite or too frightened to tell him to get lost. He just sat there drinking more cocktails while the other fellow boasted about sexual exploits. His conquests, apparently, included both men and women.

Holly was sympathetic. 'How awful!' she said. 'It must have been a nightmare... What happened?'

Jack said Brian realized he should simply have left the bar. He went to the toilet and was on his way out, but suddenly couldn't face spending the rest of the evening alone in that unwelcoming flat. He returned to the table, where another drink stood waiting for him. Of course, he did not know it had been spiked, and that he was now drinking a nutmeg-sprinkled cocktail containing not only brandy, crème de cacao and cream, but also a pulverized Ecstacy tablet. When this began taking effect, he went wild.

'The drug took away his inhibitions and at the same time made him totally paranoid', explained Jack, 'To the extent that he got up and started punching people he thought were laughing at him.'

It had not taken long for a couple of bouncers to throw the hapless Brian out on the street, where he again began aggressively accosting innocent passers-by.

'Then, as luck would have it, I arrived on the scene', Jack told Holly. 'If you believe in luck... Maybe it was fate! Anyway, I was doing some overtime in uniform that evening, which was easy to do in those days. Brian was swearing at a young woman and raising his fist threateningly when my partner, John Helmsley, and I came around the corner. It turns out he had already struck the woman once. The first thing I saw was the boyfriend charge into Brian with a rugby tackle, forcing him over backwards onto the plate glass window of a bookshop. Luckily it was reinforced and didn't break; but as the young couple backed away I could see Brian lying there pretty dazed. I went over to him while John spoke to the lovers, taking their names and contact details and asking for a statement. The woman had a fresh cut on her cheek, and they wanted to press charges, so there was nothing for it. I had to arrest Brian.'

'It must have been fate indeed', said Holly.

'He hadn't been knocked out, I don't think', Jack continued, 'But he was clearly in no state to go home; so I cautioned him, then called an ambulance and escorted him in it to A & E. When the doctors at the County Hospital found out he'd been drinking, and the X-ray showed no skull fracture, they weren't interested in keeping him for observation, so I had to arrange a taxi to take him home, once he had calmed down.'

'Was he still paranoid by then?' Holly asked.

'No… Just sleepy,' replied Jack. 'Anyway, I had booked him for being a public nuisance, drunk and disorderly, possibly also for ABH, so John Helmsley and I arranged an interview at the station a few days later. Brian, of course, was very worried about his new career in public service. He arrived with his solicitor, very sober and sheepish, and told us all about what had happened that evening. He was so apologetic. He was also very grateful to me in particular for, as he thought, protecting him, taking him to the hospital and so on. I found myself feeling a bit sorry for him. In the end, I said in my report that this was out of character, his first offence, and that he was properly contrite. I gave the opinion that the chances were he'd learned his lesson. In the end, despite her boyfriend's protests, the girl who Brian attacked changed her mind about pressing charges. The magistrate let him off the public nuisance issue with an absolute discharge and no more than a stern warning. His employers were never told.'

'But how did you actually get together then?' Holly persisted.

'He was so grateful, you see… Brian, I mean,' said Jack. 'He knew my name and had my police number, so he had no problem tracing me. Then, after it was all over, he sent me a gift. This was unexpected, and, of course, unnecessary. I knew he couldn't afford much.'

'It might also have been unethical, Jack', Holly teased him.

'Not for him to offer, but for you to accept it.'

'I wasn't going to… Until I opened it, Angel', Jack replied. 'But, after I'd seen that it was not too expensive, and that it was so special, I couldn't resist. I'll bet you've never tried 'The Botanist'. It's Dry Gin from Islay… Wonderful stuff! It's like ordinary gin but supercharged with masses of extra aromatic herbs from the Hebridean islands. A gift-wrapped bottle of that exquisite nectar was Brian's thank-you present; so, of course, I had to thank him in return. Naturally I hesitated, but I liked the lad, and felt protective towards him. I didn't expect him to fancy me or anything; and I didn't think anything would come of it, but it just seemed the decent thing to do… Anyway, I sent him a card and invited him out for a coffee. That was the start of it.'

Jack smiled, giving a small suppressed sigh. Holly noticed his eyes growing a little misty.

'We met at the garden centre by the race track one Saturday morning', Jack went on. 'There's a nice café there, and it seemed a safe neutral place. The lad seemed a bit low, so I asked him if his job was the problem; but no… The work was fine. He was doing well and already hoping for promotion; but he was upset about the terrible place he was living in. I said it couldn't be all that bad, but he challenged me to go and see for myself. So I did… And it was genuinely awful, Angel. An utter disgrace!'

'You know those elegant, white-fronted Regency buildings in Adelaide Crescent near Palmeira Square, built long ago for the gentry? Some of them are now real rabbit warrens inside. Those money-grabbing landlords have divided and sub-divided them into numerous one- and two-roomed hell-holes, many of them with no proper plumbing, just a single wash-basin within and a communal shower/toilet facility shared by four or five flats along each corridor. It's shameful, Holly! Some of them don't even have a window. They are all filled by people on benefits or low incomes, of course. Brian's flat, on the ground floor, at least had three rooms, including a small bathroom and kitchenette. It was one of the better apartments, but it was still dreadful.'

'The funny thing, when I told my Mum about it later, is that it was she who insisted we offer the boy a room in our house. She always had a good heart, my Mum. When I called him to make the offer, I don't know who was more grateful when he jumped at it: him or me.'

'My big sister, Carol, had moved out, you see', Jack continued. 'She's an architect and lives in London now. After Dad died, Mum asked me to come back and live with her for a bit, so she wouldn't be lonely, and I was still there. We had plenty of room. It's the house we still live in now, if you hadn't realized. Brian moved into Carol's room, once we'd had it redecorated.'

'And what did your Mum think of it, when you and Brian became an item?' Holly asked, friendly curiosity getting the better of her.

'Ha!' Jack chuckled. 'It was Mum who spotted it. She saw what was going on between me and Brian, our feelings for each other, before we did; well, before I did anyway… Come to think of it, I wonder if she always knew I was gay. She never said anything when dad was alive; and I never said anything either. I'd barely even admitted it to myself by then, and I'd never had any close gay friends. On the other hand, Brian didn't try to conceal it, like me. He was always open about his sexuality and, to my pleasant surprise, Mum was alright with that. She was a very warm, loving person; and she probably found it easier to show him affection than me. She definitely came to love Brian as much as me in the end. Anyway, she must have said something to him because, after he'd been living in the house just a few weeks, he came into my room one evening. I was nervous; for several reasons, as you can imagine. I must have said something like, "We'd better not, because Mum wouldn't like it"; but he just laughed, kissed me on the mouth and told me to stop worrying, "It was all her idea", he told me. "She's downstairs now watching 'Strictly' with the sound up… Told me to pay you a little visit! I don't think she could bear you not to have what we all know you really want." And, do you know, Angel? I think I cried with relief. Afterwards, when we went downstairs, Mum just made us all a cup of tea.' Jack sighed again. 'It was meant to be, Angel, don't you think?'

Holly knew the pair had been happy together for years, too late by far – even if she had wanted – to issue any words of caution. 'I think it's a lovely story', she said, 'But I can understand why you haven't told many people in the force about the relationship. They probably know, though. Don't they? I mean… You told me once about your unmentionable nickname.'

'It can come out properly when I retire', Jack offered, 'But I'd prefer you to keep the details to yourself for the time being, if you don't mind.'

'When *are* you going to retire, Jack?' Holly asked, suddenly inquisitive. 'You must be nearly fifty by now, aren't you? You could go soon, couldn't you? We only have to do thirty years on the force.'

'You're right, as usual', said Jack. 'I could go in two years, but it's about Brian again. I don't want to retire much before he does, which won't be for ages. I'll do another ten years at least…

I enjoy the job mostly. It's satisfying… And I'm not cut out for gardening, sitting at home watching daytime television and that sort of thing.'

'You could always get some voluntary work', Holly suggested; but Jack did not seem interested in pursuing that line of thought. She was silent for a few minutes, then, looking out of the window, she noticed a field full of Peruvian llamas, as well as a few sheep.

'Look at those daft creatures!' she said. 'I wonder if they're missing the mountains.'

———————

They reached the picturesque seaside town of Sheringham at about one-thirty. Finding a place to park near The Esplanade, they strolled along until finding a bench, where they sat to eat sandwiches and drank bottled water. The September sun shone brightly, but there was a chill in the breeze. Nearby, a couple of seagulls were taking turns foraging for scraps in an overfull waste bin. 'Just like Brighton', said Jack. To while away time before their appointment with Rita McInnes, he took from his pocket the crossword he'd been working on.

'Come on, Angel', he said. 'Give me a hand with this clue: "Tender working with surgeries"; two words, the first word has ten letters beginning with "r"; the second word has five letters. Any ideas?'

'I'm not very good at crosswords', Holly replied, turning her attention to a man on the beach, struggling to put up a wind-break while his wife and two small children stood by with worried looks on their faces. 'I expect it's an anagram of "tender" and "surgeries"' said Jack.

'Who do you think you are?' Holly asked, teasing, 'Inspector Morse?'

'I've got it... "Registered Nurse". How about that?' Jack was delighted. 'That helps... Now, "butter" – that's the clue: four letters beginning with "g".'

At two o'clock sharp, the duo stood outside a small, odd-looking house in the Driftway, a cul-de-sac running south-west from the seafront. Looking around, Jack noted that this strange dwelling must have started out as half of a fisherman's winter storehouse for boats, nets and tackle, a simple rectangle with corners of brick and walls of inlaid flint-stones. The frontage of the northern half of the divided building was dimpled, the flints heavily over-painted in cream. Lintels had been engineered into the original plain walls to allow insertion of attractive white-framed windows and a single, cheerful blue door. Incongruously, the southern side of the building in no way matched its twin, except in dimensions. The flints here were exposed, and fewer, smaller windows fronted the lane. The only door in that half was set around the corner into the southern side wall. Once part of the very fabric of this coastal village, the cottage now seemed sadly out of place. Modern, brick-built houses hemmed it in on either side, and opposite stood an unprepossessing 1960's four-storey apartment block. Time on that spot seemed momentarily to be holding its breath. Everything was perfectly still and silent in the roadway as Holly leaned forward and gave the bell a firm press.

The two detectives listened as the sound of chimes died away. Nothing appeared to be moving. Nevertheless, a few seconds later, the door swung quietly open. The woman confronting them with a steady gaze seemed youthful. She had short blonde hair. Her clothing, although colourful, was simple and plain. Her calm look radiated confidence; and none of this – except perhaps her hair colour – was what they had expected. Holly, Jack noted, seemed suddenly disconcerted. He was about to step forward and break the ice with introductions, when the person they had travelled all morning to see stepped back and beckoned them in.

'I'm Rita McInnes', she said in a clear, mellifluous voice. 'Usually known hereabouts though as Rita Punnett'.

The doorway led directly into a small, neat kitchen. There were fresh flowers in a vase on the dresser. The sickly-sweet scent of lilies filled the air in a way that Holly found unpleasantly stifling, reminding her of funerals. Their hostess ushered them through into the other downstairs room and asked them to sit. A wooden staircase in one corner clearly led to the upstairs apartment, where there could only have been room for a bedroom and small bathroom. The ceiling was low and Jack had to bend forward. A couch and two arm-chairs stood either side of an empty wood-burning stove, a low table between them. Jack, taking command, decided on one chair, motioning the house's occupier to the other. Holly busied herself with the tape-recorder; finding somewhere to plug it in, attaching the microphone lead, and placing the microphone stand on the table; then took her place on the couch. When all were seated, Jack conducted the necessary formalities. Without further prompting, the machine whirring softly, Rita McInnes began telling her story.

'I was unhappy in my marriage as soon as I realized my husband had never intended to remain faithful', she began. 'Soon after he left college, Wayne started working for my father. Dad had always wanted a son and Wayne knew how to play on that. He was often at our house. Mum and Dad always made a great fuss of him, which he adored. I was only sixteen when he first came into our lives. He was handsome and charming, so of course I fell for him. I don't think he noticed me at first, but later on he did. My parents trusted him, and we were quite often left alone in the house. He was the first boy I kissed; and the first I went to bed with, if you could call it that; more of a fumble on the sofa that led to something I wasn't ready for… Not at seventeen.'

She spoke in matter-of-fact tones, not like someone on the lookout for sympathy.

'Soon', she said, 'I was pregnant.'

'How did you feel?' Holly, although schooled to avoid interrupting, could not stop herself asking.

'I was angry... A bit scared. I felt too stupid for words to have let it happen... But mostly I was angry with Wayne. He should have prevented it, I thought; but it eventually dawned on me that he had planned the whole thing. His intention had always been to marry the boss's daughter; and that's what happened. My parents were a little bit shocked by the pregnancy, but I could see my Dad was secretly delighted; and Mother went along with him in this as in all things. No-one cared about my feelings or what I might have wanted. We were married, and then I lost the baby on the honeymoon. It would have been funny if I hadn't been in such a dreadful predicament.'

'I became seriously depressed afterwards', she continued after a brief pause. 'Daddy had set Wayne up as a partner in the business and given us a brand new house to live in: one of the company's latest upmarket developments. Everyone said how lucky I was; but I felt wretched inside. They insisted I see a doctor, who said I was depressed and prescribed medication. When that didn't work, they sent me to a psychiatrist, a woman as it happens, who also said I was depressed and gave me stronger medication. All that did was to make me sleep all day and go around feeling like a zombie. In the end, I refused to take the tablets. There was talk of giving me shock treatment, but I refused that as well. I said I wanted a job. I was eighteen. I needed something to do. My Dad arranged for me to start, part-time at first, for a chain of estate agents he used for selling some of his properties: Derringers. It was easy work and I found I got some satisfaction from it. Later, I went full-time, doing sales and lettings. Then Hazel came along and I stopped.'

Holly, Jack noticed, was sitting quite still, absorbed in the unfolding tale.

'Wayne was never short of girlfriends', Rita McInnes went on. 'Typical of the man he is, he blamed me for his infidelities. When I was depressed, of course, I wouldn't let him near me. Naturally, he accepted this as the perfect excuse to find satisfaction elsewhere; although I'm convinced it would have come to it anyway. When, one day, I accused him of seeing someone else, he threw it back at me. "Why wouldn't I?" he said. "I could have any woman I want." After that, he used to come home and boast of his conquests, as if to rub my nose in his stinking behaviour.'

'I tried to tell my mother about it once.' Rita looked down at her hands, folded in her lap, as she spoke. 'She said she didn't believe me. She told me that, if it were true, it was only to be expected. Wayne had been shocked by the loss of the pregnancy too. He'd told her that he'd been convinced it would have been a son. So it was my job to help him recover from this grave injury to his manhood. "You should get pregnant again", Mother said. So I did... Actually, I had enjoyed sex with Wayne at first; really enjoyed it, I mean. He can be very passionate, and very inventive. So, once I was working and feeling better, I decided to seduce him all over again, even though my enthusiasm for the physical act had waned appreciably. I kept track of my periods, worked out when I was likely to be most fertile, and gave myself to him at those times... Unfortunately, it was a long time before I fell pregnant again. By then, to my certain knowledge, he had been with five or six other women at least. After Hazel was born, he never touched me again, by the way. I dare say I discouraged him; but I think he had lost interest in me for sex. I was just there to mother his child and keep house.'

For the first time, Rita McInnes sounded bitter. Jack leaned forward and pressed the 'pause' button on the tape-recorder, suggesting they take a short break. He asked Holly to fetch water and glasses from the kitchen. By the time she returned, the atmosphere in the room had improved. Taking a sip of water, the fugitive wife indicated she was prepared to resume her tale.

'We carried on with the marriage, keeping up the appearance of being a happy family... Wayne insisted on that. He used to get angry with me and, to be honest, I used to blame myself for the problems we had. I lost all confidence in myself; stopped seeing the few friends I still had; avoided going out, except when absolutely necessary. They were dark days; but things improved once Hazel started school. Eventually, I decided to try and get a job again. That was when I went down and spoke to Mr Murry. I was so relieved when he agreed to take me on. I think that job saved my sanity; and of course it was there that I met the other Rita, Rita Punnett.'

After mentioning the Australian's name, her English counterpart brightened up, carrying on her account with a half-smile playing now on her lips. 'Rita was a Godsend. I mean it! There was a psychiatric hospital in Brighton, which closed when they built the new one at Hangleton. The frontage only was listed, so a development company – not Wayne's – had preserved that part somehow while turning the site into high-end luxury apartments. Mr Murry got the contract to sell some and rent the others. Rita was taken on to do the selling, while I concentrated on rentals. We were both part-time, but we overlapped a lot and covered for each other. Our 'office' was the show flat, and often there was just the two of us there together.'

'I wasn't comfortable with her at first. Rita was everything I wasn't. She was outgoing and confident, always laughing and joking. You couldn't help but like her, though; so eventually I, too, like everyone else, fell under her magical charm. She was a hard worker; but she wasn't one for standing on ceremony. Often at lunchtimes, if neither of us had a client, she would insist we went somewhere for lunch... on expenses; including wine, in her case! But she didn't need any alcohol to give her courage. Whether sober or tipsy, she had no qualms at all talking about herself. Quite quickly, I learned pretty much everything about her.'

'She told me she grew up in Wollongong, on the New South Wales coast, just over fifty miles south of Sydney. Like me, too, she had a rotten marriage; but, unlike me, she did something about it. Wayne only hit me once in anger. He preferred to throw things around, especially when he had been drinking, like the time he threw a whisky tumbler at me in the bedroom when we were arguing about Hazel for some reason. I cut my hand quite badly, picking up the broken shards that time as I couldn't see properly. My eyes were full of tears. Anyway, Rita's husband, Clive, in contrast, used to get physically violent with her. That was standard behaviour.

She said he was an airline pilot who she'd met while working as an air-hostess for a small freight and passenger company flying all over Australia out of Wollongong airport. His first marriage had broken down. She flirted with him, and he was soon hooked. They were married within a month of getting together... But he was the jealous type; always accusing her of becoming too friendly with other men, even if they were just customers of the airline and she was trying to make sure they were enjoying the trip. Anyway, Clive was adept at giving her bruises in places where it wouldn't show when she had her uniform on. She always photographed them, though. Once he twisted one of her fingers until it became dislocated, and she had to go to the hospital, so she got one of the doctors to write her a report about it. As soon as she had enough evidence, she took it to a solicitor and, by threatening Clive with the police and charges of assault, quite quickly obtained her divorce and a very good settlement. That was when she decided to come over here to look up her British roots.'

'I see why you and she might have hit it off', Jack intervened. 'Did she help you deal with Wayne?'

'Not at first', Rita replied. 'I wasn't ready to tell her about the problems in my marriage. I suppose I was still hoping that somehow they would improve... Silly really! I was too much under Wayne's control to think I could do anything about the situation. That's where Rita helped me most. She showed me what might be possible.'

There was a long pause while the betrayed wife continued reminiscing in silence. 'Please go on', Holly broke in after a while.

'Well... I'm not sure how it happened exactly', she said. 'Rita used to talk about her freedom, how wonderful it was to have cash in the bank, to travel and everything. As well as admiring her, I suppose I began to feel envious. "You are lucky!" I think I told her one day; and she must have picked up my change of tone. She immediately asked me why I said that. Up until then she seems to have swallowed my lies about being a dutiful wife with a perfectly happy family. Anyway, I remember sitting in the sun, in the garden of a lovely country pub somewhere, suddenly crying my eyes out. Rita went and bought me a large glass of wine, and we sat there for ages, long past when we should have been back at the show flat, while I poured out my sorry list of troubles... Do you really want to hear about all this?'

Jack simply motioned for her to go on.

THE 7TH CHAPTER

They were travelling back. After doing his stint at the wheel, Jack was dozing in the passenger seat when Holly, driving the Mondeo with more care and attention than formerly, felt compelled to break the silence.

'Have I got this right, Jack?' she started. 'When Rita McInnes told her Aussie namesake she was unhappy in the marriage, they became accomplices… Together they organized her escape from Wayne.'

Sleepy, her companion remained silent for a few moments, collecting his thoughts. They had remained in the cottage listening for almost two hours, and there had been a lot to take in.

'Yes', he agreed eventually. 'It seems Punnett was so incensed by McInnes's story that she persuaded her to run away again, convincing her that with careful planning, a successful getaway was possible.'

'And our Rita was doubtful because her first attempt had failed so badly', Holly added.

The woman had told them how, the first time, she had asked her boss Mr Murry for a month's unpaid leave. She had also withdrawn a thousand pounds in cash from the couple's joint bank account; then she had gone to Eastbourne, checking randomly into a nondescript B & B a few streets away from the seafront. 'I needed time on my own to think things through', she had said. 'I just left… Went by train! It seemed so easy; but then, as time passed and the money began to run out, I didn't know what to do.'

A lawyer she consulted had not been very encouraging, saying that she had few grounds for divorce, giving her the unwelcome advice to go home and patch things up with her husband. Foolishly perhaps, she had then contacted her mother, hoping she would send some extra money to tide her over for a bit longer; but her mother straightaway telephoned Wayne, who drove immediately to Eastbourne to collect her.

'I felt so sorry for her when she told us about that', said Holly. 'She must have felt properly trapped… And things didn't get easier.'

'I often feel sorry for people', replied Jack, 'But you can't let your feelings rule your mind, especially if crimes have been committed.'

'But has a crime been committed?' Holly asked. 'It only counts as fraud if you adopt another name with the intention of profiting at the expense of another person or organization. In this case, Rita McInnes became Rita Punnett with the help of the original Mrs P. She did not use the new name for financial gain at all.'

'You have to admit it was a clever scheme', said Jack, recalling to mind some of the details.

Rita Punnet's grand-parents, her father's parents, had apparently lived all their lives in Sheringham where her grandfather had been a fishmonger. The couple had two sons, but one – the elder – died of diphtheria when he was still a toddler. The other, Rita's father, emigrated, leaving for Australia on the government-subsidized scheme for just ten pounds, in the days before Australia changed over to dollars. He was lonely on the ship, but he met a girl in Melbourne. They moved to Wollongong where he found a job. The couple were soon married and their daughter was born, but the marriage soon floundered. Rita had told her English friend the story of her mother like this: "The Sheila didn't stick around… Went back to Melbourne!" "And when I grew up", she had added, "I was the same… Itchy feet! I left school at seventeen and went up to Sydney as soon as I could… Hung around The Rocks and King's Cross, dossed down in Centennial Park… It was fun!"

Back in Sheringham, at some point, Rita's grandfather had bought the fisherman's building in The Driftway and converted it into a refrigerated cold-store for fish and seafood. He was supplying a good number of restaurants and hotels around Norfolk by then. Unfortunately, he soon after developed a devastating neurological disorder. When the illness struck, and when the inevitable prognosis of continual deterioration, the gradual and cruel loss of essential functions until a premature death, was explained to him, with no prospect of successful treatment, he had the cold-store converted into two dwellings: one to move into, and one to let out, so that his wife would continue to have some kind of income after he'd gone. Then, weakening steadily, he sold off the original family home and the business.

The unfortunate man's granddaughter, Rita Smith, who became Rita Punnett, knew about this only in the vaguest outline, however. She did remember that her father's aged mother used to send her birthday and Christmas cards every year when she was young; but she had never taken the opportunity to ask anyone much about her forbears. When her father succumbed at forty-five to the same tragic condition that had taken his father at fifty-five, it was too late to enquire. Only when the solicitor read her the brief 'Last Will and Testament', leaving her everything, did she discover that, in addition to modest savings, only a few thousand dollars, she also owned a property overseas. Her grandmother, Mrs Smith, in advancing years, it seems, had sold off the second half, but retained one side of the building as her own to live in. On her death, the deeds had been transferred to Rita's dad, and now they had become hers.

There was no question of her inheriting the family illness, she discovered. It passed down the male line only. Nevertheless, the unexpected windfall had helped prompt her decision to leave Clive Punnett and eventually visit the home country; not that she felt particularly British. There was clearly no chance of work for her in Sheringham, a small town, she felt, so she had come to Brighton after once enjoying a day-trip there from London. While working at Murry's, she had continued to use her New South Wales driving licence, and this had given her an idea.

'It was Rita who finally persuaded me to leave Wayne once and for all', Rita McInnes told Holly and Jack. 'She said divorce would be easy if I left and we stayed separated for a couple of years. I just needed to disappear; and the best way, she said, was to assume a new identity for that period. That's why she offered to let me become Mrs Punnett.'

It sounded very strange at first, but when her new friend explained how they could bring it about, she had agreed. Rita P then went ahead and applied for a UK driving licence using a photograph of Rita M, getting her to sign the application form. They did puzzle about how to get someone to countersign the photograph and application. Mr Murry was a possibility, but it would put him in an awkward position later, they agreed, and McInnes vetoed the idea; so then they decided that they probably had to try bribery.

Rita Punnett had been seeing a local businessman she had met one night in a pub. She and the bloke both knew it was a fun relationship, but not one that either expected to last. Because of his gambling addiction, nothing lasted for Percy Edwards anyway. His first wife had tried to stay loyal, but the losses and the lies had strained the marriage past breaking point after fifteen years; and, as for his second wife, she had not even endured the grief he put her through for as much as fifteen months. Percy was lucky, though, to have inherited a printing business, which was basically run for him by a competent manager. Money came into his account on a regular basis, although it was seldom enough to keep pace with his appetites. He was especially vulnerable to the risk – and only occasional reward – dished out by the greedy and impersonal fixed-odds betting terminals to be found in every bookmaker's in town. When Rita explained that her friend needed a favour, and was willing to pay £200 for a couple of signatures, Percy did not think twice.

They used the address of one of the still empty flats in the new development, and Rita P had her utility bills redirected there for a short period. That enabled Rita M to use the driving licence and some electricity statements to set up a bank account for herself in the name 'Rita Punnett', an account which she began topping up with cash removed in unsuspiciously small amounts from her joint account with her husband. Mr Murry was in the habit of paying his staff a generous bonus every year, and Rita asked him for once to give it to her in the form of a cheque made out to Rita Punnett, explaining that it was to repay a loan that she did not want Wayne to know about. It was a large sum, but Andrew Murry complied without asking awkward questions, as she knew he would, and she paid it directly into her new account.

Rita Punnett had been to Sheringham to inspect her property before coming to Brighton. It had remained unoccupied for a number of years and was full of antiquated furniture, all of it covered in cobwebs and dust. Now she hired some cleaners, a clearance firm, a plumber and an electrician, bought some new furniture, and soon had the place quite habitable; a suitable bolt-hole for her friend. Rita McInnes bought a suitcase, some new clothes and toiletries, and stashed them in a cupboard at the show flat. Everything seemed to be ready, except that she did not feel she had put enough money into the new account to last until she could get work, and this gave her an excuse to hesitate. Despite her Australian friend's confidence, it still seemed an enormous risk to be taking. Wayne could be very vindictive, even violent, and there seemed so much that could go wrong.

Mrs Punnett was of the firm opinion that her friend should go ahead and scarper as soon as possible. The flats were being let or sold in increasing numbers, and it seemed likely that Mr Murry would soon give his temporary employee her notice. Mrs P urged Mrs M to leave before that happened, particularly because she had also decided to return to her home country, which she was missing. She tried hard, with the assistance of copious amounts of Chardonnay on several occasions, to persuade Rita to make her break and run for it, but the frightened woman continued to resist.

'I worked out why later', McInnes told Jack and Holly. 'I didn't see it at the time, but there was a deep-seated block in my brain against abandoning Hazel. Fear of failure and dreading Wayne's reaction were the obvious reasons for hesitation, but there was part of me that simply could not leave that child behind.'

'So Rita went home to Australia, but we kept in touch. She bought us both one of those hand-held computers so that we could speak to each other face-to-face. It's very odd, you know, speaking to someone who has just got up when you are preparing for bed. This was the most convenient time for me, though, when Hazel was asleep and Wayne was still out working or whatever he was doing. We spoke nearly every day.'

'So, what changed, Rita?' Jack finally asked. 'What made you leave when you did?'

'Well, it was Hazel', Rita replied, reluctant to admit it. 'I just got so angry with her one day; and then I finally realized that she wouldn't care if I was there or not. Wayne has always been very lenient with her, and I've always been the disciplinarian... Not that I've been very effective. She has her father on a string, if you ask me, indulging her every whim; so she started standing up to me. We had some wonderful times together when she was younger. I suppose I had been hoping we could find that happy harmony again... Anyway, shortly before I left, Wayne started bringing one of his young employees to the house on one transparent pretext or another. Susie, her name was.'

'Ah!' Holly could not hold back the exclamation. She looked up quickly at Jack, whose glance up at the same moment seemed to confirm her own thoughts. 'Wayne McInnes had lied to them.'

'Do you know something about this?' Rita asked, catching the unspoken communication between the two.

'We've met her', Jack replied, retaining as best he could the look of a poker player. 'But please carry on.'

'Well, Wayne clearly had the hots for Susie. It was shameless. This kind of thing had happened before, but it was never so blatant. I walked into the living-room one day and they were sitting beside each other holding hands, looking very much like I had interrupted them kissing. I was angry, of course, but what I said was, "Please don't take the risk of making such an exhibition of yourself in front of your daughter", and at this point Hazel followed me in. I hadn't realized she was behind me; but what surprised and hurt most was when she said, "I think it's rather nice when two people like each other". She was so bold about it. I don't know if you can imagine how I felt. It was dreadful... She obviously knew Wayne and Susie were carrying on, and she evidently approved of it. Even worse, she blamed me for it.

"You're always so cold, Mum!" she said to me once, "No wonder Dad looks elsewhere for affection".'

'I tell you, I ran from the room that day. I just fled upstairs and wept. My heart was broken... That's when I decided to leave. Rita had left me her car to use. It was in a lock-up garage in Hove, and I had transferred my suitcase and a few other things there before she left. When the day came, I disguised myself from any CCTV cameras with a big floppy hat and just strolled down with the key, got in the car and drove north. I was in Sheringham, here in this house, by teatime... It was such a relief!'

'How are you feeling, Angel?' They were approaching the Dartford Crossing. The evening light was fading and the Ford's automatic headlights had just switched themselves on.

'What do you mean?' Holly sounded ruffled.

'Well, there's quite a pattern going on, isn't there; of Mum's betraying or abandoning their daughters? Punnett's mother left her. McInnes' mother informed Wayne of her whereabouts when she was trying to escape him. Rita herself finally left Hazel after Hazel made it clear she supported her father. And your Mum left you and your Dad when you were little. I was just wondering if you're okay...'

'I haven't been thinking about it', replied Holly glibly. 'Now that you mention it, I suppose it makes it feel better somehow. In a strange way, it's good to know that this kind of thing happens to others too.'

Jack realized she didn't want to pursue the subject. 'Let's take a break soon', he said. 'Are you hungry?'

Not long afterwards they pulled into the Clacket Lane service area and went inside for cheeseburgers and fries. When they were seated, Jack pulled out his crossword. 'Goat', he said,

looking up. 'That's "butter"... Four letters beginning with "g".
It's nothing to do with what you spread on toast. The answer's
"goat"; get it, Holly?'

'How do people think up those things?' she replied,
unimpressed.

'My father used to do crosswords', said Jack. 'I'm not like
he was in many things, but he did teach me to love the play on
words. I'm grateful for that.'

Holly did not reply. 'What next?' she said later, nursing a mug
of tea while Jack ate a portion of cheesecake. 'I'm on a training
day tomorrow: "control and restraint" in the morning, and "first
aid using defibrillators" in the afternoon. I could come in early
to do the report with you, if you like.'

'No. I can do it, Angel. I'll re-register the case from "crime"
to "non-crime" while I'm at it. I think I'll do it tonight after
dropping you off, while it's fresh in my mind. And I'll set up a
meeting with Wayne for Friday. I know you want Thursday off.
Give my regards to your Dad.'

It was late when Jack finally arrived home. Brian, in his dressing
gown, was sitting at the felt covered dining table where he was
attempting a challenging 1,000 piece jigsaw. The picture was of
King Tutankhamun's funeral mask on a black background. After
working at the task for several evenings, with less than a third of
it complete, he was beginning to feel stumped when he heard
Jack's car in the driveway. Quickly, he went into the kitchen and
filled the kettle, setting it to boil, returning to the hallway as Jack
was removing his jacket and loosening the knot of his tie.

'You must be exhausted', he said, giving the taller man a
quick friendly hug. 'Come and sit. You've rescued me from the
deadly boy Pharaoh... I've put the kettle on. Do you want tea?'

Jack said he'd prefer a cup of hot chocolate, so they went into the kitchen together. While Brian busied himself with heating the milk, Jack sat at the table.

'You look worried', said Brian. 'Don't fret. Was it a difficult interview?'

'Not especially', replied Jack. 'Actually, I was thinking about Angel.' And he related, without giving names or precise details, the triple saga of mothers disloyal to daughters. 'I had the feeling that this was getting to her', he explained, 'Or rather, that it should have been, more than it appeared to be. She's never spoken about it, has she? I don't think she's ever got over the pain of feeling abandoned.'

Brian's next comment baffled Jack. 'You think she's been for a swim up at Luxor?'

'Whatever do you mean?' he said.

'What I mean, dear man', Brian elucidated, 'Is that maybe our charming, lovely and wonderful friend has ended up in "de Nile"!

'Oh!' He chuckled. 'So she's in denial, and we need to be patient. Is that what you're saying?'

'I'm sure you're right that she was pretty deeply traumatized by her mother's infidelity and departure, and that she still has a lot of work to do to assimilate it, to grow through it… But she's not short of courage, that girl. She'll face it when she's ready, which will probably be when she feels safe enough to do so and not before. That's usually how it works. So, yes, our job is not to force the issue but simply to help her feel safe and appreciated for who she is, not necessarily for what she does.'

'I can see three years of therapy haven't done you any harm ', Jack's sarcasm was distinctly playful, but sounded to Brian as if it had a serious edge. 'You've become quite an expert on human psychology lately.'

'I'm glad you've noticed'. Brian, while trying not to feel undermined, was also genuinely gratified. 'You do realize, I have been working at it; and it's not just all about me. People are put off by Freudian ideas and such like, I know. Well, he did go overboard about sexuality, I admit; but I've been studying the defence mechanisms people use and it is a fascinating subject. It comes in very handy at work, I can tell you, knowing a little bit more than others about what makes them tick.'

'I bet that's true', agreed Jack. 'It would come in right handy in police work as well.'

'Yes', Brian continued, rather breathless with enthusiasm for his subject. 'And one thing I've discovered is that everyone is in denial about something... Usually quite a lot! For instance, pretty well everyone is in denial about death.'

'Now you're growing morbid', said Jack. 'And I'm bushed; so I'm just going to finish this drink, try and help you with that impossible jigsaw for a bit, and then I'm off to my bed.'

Jack's sleep that night was deep, and included exotic dreams about Pharaohs, pyramids and Cleopatra's Needle, which he decided not to mention to Brian the following morning. Now, three days after the Norfolk trip, it was Friday. Holly had just arrived from Chichester, and the two detectives were at the door of Wayne McInnes's mansion, completely unsure as to how he would react to their news.

The property developer came to the door this time in a tailored, red white and blue striped shirt, open at the neck revealing a heavy gold chain. His cuffs were not yet done up; his golden cuff-links trailing. Below the shirt he wore neat grey-flannel trousers and a pair of soft, hand-made, black leather house shoes. As he ushered the detectives directly into the living room, the whiff of his expensive after-shave trailed behind.

As she entered the rather stark room, Holly was struck by how masculine the décor was. Shades of light and dark grey dominated, with black leather upholstery on the armchairs and couches, a modern gas fire recessed into the chimney place, and above the mantel the only colour to be seen: an abstract painting, a kind of nondescript grey and white cloudscape, with a pale yellow-brown wash towards the top left, a small vivid ovoid vermilion blob positioned just below the painting's equator, shifted a few centimetres off-centre to the right, and a brilliant turquoise teardrop on its side towards the bottom left. It had an astonishing effect. Holly didn't think she liked it at all, but she had to admit the power of those bright blue and reddish spots to draw and hold one's attention. It was mesmerizing.

Fortunately, Jack was immune to such visual niceties. Ready to begin as soon as the three of them were seated, he was however forced to pause when the door wafted quietly open again and young Hazel entered the room.

'Hello Dad', she said coyly. 'Is this about Mum? I want to listen too please.'

'Of course, Sweetie', her father replied. 'Come and sit here with me.'

Holly could now see what Hazel's mother had earlier described. Father and daughter were bonded almost umbilically close. Without thinking, Wayne was holding out one arm and Hazel automatically began skilfully threading the links through the cuffs as if she had been doing this for him for years. Such a hand-maidenly vision helped Jack decide to say what he had come to say without trying to sugar-coat it for the fifteen-year-old. Rita McInnes had given full permission for him to tell Wayne her story, so he launched right into it without frills, judging now that a brief account would be best.

He told father and daughter little more than that Rita had been unhappy. She had planned her escape. A friend had offered her a place to stay, more or less rent-free, in another part of the country, and had also made available a small car for her to use. She had set up a separate bank account and was using a new identity for the time being.

'From the police perspective', he concluded by saying, 'This is now a domestic rather than criminal matter. Do you have any questions?'

Apart from switching hands, so that Hazel could fix his other cuff-link, Wayne had remained remarkably still while Jack was speaking. Now, neither he nor Hazel enquired about Rita's state of health or well-being. Holly was shocked, too, by how little interest they showed in the reasons for her departure, or in the means by which she had carried out her escape. Wayne McInnes simply said, 'What is she going to do now?' He did not seem unduly upset. Hazel, her father's attire satisfactorily attended to, simply sat there hugging her knees, with her feet curled up on the couch, an unsettlingly smug little grin playing about her glistening lips. Holly took to gritting her teeth to avoid revealing the disgust she couldn't help feeling.

Responding to Wayne's query, Jack took the opportunity to pass on the message from Rita that he would shortly be hearing from her solicitor about a divorce.

'I won't have to go and live with her, will I, Daddy?' Hazel piped up in alarm.

'I shouldn't think so, Darling', her father replied soothingly. 'Not if you don't want to… She will get a big settlement from me, of course. I may have to sell off, or make over to her, one or two properties. She'll be very comfortable if her lawyer's any good; but at least we won't have to move out of this lovely home. I'm sure of that. The divorce courts will look favourably on the idea of you staying put because, after all, any house move would threaten to interrupt your education, and no court would allow that to happen.'

'Thank you, Officers', he said, turning to face them with an air of dismissal. 'I guess it's up to us to take it from here... Would there be anything else?'

As one, Holly and Jack rose immediately to leave.

THE 8TH
CHAPTER

Without ever saying so, some of her colleagues tended to think of Detective Inspector Laura Garbutt as heavy. This was not only in terms of physical bulk, but also in the sense of being a relentlessly serious person. She exuded a tiring kind of desperate 'gravitas', having no time or patience for levity or distraction. Unconcerned with appearances, she usually wore an unflatteringly tight-fitting tunic and little make-up. Her steely-grey hair was cut short 'en brosse' as the French say, which means standing up like the bristles of a brush. She wore plain, steel-rimmed spectacles atop her somewhat fleshy nose, below which incongruously thin lips encircled a slim mouth that sat enfolded by what, being somewhat pendulous, were better described as jowls rather than cheeks.

In keeping with the no-nonsense personality, her office at Sussex House suggested nothing of a personal nature. There were no pictures, no photographs, no knick-knacks or other items betraying any individuality. There was only a desk bearing a telephone and a computer, plus a rectangular maroon coloured plastic laminate-topped table and six black plastic chairs on the opposite side of the room. Three filing cabinets stood against one wall, and a large bare pin-board hung on another. There were venetian blinds but no curtains on the two south-west facing windows, at one of which the career policewoman now stood, gazing sightless at the rooftops below, the sea in the distance, her mind in uncharacteristic turmoil, too disturbed to take in what she saw.

Thirty minutes earlier, she had received a disturbing call from the Chichester pathologist. Dr Narayan had failed to get through to Holly, who had switched her phone to silent while at the McInnes house that morning and did not notice the vibration signals, the phone being in her bag rather than on her person. He wanted urgently to tell her that his continuing examination of the female corpse from the golf club had led to an important discovery. Needing to tell someone, the obvious person was, he thought, Holly's boss.

'The woman's cricoid cartilage has a faint horizontal hairline crack in it', he informed the DI. 'Most likely this means someone applied pressure on it'.

'Therefore she was murdered', the DI interrupted. 'Is that what you're saying?'

'Well... Unlawfully killed... Yes', he replied. 'As you know, the cricoid is a circular ring of cartilage at the top of the trachea, holding it open. Press on it and you occlude the airway, so the person suffocates; but it could only have been pressed very gently, because it appears to have sprung back into place. That's why I didn't spot the fissure or notice anything else wrong when I first examined it externally. Perhaps the cartilage was weaker than usual because of the under-nourished state of the victim. Perhaps the perpetrator also used a pillow...'

'Oh yes!' the DI interrupted again. 'I remember the Home Office pathologist Sir Michael Cherry, years ago. He always told his students that committing murder undetected was easy. "You can't beat a skilfully placed pillow!" he used to say. Do you agree?'

'I think I do. I did not, in this case, detect any bruising, petechial haemorrhages or other external signs of either violence or suffocation. Anyway, I'll write up my preliminary report and send it to you and the Coroner.'

Standing there at the window, the heavy woman was in her heaviest mood, thinking she could have made a colossal mistake. The image of a clothing shop manikin arranged in the red leather chair, giving her the idea of nothing more than a schoolboy prank, had filled her mind the day before, rather than the corpse of a woman indicating a possible murder. She had not taken the case seriously enough. 'Instead of calling in Angel, I should have put a murder squad together there and then', she was thinking. 'Let's hope the delay won't make too drastic a difference.'

She had already told the Chief Inspector, who had immediately taken her to see the Superintendent. He had decided to set up a full investigation squad, meeting later on when all the necessary personnel could be mustered, some of them having to come across to Brighton from Chichester. The Chief Superintendent would be informed, but would probably not intervene directly himself. Holly had also been summoned, of course, by text message. Laura Garbutt, known throughout the force for her steely-eyed efficiency, was now feeling strangely and uncomfortably inept.

Holly had always planned to visit her boss at Sussex House after going to the McInnes house with Jack. On arrival, though, she made her way first to the canteen, ordered tea in a proper cup, also a sausage roll, took her tray, made her way to an empty table, sat herself down and took a welcome bite of the roll before she remembered her phone. Retrieving it from her bag and switching off the silent mode, she was surprised to see she had missed three calls and had four text messages. At the same moment, an officious officer, looking in at the door of the canteen, spotted her and made his way across the room.

'You're wanted upstairs', he barked unceremoniously. 'DI Garbutt's office... Quick-fast!'

'Of course', Holly replied respectfully, unsure why she had been spoken to so rudely, eyeing the gruff bearer of such questionable tidings as he stood a moment, turned abruptly and began walking away like a Sergeant-Major on parade. Shrugging mentally when he had gone, she took a quick gulp of the tea then wrapped the rest of the sausage roll in a paper napkin, putting it cautiously into a compartment of her capacious bag. She stood up then and went quickly to the counter for a disposable cup, pouring the remains of her tea into it, slamming a plastic lid on top. Then, swivelling round, she sat down again at the nearest table. 'I'd better phone Narayan first', she was thinking. 'It's no use going to the boss unprepared'.

Luckily, she got through right away. The doctor told her what he had said to her boss, then added that he had thought of something else. 'The thing is', he spoke hesitantly, 'I don't know what happens to human cartilage if you freeze it and then let it thaw. It's possible it could fracture spontaneously'.

'What are you saying?' asked Holly. 'Are you saying it's not murder now?'

'I'm less sure than I was an hour ago', the pathologist replied. 'Let's put it that way.'

'Have you told DI Garbutt?' Holly was shocked at this new revelation. They had to know for certain that they were dealing with murder.

'Well, I tried telling her', Narayan continued. 'I phoned a few minutes ago, but she didn't want to listen. I think she's made up her mind that the woman was unlawfully killed and that's that.'

'She can be a bit stubborn', Holly commiserated. 'Thanks anyway... I'll see if I can pass on what you've said'.

As it turned out, though, she did not get the chance either. On reaching her boss's office, she was hurried brusquely along the corridor and upstairs to a briefing room where almost forty police officers, technicians and admin staff had gathered. The Coroner's officer from Chichester had also just arrived. When Holly entered, the room was quiet, Detective Chief Inspector Holroyd already on his feet.

Hugh Holroyd had degrees in both law and criminology from Cambridge, explaining why he had quickly been promoted above others with significantly more years of service, including DI Garbutt. Few begrudged him this, however, mainly because he had proved himself capable, friendly and reliable. He smiled a lot, spoke little, listened well, and had the happy knack of making people feel they were as intelligent as he was. A lean figure of medium height, often dressed in grey flannel trousers, dark-coloured shirts and a yellow-brown corduroy jacket, his auburn hair thinning prematurely, he never appeared to offer any kind of threat to junior colleagues, only encouragement. With criminals, though, he had a reputation for being more than tough when the occasion demanded.

'Welcome', and, 'Thank you for coming', he was saying when Holly entered the room, fussily shepherded forward by her boss. 'This is the case of Jane X. DS Angel will now bring you all up to speed... Come on Holly!'

When beckoned, Holly put her plastic cup on a nearby desk and walked over. Holroyd simply waved his right hand forward, this simple gesture serving to both present her and prompt her to speak at the same time. Holly introduced herself again by name, then gave a brief account of the discovery of a naked anorexic woman's body in one of two red leather arm chairs placed on the fifth fairway of the Sussex Royale Golf Club. Photographs and other bits of useful information were already on display. DCI Holroyd announced that this was to be a murder enquiry, then motioned DI Garbutt forward to take over the meeting, while he sat down to observe. The DI then explained that an incident room would be set up close to the golf club's location within a day or two, and began apportioning jobs.

Holly was given the task of liaising with Club Secretary, Peter Harding, and asked to make contact with the club's founding president, Jamie Royle. Missing persons review; local and national publicity; telephone and further face-to-face interviews with club members and staff; house-to-house enquiries; chasing up hospital and dental records; locality CCTV footage examination; further forensic testing: all were considered and each task allocated. There were questions, mostly answered in the negative by the DI, and some discussion. The most helpful suggestion was that they concentrate on removals firms in the area, one of whose vehicles might have been used on that fateful Wednesday night.

After almost an hour, DCI Holroyd took over again, thanked Holly and her boss, delegated two officers to look into fingerprint matches and unsolved missing person cases, then summarized priorities for the whole team. Who was this woman? Who killed her, and who transported her to the golf club? How was it done, and why?

'The motive for the killing is one thing', he said quietly. 'More important, because it will help us solve this case, is the motive for dumping the body where it was, and the manner in which it was positioned very deliberately. This was a message for somebody. We want to know who the message was for... And what it was trying to say.'

That was it. The meeting was over. A few people made their way between the desks to speak to Holly. Some were colleagues she had worked with before wanting to say Hello, and some had more specific questions to ask. Holly's tea was cold by the time she went to retrieve it. Leaving the briefing room, she stopped off in the lavatory to pour the rest down the sink. On emerging, she was slightly disconcerted to find her boss in the corridor, waiting for her.

Back in the barren office of her senior, Holly quickly spoke up first, spending a few minutes relating details concerning the outcome of the McInnes case. After this she picked up her bag, hoping to leave, when she was bluntly instructed to wait.

'We have a new DC starting with the team on Monday', her boss said sternly. 'I want him to work with you, Holly. I think you will be a good teacher. His name is Richard Baum. I think the name may be Dutch, but he's been with the Kent force and comes from Maidstone. Apparently his parents live near here and he wants the transfer to Sussex for that reason.'

Holly remained silent, taking the news on board thoughtfully. It was obviously not a request. On the one hand, it showed that her boss had confidence in her. On the other, she wasn't sure she wanted an inexperienced sidekick hanging around at the start of a murder case.

'I've not met him yet', the DI continued. 'He'll be coming here first thing on Monday. I'll release him to you in the afternoon. Make sure you let me know where you'll be and I'll send him along.'

A few minutes later, Holly found herself in a heavy downpour as she made her way swiftly across the car park, jumping once or twice to avoid the puddles. Despite being uncomfortably wet, she sat still briefly as the Micra's windows immediately steamed up. Having to wait for them to clear before she could head back to Graffham, she removed the neglected sausage roll from her bag and took a bite. It was unappetizing, dry and hard to swallow, but hunger made her persevere. The food felt like lead in her belly. She was thirsty, but had nothing to drink. She found a bag of peppermints in the glove compartment and took one. Starting the engine and turning on the air-conditioning helped clear the windscreen, but still she sat motionless for a while, her mind drifting back to the pathetic corpse she had seen again that morning. 'Who was she? What terrible things had happened to her?' Holly wondered as a decision formed, taking firm hold in her mind: 'I am definitely going to find out'.

Emerging onto the by-pass a few minutes later, she turned on the car radio, tuned to a local station. Someone at the briefing had got quickly down to work. After an item about another train strike on Southern Railway, the announcer stated that the body of a woman in her thirties or forties had been found in countryside near Graffham, and that Sussex Police were requesting anyone with possibly helpful information, for example about a missing person, to get in touch. The next item concerned the breaking up of a protest against fracking somewhere in East Sussex that had already been going on for several days, blocking roads in the area. Uninterested, Holly switched from the radio to the CD player, and soothing sounds soon filled the car. Holly's current favourite was the Shoreham-based 'Guitar Whisperer', Richard Durrant, the recording featuring tracks of cheerfully evocative music from Latin America. Pressing down on the accelerator, Holly was soon humming along with the tune.

At much the same moment over at the golf club, Peter Harding lifted, then abruptly put down again, his mobile phone. There had been a text from Jamie Royle in Chicago: 'The golf has started. Do not call me again until Monday. I do not want to speak to the police.' He decided he would say nothing about this to Holly, only that he was still trying to make contact with Jamie.

It was almost four-thirty, by which time the rain had stopped, when the detective arrived at the club. Holly was a little surprised to see the car park more than half full. She could see no-one playing on the course; but when she went inside the building, the mystery was explained. A large flat-screen television in the member's lounge was tuned to the Ryder Cup golf in America. A good-sized crowd was watching the action. She noticed Mark Berger and Kyle Scott sitting at a table with several others, but before they spotted her, she button-holed the Colonel who was standing near the bar. 'Can we talk?' she enquired. 'I've got a few more questions to ask'.

Peter Harding led the way to his office, repeating before she broached the subject that the club founder was still unreachable. 'Can you give me his wife's address and phone number then, please?' Holly asked. 'She lives nearby, doesn't she?'

Georgina Rosemary Royle, was known to her husband, not always affectionately, by her initials, 'GRR'! She was said to be a tough nut. Harding gave Holly the number, saying that she lived at Rose Cottage, near Duncton, just a few miles from Graffham. Holly phoned immediately, and was eventually informed by Mrs Royle's assistant that she would be expected the following morning at ten o'clock. Speaking to the Colonel again, Holly then broached a different subject. She said her bosses were looking for a building nearby, or part of one, that they could rent and use as an incident headquarters for the next few weeks.

'You might be in luck', he replied. 'The club owns a property, 'Greenings'. It's a three-bedroom house in Graffham village, purchased more than twenty-five years ago when houses were much cheaper than today, for the use of our then head professional, Alex King. It was an incentive. Jamie wanted the best teaching pro he could attract and set out to entice Alex over from Betchworth Park, a golf club near Dorking, where he had already established himself. King was teaching the English

Amateur Women's team, among others, at the time, and his own career also held a few highlights. He was not in Arnold Palmer's league, but Jamie was still very pleased to get him.'

'In fact, I was reading about him in the club's archives the other day, after somebody rang up enquiring about him; a relative, I think', Harding continued. 'In July 1963, for example, King qualified for The Open Championship at Lytham by playing two qualifying rounds. Remarkably, he scored a course record 66 at the nearby St Anne's Old Course in the process. Then he went on to come equal tenth or eleventh in the tournament itself, one of the two top British players in the event.'

Holly wasn't sure what all that that meant, reminding the Colonel that she was hardly an aficionado of golf.

'Well, if someone did that today', he responded helpfully, 'A club professional, not a touring pro; he would be instantly famous and set up for life. He would get many more tournament invitations around the world, also advertising contracts and such. You name it, in fact! He would have got a lot more prize money, too. But Alex, by all accounts, was a modest guy. He came originally from Rothesay, on the Isle of Bute, where his father was the post-master. I never met him, though. He retired in the late '90's and died a few years ago.'

'What happened to the house?' Holly asked.

'Oh, yes...' said Peter Harding. 'I was forgetting... Well, when King left, the new club professional didn't want to live there, so our head green-keeper, Ted Brough and his wife Martha, took it over. They had twin sons and it suited them fine; but he eventually left, and when John Tranter came, we didn't need it. John's single, you see. This was in my time. I think I'd been here about a year then. Anyway, the Board decided to keep it, in case we needed it to use as an employment incentive again, but to rent it out. Now, as it happens, the most recent tenants have just left, only a few weeks ago, and I've been arranging re-decoration and a bit of re-furbishing before we advertise the tenancy again through Smith and Wessons, the local estate agents. I can show it to you now, if you like.'

'Smith and Wessons... Really?' exclaimed Holly. 'I don't believe it'. 'Son of a Gun!' she was tempted to add.

———————

They went quickly in the Colonel's Audi, and were back at the club less than twenty-five minutes later. On brief inspection, Holly thought the house was perfect for the job. She telephoned her boss immediately. Harding said he would arrange it with the agents, and someone authorised by Sussex Police could go through the formalities of renting by the month and collect the keys from their office in Midhurst the following morning.

Back in his office, Holly asked the Colonel to clarify the relationship between Jamie Royle and the club. 'When you said the Board decided not to sell, I was wondering who exactly makes the decisions here.'

'It is a bit complicated', Harding agreed. 'Royle bought Graffham Golf Club, including the existing land, through a company he set up called Regal. It was a subsidiary of Royle Enterprises. In fact, Regal stands for "Royle Enterprises – Golf and Leisure". He also bought the additional farmland through Regal. Sussex Royale Golf Club Limited is, at least nominally, an independent company, rather like any other private members golf club. It has a Chairman, a Treasurer and a Board who are all financially responsible and who therefore make the important decisions. There are also a number of committees: general, membership, handicap, house, and greens committees, for example, with different areas of responsibility, answerable to the Board. All these people are elected by the club's members at the Annual General Meeting in April. I and other staff here are employed by the Golf Club according to a written Constitution. The complication is that the club leases the land and the clubhouse from Regal, and therefore from Jamie Royle. He is also Life President and has full playing membership of the club, as of right. He's a powerful figure, and he likes to get his way so, of course, he tends to be co-opted onto the various committees when he wants to be, and asked his views on anything and everything important.'

'Doesn't that sometimes leave you with a sense of split loyalty?' Holly's question was highly perceptive and took the Colonel aback. He found himself thinking that he often felt more like Jamie Royle's employee than the club's. 'The lines are a bit blurred sometimes', he admitted while blushing. 'Most of the time what Jamie wants is also what's good for the club, so there's no allegiance problem. I occasionally get the impression he would like me to be his agent here; not exactly his spy, but he does like to know what's going on, especially when he's away, as at present.'

'It seems odd to me, then, 'Holly interrupted swiftly, 'That you haven't been able to reach him for the last two days!'

The Colonel blushed again under the detective's steady gaze, but simply shrugged in reply. 'I don't control him, you know', he finally managed to say.

'I don't suppose anybody does', replied Holly. 'Tell me what you know about his business affairs. How did he get to be so rich? Regal are massive now, aren't they? Electronics, computers, music, publishing, clothing and sporting goods shops, sports academies... What else?"

'I don't know where his wealth came from', said Peter Harding. 'I've never discussed it with him. He has an office for Royle Enterprises in Horsham with a secretary I've spoken to once or twice. I can give you her details, if you like. But that's not the main office of Regal, and anyway, I think he leaves the main running and development of that company to his business partners. Some of the companies using the name Regal are franchises, companies set up by Regal and either sold on, with the new owners paying royalties for use of the name, or managed as independent subsidiaries.'

'You seem to know quite a lot', Holly remarked, making a mental note to investigate this further. She was always suspicious of people with enormous wealth. Changing tack, though, she asked, 'What about the new professional? Gary Brooker is it? I saw his name outside the professional's shop downstairs. Is he around? I haven't seen him yet.'

'Well, firstly, he isn't the one who followed Alex King. We had someone else for a few years, until he decided to go back to Germany. Erich Wessell was his name. It didn't work out too well, I'm afraid... Not one of Jamie's better picks. Apparently Wessell cured him of slicing all his drives or something when he was visiting Germany one year, so Jamie signed him up; but the members didn't take to him, I gather... Too serious! Gary is very different.'

'Where is he?'

'Oh!' Harding was again startled by Holly's abrupt tone and direct manner. 'Gary's with Jamie in Chicago', he said. 'He likes to take him on a trip from time to time. It's something of a reward for his services here. Also, I think, Jamie uses it as an opportunity. Gary is such a terrific match golfer, and Jamie is very useful off his handicap of five. When they team up, they are hard to beat. I've heard them boasting about it together in the bar downstairs on occasion. They take on opponents for money, and I imagine the stakes are quite high.'

'He likes to win, then... Jamie?'

'I think that's fair comment. Yes!'

Holly left the Colonel alone to tidy and lock up his office. She had reached the bottom of the stairs when she heard cheers and some clapping through the open doorway to the member's lounge. Investigating the applause, she was just inside the door when Kyle spotted her from across the room. Standing up, waving excitedly, he called out with typically cheerful Caribbean cheek. 'Hi there, Missy!'

Holly steeled herself not to react, but then another voice whispered the same phrase softly in her left ear: 'Hi there, Missy'. A shiver ran down her spine. This was not a welcome sensation, but it was not entirely unpleasant either. The voice belonged to Mark Berger who, taking advantage of a commercial break, had taken a comfort stop in the men's room, creeping quickly and quietly up behind Holly on returning to the lounge.

'Oh… Sorry!' He said, seeing her jump, putting a hand gently round her shoulder. 'I didn't mean to scare you… Can I buy you a drink?'

Holly let the hand remain in place for a few seconds. Under circumstances like these, she would normally yank the arm away and possibly also apply a painful wrist-lock, or at least tell the chap to get lost. This time, however, on reflection, she decided she quite liked the attention. She even agreed to a drink. 'It'll have to be a soft one, though', she added. 'I'm still on duty, you know.'

'What can I get for you, Mr Berger?' The barman said courteously, his accent unmistakeably Irish. Mark looked across at Kyle who, still standing, telegraphed his preference by sign language, holding up an empty glass. 'Two pints of Sussex Ale, please', he replied, 'And… What will it be, Detective Angel?'

'What do you suggest, Frank?' she asked the barman, whose name she remembered from interviewing him the day before. 'This apple and mango juice is very popular, Madam', said Frank. 'You can call me Frankie, by the way', he added. 'Everybody does.'

'Thank you, Frankie', Holly answered. 'I think I'll just have mineral water this time.' Frank reached into a fridge behind him. Turning, he held out two bottles. 'Still or sparkling?' he asked. Holly just pointed to the one with the bubbles.

Moments later, Mark led her between tables to where Kyle was sitting. He was about to introduce her to the others when the man sitting beside Mark's empty chair got to his feet and offered Holly his seat, then ambled back across to the bar. As Holly sat down, the lady opposite leaned forward with a smile. 'Hello, Dear', she said. 'I'm Marjorie Willis, and this is my husband, Dick. How lovely to meet you… But what a terrible job you have. I don't know how you do it.'

Holly gazed at the grey-haired woman across the table, taking note of the wispy hair, light eye make-up, face powder and slightly smudged lipstick that failed adequately to camouflage the heavily wrinkled, blotched face of a lifelong outdoor addict and cigarette smoker. She noted too the slicked-down, darkly oiled head hair and luxuriant accompanying growth on the upper lip of the man sitting beside her, dressed in a faded tweed jacket with a similarly faded brown choker at his neck. Although the pair looked elderly, and decidedly 'gone-to-seed', something about them strangely lifted her spirits. The couple seemed to give off a natural and genuine warmth of feeling that made you like and trust them immediately.

'Don't embarrass the girl, Marge!' Dick Willis immediately cut in. 'I'm sorry!' He started to apologize.

'No… Really', replied Holly. 'It's alright.'

'I was thinking of that gruesome case a few years ago', Mrs Willis persisted, 'When that little girl's body was found in woodland near Pulborough. It must have been awful to be involved in that one… Such a heartbreaker!'

'You mean Sarah Payne', Holly said. 'That was twelve years ago. I was still a probationer then, not a detective. Like you, I only heard about it from the news. She was eight years old, much younger than the woman we found here, by the way, and she was abducted by a known paedophile. He's still in prison, and likely to stay there for a long time to come.'

'So you can definitely rule him out!' Mrs Willis replied. 'It makes you wonder how anyone could do such a dreadful, dreadful thing. It's so wonderful that people like you want to catch evildoers like that.'

Holly was about to thank her, but Dick Willis was up on his feet. 'Come on, Marge,' he said. 'That's enough bothering the detective. Drink up! The morning games are over. If we go home now and get some tucker, we can watch the afternoon matches there.'

'Oh, yes!' said Holly, who had barely glanced at the television since entering the room. 'How are things going in the Ryder Cup?'

'Thank goodness for Poulter and Rose', said Mark, relieved to be back in the conversation. 'We... Europe that is... Were two-one down until that pair managed a fine win over Woods and Stricker... so, it's two-all at the halfway stage today. The afternoon fourball matches have already begun though, and unfortunately we're already a couple of holes down in the first match... Of course, there's plenty of time...'

His voice trailed off. After the Willis's left, Kyle made his excuses as well. Unable to think how else to keep Holly entertained, but keen that she should stay, Mark started to tell her about Dick Willis. 'He's a remarkable man', he said. 'With that great walrus moustache, he looks just like the famous James Braid. Braid was a champion golfer and later a wonderful golf course designer. Between 1901 and 1910, he managed to win The Open five times. Originally from Scotland, he eventually settled down as the club professional at Walton Heath in Surrey. If you go into the main lounge in the clubhouse there, you will see a near life-size, full-length portrait of Braid in pride of place; and the thing is… He's the spitting image of Dick. I couldn't believe it when I first saw it.'

Mark looked up, glad to see that Holly was at least faintly amused by the astonishing resemblance he was describing. 'Anyway', he continued, 'Dick's eighty-six now and still walks round the course, playing a few holes at least twice a week, carrying his little set of six clubs in a lightweight bag on his back. He still manages a pretty good game, being particularly wizard with the putter. And we know his age precisely because a week or two back he went out for a game with a new member who, impressed by Dick's wondrous skills, asked how old he was. This fellow is in his early forties and, when Dick told him the answer, he replied, "I don't think I'd like to live to be eighty-six". Quick as a flash Dick's answer was classic… "I'll bet you would if you were eighty-five!" Isn't that something?'.

Holly laughed. 'That's wonderful', she said. 'But I must be going now, Mark.' She had finished her drink and was beginning to realise that she was very tired and very hungry. She wanted to go home. It was tempting, momentarily, to accept Mark's immediate offer to buy her dinner, but she knew she had to decline. 'I don't think that would be appropriate', she said, pointing out that she was still involved in the early stages of a murder investigation that might have something to do with one, some, or all of the members of the club, including Mark himself. 'Besides', she said conclusively, 'I'm sure you don't want to miss out on the rest of the golf.'

Unable to think of a suitably witty reply, Mark just shrugged and made a sad clown's face. As he hoped, once again, Holly laughed.

THE 9TH CHAPTER

When she awoke the following morning, Holly was still caught up in a dream. Lying on her side, she experienced the clear sensation of someone, a man, enfolding her from behind in a warm loving embrace. Without moving or opening her eyes, she basked, lingering in the glow of the moment. She was surprised but pleased, and her thoughts turned immediately to Mark; to his whisper in her ear the evening before, and to the time he enveloped her gently to demonstrate the golf swing by the pond out on the course. 'Why not?' She thought. 'I've not been close to anyone for a long time.' But then, abruptly throwing back the bedclothes, experience prevailed and she told herself to grow up. She wasn't a romantic juvenile any longer.

On returning home the night before, she had put a supermarket fish pie in the oven to heat up, then turned on her computer to review the Payne case. Satisfied that there was no likely link to the present situation, she then looked up the murder of Maryanne Fisher, who had been strangled in Worthing in 2002. Her body had been kept for several weeks by her murderer, who later dumped it, partially burned, in woodland on the edge of the Downs. Thinking that this crime had more in common with the golf club case, Holly discovered that here, too, the perpetrator was locked securely away in a High Security Prison for a very long time. It could not be the same man.

Hearing the 'ping' of the timer in the kitchen, Holly broke off from her deliberations to put frozen peas in the micro-wave. When the food was ready, she poured a glass of Picpoul de Pinet, a new wine she was trying out, recommended by her father, and sat in her favourite comfortable chair. She always recorded the six o'clock news and the local news on television, and thought about watching these programmes, but instead started flicking through the sports channels until she came to the golf.

'Why do I care about this?' She thought, watching a crowd of fans cheering on one of the American players who, hands in the air, was egging them on. 'I'm not really interested.' But she was losing the argument with herself and continued to watch. Unfortunately, the European Team were struggling. Late in the day at Medinah, of the four Ryder Cup pairs, one had already lost their match. Two more were close to losing. The final game of the afternoon was even. That result could go either way.

After twenty minutes, a new thought struck Holly and, distracted by it, she switched off the set, returning to her computer. She wanted to check whether or not it was a crime simply to conceal somebody's death, just in case Jane X had died of natural causes after all. She found herself reading on the internet about two types of situation. Firstly, there were stories of young single mothers, ashamed of their pregnancies, delivering their babies frightened and alone. When the baby dies, at or soon after the birth, some of the unfortunate women hide or dispose of the little corpses without telling anyone.

In other instances, it is elderly folk, grief-stricken men and women who, from denial, confusion and a kind of terror of loneliness, hang onto the corpses of their deceased spouses for days or even much longer. One woman in her eighties was reported as having gone to bed each night and slept beside her dead husband for more than two weeks, until the smell of decay forced her to make up a bed downstairs and sleep there. It was a month or so later that a neighbour called on some pretext, concerned for the couple. By this time the smelly tentacles of putrefaction had spread all the way throughout the house, reaching the front door. Her fears confirmed, the neighbour called the police.

Only rarely did the bereaved person deliberately and fraudulently conceal the death of their partner, usually with the intention of continuing to receive their pension for as long as possible. Accordingly, very few elderly folk were prosecuted; the police and Director of Public Prosecutions taking a lenient view in most cases. Where a trial was held and someone found guilty, a brief suspended sentence or a few months probation was the usual outcome. Holly hoped that some form of grief counselling was also on offer.

This case was obviously different from those she was reading about. Holly's researches confirmed that there is a common duty upon all citizens to give information that will inform a Coroner of circumstances requiring an inquest; in other words, if somebody dies. It is therefore a common law offence to obstruct a Coroner by disposing of a body before a Coroner can openly inquire into the circumstances of a death. The offence would have to be tried on indictment, and carries a maximum penalty of life imprisonment and/or a fine. A lesser, but similar offence called 'preventing the burial of a body', is also possible. This does not involve proving any attempt to obstruct a Coroner. Holly was still not sure which, if either, might apply. The body of Jane X had not been concealed. Quite the reverse! It had been deliberately left in plain sight.

Back at SRGC, one or two members had stayed to watch the end of play, at which stage the US Team led the Europeans by five points to three. It was not a disaster, but the Americans had all along seemed to be the more convincing side, very much in control.

'We'll be needing the luck of the Irish tomorrow, then, Mr Patcham!' Frankie called out to one of the departing members, as he set about closing the bar.

'I don't think it's working', replied the member concerned, impressed that Frank had remembered his name. 'McIlroy and McDowell went down badly to Mickelson and Bradley this afternoon. That's two Irish together.'

'That Bradley must have Irish blood in his veins then, to be sure! That's your explanation', Frank called out. He had made it up, but took pleasure in having the last word anyway.

In the morning that Saturday, drinking tea and eating toast, fully recovered from her nocturnal dream-state, Holly was watching the local news she had recorded the evening before. A brave reporter at the site of the proposed fracking plant was asking rhetorical questions of those protesting, like whether they drove a car or had central heating in their houses. They did, of course, so he would ask where they thought the fuel would come from in future? Were they prepared to pay the much higher prices that petrol would probably cost? Things like that. Complaining about bully-boy tactics and 'the rape of the countryside', most of the people he spoke to gave him short shrift, but one white-haired gentleman did admit there was a dilemma. 'You can have one thing or the other thing', he agreed, 'But you can't have both.' 'In this case', he added, 'We need more information about the possible destructive effects of fracking. My protest is against the rush to go ahead without a more careful analysis of the probable outcome, including risks as well as benefits.'

The eager reporter continued holding the microphone in front of him expectantly. 'Everyone seems to be in such a hurry these days', the older man concluded, with a shrug and a wry smile. 'I think we all need to slow down.'

As if to prove the point, the next news item concerned a woman cyclist knocked down by a van driver travelling too fast in a built up area near Eastbourne, while he was at the same time trying to text his girlfriend on his mobile phone. He had wanted to tell her he was going to be late home. Fortunately, the cyclist's helmet seems to have saved her from joining that month's road death statistics.

Finally, Holly watched as DCI Holroyd and DI Garbutt faced the spotlights and reported the discovery of a body in West Sussex, asking for members of the public to come forward and contact the police with any possible information that might prove useful, particularly in identifying the deceased person. A photo-fit image, an artist's impression of what she might have looked like when alive and relatively healthy was displayed. It was based on computer manipulation of photographs taken in the forensic suite in Chichester, and Holly found it barely recognizable. They had given Jane X a lot of extra weight. The piece was accompanied by a clip of a reporter standing in front of SRGC, followed by a brief telephone interview with Peter Harding saying that staff, officers and members of the club were co-operating fully with the police, but that no connection between the dead person and the club had been established. Quite deliberately, by prior agreement Holly suspected, no-one mentioned either the red chairs or the message one of them held. It was too early to give out the idea that this could have been a murder, much less that there might still be 'Murderers' about.

Holly was slightly ahead of time for her appointment. Approaching the impressive black and gold wrought iron gateway of Rose Cottage just before ten o'clock, she noticed something shining brightly back at her. This was the bright sun, reflected back from the steel grille of the intercom, into which she had to speak to gain access. Soon after, the electric gates slid quietly open, and Holly could see the beech-lined driveway curving uphill, concealing any view of the house from the main road.

Making her way up the long S-bend of the approach, cresting the avenue's gentle rise, she soon saw that the building was less of a cottage and rather more of a mansion. The large forecourt was paved, rather than gravel, oval in shape with an ornate central fountain from which water bubbled rather than spouted. Behind it, the foursquare Georgian house rose up splendidly before her. The yellow painted front door had a ramp leading up to it, she noticed, as well as a stone staircase. Either side, carefully colour-matched yellow Mountbatten roses climbed high on the walls between the two tall sets of ground-floor windows. There was an additional window above the front door, making five on the second storey. The yellow-grey stonework was offset by the angled red-tiled roof, interrupted halfway up by one dormer window on either side. Brick chimneys rose above the whole, completing a pleasingly symmetrical vision.

To her left, Holly noticed a red-brick stable-block; and, on the right, a more modern, low-rise garage, sizeable enough for three or four cars. Large, well-established trees could be seen towering to the side and behind the house. Having parked up and got out of her car, there was no time to take it all in before the front door opened silently. A tall, severe-looking grey-haired woman with black spectacles, wearing a navy-blue blouse beneath a black jacket and long skirt, stood patiently in the entrance.

'Mrs Royle?' said Holly, as she climbed the few stairs.

'Is inside', said the apparition, in the same metallic voice that she had used to answer the driveway intercom. 'I'll take you to see her, Detective.'

Glancing round the wood-panelled hallway, Holly became briefly aware of the curving carpeted stairway, the portraits on the wall, the elegant grandfather clock now ringing the last of its ten chimes, and the enormous flower vases on tall pedestals filled with fragrant blooms, before being whisked forward into another room, which held not one surprise for her but two.

The panelled entranceway led into a normal dining-room, entirely at one with the architectural period of the house, containing a large oak sideboard, wall cabinets, old master landscape paintings on the walls and, placed crosswise, an elongated, twelve-place dining table complete with high-backed chairs bearing two solid silver candelabra. Originally, this room would have felt rather dark and sombre, except that now the opposing north wall had been entirely removed, so that where oak panelling ended, steel and glass supervened. There was also a slight downward incline for two or three paces at that point, then a drop of three or four feet to a large, open, contemporary-style living space. The whole effect, of sudden light and expansion, was breath-taking.

Holly stood still and blinked. Only when she moved forward, towards a ramp leading from the higher to the lower level against the side wall, did she notice that the space below was occupied. This was the second surprise. Georgina Royle was in a wheelchair. No-one had thought to tell Holly that she was disabled.

The grey-haired spectre was still silently ushering her forward from behind, urging her to descend the short staircase to the right. The woman in the wheelchair, alerted by the sound of her tread on the steps, swivelled round and looked up.

'Welcome, Detective', she said. 'Please do come and sit down.'

The dark-clad humanoid apparition melted silently away as Holly reached the bottom of the stairs, taking the chair indicated.

Her hostess, she noticed, was an Englishwoman of about sixty, who looked both healthy and alert. Her beautifully kempt dark hair framed a still attractive face into which were set deep blue, almost violet eyes, flanked by the kind of creases you get if you smile a lot. There was a single string of pearls at her neck, and she was wearing a bright vermilion cashmere cardigan over a cream-coloured blouse. A soft grey rug lay over her lap, concealing her legs.

Jamie Royle's wife, aware that Holly was studying her, remained silent and passive for a few seconds, then – as if to convey the message, 'I have nothing to hide' – whisked aside the rug, revealing her withered, trouser-clad limbs underneath. Restoring the camouflage moments later, smoothing the rug with both hands, she began speaking in a clear, steady tone of voice without any need to be prompted.

'It was a riding accident', she explained. 'We had been married a couple of years. Jamie had scoured the land for a suitable house and we'd moved into Rose Cottage a year or so earlier. I've always ridden, and loved having the stables; and I'd a new hunter to ride: Gulliver. He was a grey; not a large horse, but game, fearless. I loved riding him; and when the local hunt asked to hold a meet here, I decided to ride with them. Perhaps I should have got to know the local terrain better, but I was a confident rider in those days.'

Holly had taken a notebook from her bag, now sitting beside her on the floor, but she was not writing in it, only listening. Outside, through the glass doors ahead, she could see sunlight and occasional dark cloud shadows passing across the spacious lawn surrounding the massively majestic Cedar of Lebanon. This wonderful tree, she later discovered, had been planted when the country was still at war with Napoleon, when the house's foundations had also been laid.

'It was March', Georgina Royle continued. 'There had been a hard frost in the night and, in the morning sunshine, everything looked sparkling and beautiful. I remember the feeling of exhilaration just to be alive. However, we were disappointed. At first and for ages, nothing much happened.... No foxes! Later on, a bunch of us were milling around by a small copse, thinking of calling it a day, when suddenly we heard the hounds and the bugle far off to the south. I was facing the wrong way and, by the time I got Gulliver turned, there were about thirty horses and riders in front of me, all heading fast for the same small gap in a high hedge between two fields. On impulse I set Gulliver at the centre of the hedge to the left of where everyone else was going. I knew he could jump it, and that if he hit some of the topmost fronds, he would just barrel-charge through. Unfortunately for me, though, as I found out later, some hunt saboteurs had strung strong wires along inside the hedge. These caught Gulliver's hooves, and he went down with me underneath him. If the ground had been softer, I might have been alright, but it was still firm as concrete. My pelvis was smashed and my lower spine broken beyond repair. I don't remember anything of it, but I was rushed to St Richard's in Chichester by air ambulance where I had my spleen and a third of my damaged liver removed that afternoon. Both had been ruptured when the horse fell on me. They told me later that I lost a lot of blood and was lucky to get there in time.'

Holly was impressed with the matter-of-fact way the tale was told, with no sense that the impressive woman recounting it might be feeling sorry for herself, only grateful.

'I was left paralysed from the waist down, as you see', Georgina Royle went on. 'But harder to bear, in a way, was that I lost the pregnancy I was carrying. It was still early days, and I hadn't even told Jamie about it, but I was sure, and the surgeons confirmed it after also removing my badly damaged womb... It took me a long time to get over that.'

Although this was not what Holly had come to hear, she later somehow felt glad that this was where their conversation had begun. Her interviewee's disability was the most obvious topic. She had not thought much about having children herself at any point, but realised forcefully now what a blow it would be if that option were suddenly closed off. Although the woman across from her was not looking for sympathy, Holly experienced immediate heartfelt compassion for her nonetheless.

At this point, Mrs Royle stretched across the table between them, picking up the small hand-bell resting there. When she raised and rang it, more or less instantly, robot-like, the grey apparition re-appeared above them.

'Monica, dear', said her employer, 'Please bring us some tea.'

Turning back to Holly, she explained, 'That's Monica… Miss Kidd. She is my assistant. I know she doesn't say much. We think she's probably on the autistic spectrum, Asperger's syndrome or something like that. All the same, I don't know what I would have done without her help all these years… After the accident, when I was in hospital recovering from the operations, and afterwards in the rehabilitation centre where I spent three months, Jamie had people come here and adapt the house for a wheelchair user. There's a lift now, so I can still get upstairs, and the stable block was partly converted to house a small hydrotherapy pool and a mini-gym for my use. This extension was done later. He also hired a physio to come twice a day, every day, to put me through my paces; and Monica came at the same time, to live in and manage the household. She's been with me ever since.'

That same person, the subject of discussion, now re-entered the room, manoeuvring a tea trolley efficiently down the ramp, bringing it close to the table nearby the other two women. As she began to pour the dark aromatic liquid through a strainer into the elegant white bone china cups, Holly heard her hostess explain, 'This is orange pekoe tea, Detective Angel. I hope you like it. It's a strange name, I know; and not one that I can explain because, unlike Earl Grey, which has a citrus fruit extract added called 'bergamot', it does not taste remotely of oranges. This one is from Sri Lanka, a simple black tea of top quality, made only from the 'pekoe'; that's the tender-most new leaf buds. It can be made strong, as some people prefer, but I like a more delicate flavour. I also drink it neat, sometimes with lemon, but you can have it with milk if you like.'

After putting milk in and tasting it, Holly would have liked half a spoonful of sugar to offset the bitterness, but hardly dare ask. Miss Kidd had, in any case, already gone back up the steps.

'I went there once', her hostess was talking again. 'It was still called Ceylon in those days. That's when I developed an abiding taste for this tea. I was visiting a school friend whose parents managed a plantation in the beautiful Ceylonese hills. We often watched the native women picking the delicate leaves, as they did every day on the estate; and we were given a tour of the factory where the young buds were dried and processed. Did you know that in India and Sri Lanka, what most people in England drink, the stuff that goes into most of the tea-bags people buy, is known simply as 'dust'? That's the lowest grade of tea, almost the leftovers; so this is one thing I do admit to being a snob about… How do you find it?'

Holly, who would quite happily have enjoyed basic builder's tea, did not know how to reply. The tea, to her, was fine, now that she was getting used to its unusual flavour, perhaps even a taste she could acquire, but drinking it was not an experience she would be in a hurry to repeat. 'What happened to the horse, Gulliver?' she asked, changing the subject as a ploy to avoid further awkwardness.

'He was unharmed, thankfully. Soon afterwards, he was sold, along with the other horse and two ponies I kept at the time', Georgina sniffed sadly. 'I never saw him again… But we did re-open the stables eventually. The pool and gym weren't getting as much use, and there was still room anyway for a few stalls, so we bought a mare and three more ponies. I don't ride, of course, but we invited the charity 'Riding for the Disabled' to get involved, and they have been visiting twice a week now for almost ten years. They have their own animals too, which they bring along for people to ride as well as ours. This is one of the big things that keeps me going, the feeling that, disabled as I am, I can still do something for others.'

Holly, the tea ordeal over, had started absent-mindedly fingering her notebook.

'But you want me to tell you about my husband, don't you, Detective?' Georgina enquired, noticing her impatience.

'Yes', said Holly, taking her cue. 'This is a very unusual investigation. It may well have nothing at all to do with Mr Royle, but we are in the dark and anything we learn may help solve this mystery. When and how did you meet?'

'I was about nineteen. Jamie was twenty-two, the same age as my brother, Patrick. It was Paddy who introduced us, at one of his parties. They had met as undergraduates in Oxford where they were both reading law. Jamie had excelled at maths and physics at school, but his father had been a high court judge and insisted he take a classical subject while there. Then, obedient to his father, as I say, at Exeter College he read law. He and Paddy instantly became great mates. It was all a bit 'Brideshead revisited', I must say. They did everything together: studied, played golf, partied... everything; and Jamie loved coming to the house.'

'We are not proper aristocracy, I don't think, not in the higher echelons of Dukes and Earls, but my father was a baronet: Baronet Ernest Gryllock of Martsey... It used to be spelt '"Greylock" a few generations back, according to the records, denoting age and wisdom, of course, but I suspect people started saying it as 'Gryllock' and the spelling changed. Who knows? Anyway, Paddy and I come from the Baronet's second wife, Deborah, after his first wife, Rowena, died. The inheritance and the title all went to our half-brother Richard, but we were still both called 'Honourable' in those days. I was 'The Honourable Georgina Gryllock', which always sounded to me like a contraction of 'grill' and 'haddock', something you'd serve up for breakfast... But Jamie was quite taken with it when we first met. He kept calling me "My Lady". It was very flattering... He was such a terrific flirt.'

Holly watched as Georgina, a smile hovering, closed her eyes in reminiscence.

'He had lots of girlfriends', she continued. 'I always knew that... But we had something special, which I can't explain. We were always so good together, not only in bed... And we made each other laugh. I think that was the real key... I say in bed but, to be honest, we had sex everywhere, indoors, outdoors, in the stables, in the attic, you name it! We were just so hungry for each other. The first time, I remember, was during a party at Martsey House, in the swimming pool after I'd had too much champagne. Jamie was always one to spot an opportunity; but it would have happened anyway. It was the seventies. 'Love was in the air', with a whiff or two of marijuana thrown into the mix, I dare say. "Mandies make you randy" and all that! I was on the pill. It was a great, carefree time. Lots of couples came together and broke apart on a weekly basis, more or less, in those days; but somehow we eventually, after orbiting each other for a year or two, finally stuck together. Jamie and Patrick were in business together by then, and they were beginning to become seriously rich young men. I think that was also an important factor. When you are rich like that for the first time, it helps to have someone around who knows how to help you spend it, and I was good at that then.'

'How did they get rich?' Holly asked.

'One of the bonds between Jamie and Paddy, and me to some extent, was that our fathers both died at roughly the same time. When the judge died, Jamie immediately gave up reading law. He switched to engineering, for which he was better suited, and in particular to electrical engineering. One day, apparently, on a trip to the College library, he came upon Alex Kachaturian, or 'Catch' as Jamie always called him. Alex was another, very gifted, electrical engineer, a year or two older than Jamie. The story goes that they got chatting and Jamie discovered firstly that Alex was flat broke. He was Armenian, and for some reason he didn't get a student grant. I suppose his family were poor too. Anyway, he couldn't even afford to heat a room at his digs on the other side of town, which is why he came into college every day, camping out in the library to stay warm. He was also always hungry, so Jamie immediately offered to take him round the corner to the pub for a meal and a pint. It was there that he also found out that Alex had just invented a wizard little gismo for computers which, of course, were still in the early stages of development back then.'

Holly, scribbling a note in her notebook, was still listening.

'It was still at the theoretical stage', Georgina continued. 'Alex was in despair because he couldn't afford to develop the idea, build prototypes and so on, and he couldn't get a full patent until this happened. Obviously, he didn't want to sell the idea, even if he could. It wouldn't have been worth much without further testing anyway. So that's when Jamie contacted Patrick and together they made him an offer. Both had inherited some money, and Jamie was in the process of selling off his father's big house somewhere near Ewhurst, so the three of them formed a company – JAP, from their initials: Jamie, Alex, Patrick – and took the idea into development. I think it helped that people thought JAP came from Japan, where electronic wizardry was commonplace. Anyway, they completed their testing, got their patent and went into production, with the result that the latest version of Alex's gizmo is now in every computer and every mobile phone on the planet. That's how those boys; who still work together, by the way – Regal, for example, is a subsidiary of the original JAP. Anyway, that is how they got rich.'

Coming back from these memories to the present, the older woman began apologising. 'I'm sorry', she said to Holly, 'I didn't ask if you'd like more tea.'

When Holly declined, she leaned down and released the brake, moving her wheelchair slightly. 'Come on, then', she said cheerfully, 'I'd like to show you something.'

Holly got up, stowed her notebook and lifted her bag onto her shoulder while her disabled hostess worked the electric wheelchair's controls, propelling herself gradually forward towards the glass doors, which slid open in response to a hidden trigger. 'There are electronics everywhere in this house', she said, gliding to a halt. 'But let me introduce you to Henry.' She had stopped in front of a full suit of armour from the Tudor period, standing incongruously on the laminate floor amid the tasteful collection of contemporary furniture. 'I keep him as a reminder of the days, not so long ago, when everything was mechanical.'

Statue-like, Henry was adorned frivolously with a long turquoise feather boa wrapped once around his neck, the longer end trailing down to his knees. Holly, stepping forward, raised his visor to peer into the dark empty cavity within. 'Nobody seems to be home', she said, for some reason wanting to giggle.

'And I know a few people like that', Georgina Royle replied. 'Don't you?'

The two women were still laughing as they emerged, side by side, onto the terrace moments later.

'You need a sense of humour in this life,' Georgina said thoughtfully, as they recovered from their fit of mirth. 'But I can't get Monica to laugh, no matter how hard I try. Jamie is the only one who can do that.'

'Do you see him often?' Holly asked.

'No. After the accident, things changed. We became more like brother and sister than lovers, of course. We tried once or twice, but it was no good. With no movement and no sensation below the waist, I couldn't respond to him. And knowing I couldn't get pregnant, he must have been wondering, "What was the point?" He tried not to show it, but I think his self-esteem took a massive blow.' She paused, thoughtfully. 'He must have wanted a son and heir. Men do, don't they? These were dark days; and I suspect something else was going on, something Jamie never told me about; but sitting around with nothing to do, day by day, eventually did something for me that was beneficial. It made me much more sensitive to other people, to how they are feeling. I think that's a great blessing... Sometimes, it is as if I know even better than they do if they're sad or angry, anxious or ashamed. You've no idea how much sadness people carry around that they are not properly in touch with... And anger! It can be awkward at times, this secret knowledge about a person, but I do value it... Nevertheless, as I say, we had to go through some dark times to get there.'

Georgina was leading Holly down another ramp, running from the terrace to the west side of the great lawn. Then they moved forward along paving stones towards the entrance of a brick-walled enclosed garden. Entering it first, Holly's eyes met an extravagant scene, a feast for her eyes, and for her sense of smell too. Spreading before her was a beautiful, multi-coloured rose garden, the fragrant blooms radiant in the continuing sunlight. 'Oh', she exclaimed, 'This is heaven!'

'These roses were what saved my sanity, and probably my life', said Georgina. 'The soil here is excellent for them. I have gardeners, of course. But the development planning, hybrid creation, and quite a lot of the actual work, the dead-heading and end of season pruning, I do myself. This one here, for example', she said, rolling forward a few yards and pointing to a bush at her shoulder height bearing multiple clusters of tightly furled crimson and white striped blooms. 'It's called the 'Martsey Damsel', one of our successes. Smell it! You rarely get a hybrid that maintains the strength of fragrance of the original plants, but this one exceeds them, and regularly wins prizes to prove it.' Holly was impressed. The scent of the roses was delightfully heady. 'Congratulations!' she said.

The two women moved up one smooth pathway between the beds and started down another when something out of place, a particularly bright patch of greenery in the corner, caught Holly's vigilant eye. 'Is that what I think it is?' she asked, pointing.

'Oh dear... You've caught me!' exclaimed the rose expert. 'Yes. It's cannabis sativa, "Sweet Mary Jane". I don't expect you to believe me, but I grow it for medicinal purposes. I get such painful cramps in these useless, withered old legs of mine, especially at night. It's weird, because I can't feel anything down there most of the time, only when they go into spasm. But I have found that if I smoke a little pot before bedtime, it really helps... Are you going to arrest me now?'

'No fear!' Holly replied. 'I'm not from the drugs squad; and you're alright with me, as long as I don't catch you selling it. And that goes for your staff as well.'

'What a relief, Sister!' Georgina was smiling. 'I'm too old and decrepit to go to prison now. And the staff here know that they all face the sack if any one of them either tells on me or harvests any of the plants for themselves. I may lose a few seeds every year, if one or other of them want to grow a plant or two at home, but I can't be held responsible for that, can I?'

Holly decided it was better to stay silent on the matter. She did not approve of recreational drug use under any circumstances, but this was not the moment to say so. 'Don't these roses need to be in a greenhouse?' she asked by way of a diversion.

'That's what those overhead wires are for', said Georgina, pointing skyward. 'We have another electronic solution. Whenever the temperature drops below a certain point, a thick, transparent plastic cover gets pulled across to make a kind of ceiling. It's housed

behind that wall there. The cover protects the plants from any risk
of frost damage... We think of everything, you know.'

'And do you make a profit from the roses?'

'Well it depends how you do your accounting. Probably not,
is the answer; even though we have another ten acre site down
the road, on even better soil closer to the Downs. That one is
covered by hothouses, and run on a much more commercial
scale. But we don't focus on making a profit. We don't need to.
Ever since the accident, Jamie has always picked up all the bills.'

The women made their way back towards the main house.
Georgina stopped beside another Martsey Damsel and, leaning
across, deftly cut one of the flower-bearing stems with secateurs
from a pouch on the side of her wheelchair. 'This is for you',
she said, handing the sweet-smelling rose to Holly, who took it
without a word. 'Now, to answer your earlier question, "Do I see
him often?" It's like this... Jamie keeps a room here, next to mine.
He uses it whenever he wants to, usually if he's going to play
golf at the club. He was here a lot, of course, when he bought it
and during the development phase, but not so often these days;
although he does make a point of being here for my birthday in
March; sometimes for Christmas too... But, truthfully, I sense
he's uncomfortable here. And, anyway, he much prefers London.'

Holly was grateful for the older woman's candour, and
delighted with her gift of a rose. This was what she so liked about
her job: not only solving difficult cases, but meeting fascinating
individuals and hearing their stories, connecting with people, as
she felt she had done that morning with a woman she might have
considered unfortunate, until she actually met her. Bringing her
nose up from the petals in which she had buried it, looking up,
she caught the motionless dark figure of Monica Kidd, standing
on the terrace, looking in her direction.

Mrs Royle had noticed her too. 'Come along', she said. 'Let's
go back inside.'

Sitting in the Micra, Holly was surprised, when she looked at her watch, at how much time had passed. The rose, with its stem now carefully wrapped in moistened tissue paper inside a plastic sandwich bag, lay on the seat beside her, its perfume filling the air. About to turn the key, looking up, she also noticed that a multicoloured minibus from 'Riding for the Disabled' was parked in the forecourt, together with a Land Rover and two-berth horse trailer. A smiling young woman with the unmistakeable facial features of Down's Syndrome stood near the stable-block, holding the bridle of a pony that was munching grass from the verge. Cheerful sounds emerged from inside, but the detective in her was suddenly paying attention. 'Of course', Holly thought. 'It could have been some form of animal transport that conveyed those red chairs to the golf course, not only a delivery vehicle. We shall have to widen the enquiry.'

Setting off down the driveway, the sun shining into her face, another imperative struck her. 'I'm going to track down Jamie Royle. I definitely need to speak to that man.'

THE 10TH
CHAPTER

At the same time Holly was leaving Rose Cottage, due to the time difference across the Atlantic in Illinois, early-riser Jamie Royle was eating a breakfast bowl of cereal. Tall and tanned, younger in appearance than his sixty-something years, with no spare flesh and a full head of golden-blond hair, elegantly clad in the royal blue and bright yellow colours of Team Europe, a souvenir from the previous Ryder Cup in South Wales two years earlier, he was feeling fit and looking strong.

The patio door open, he could already hear Gary in the pool outside, the forty-eight year old SRGC golf professional swimming the fifty laps he liked to complete every morning. As befitted a man of Jamie's extensive resources, they were staying in a luxury house close to the Medinah Country Club, rented for the whole week at enormous cost. The other two occupants were Catherine Pokorny, Jamie's personal assistant, with a room of her own, and Louise Broad, Jamie's physio, masseuse, personal trainer, part-time cook and occasional bedfellow.

Catherine, a highly intelligent young woman from Slovakia,

whose name Pokorny, when translated means 'tame', presented herself to the world as anything but, rather as a tough, passionless ice-maiden, unreachable and dismissive. Louise, on the other hand, was light-hearted and full of fun. Jamie sometimes spoke of her as 'a good sport'. To anyone else, Louise might have seemed used, her loyalty to him abused even, but she was very content with the role he gave her. Thirty-seven years old, in good physical shape, and with a marriage behind her that failed due more to inertia than discord, she often asked herself who else could have such a good life.

She was the moll of a multi-millionaire, a good-looking and courteous fellow who took her to many wonderful places and who, except when they were travelling, left her more or less free; so she felt she had much the better of the bargain. His demands on her, even in bed, she reflected, were remarkably light. She gave him what he wanted in the sack as elsewhere, her highly-toned pelvic floor muscles ensuring mutual pleasure; also that she stayed in control. She only hoped he hadn't realised how often recently she was faking a counterfeit climax.

Still in the bedroom that morning, Louise was preparing to go to the mini-gym in the house's basement for a warm-up session when the insistent tones of Jamie's mobile attracted her attention. By the time she took the phone through to him, though, it had stopped ringing. They both said 'Good Morning'. Louise turned to leave. She was on her way, and Jamie was putting the phone down on the table, when it started ringing again. Seeing the call was from Paddy Gryllock, waving Louise out, Jamie accepted it, putting the phone onto speaker.

'Morning Jamie', said the well-remembered voice of his friend and business partner. 'How are you feeling?'

'Cut the crap, Paddy.' Jamie's reply was terse. 'It must be bad news if you're phoning me at this time on a Saturday. You know I've got a ringside seat at one of the greatest sporting events of the year.'

'Okay, Jamie... No more bullshit then. It's this... The Guangzhou people are causing problems. They want to renegotiate the contract... Put the prices up!'

'Can't I deal with it when I go to Hong Kong. I'll be there in ten days?' Jamie was irritated, but not especially alarmed. 'What's the rush?'

'The issue is that they are not in China right now. The main negotiators are in Europe. They've been in Latvia, buying up the factory there that we've been using; and now they're in Germany on a mission to acquire as much of the competition as they can, paying top-dollar too.'

'I see', Jamie was thoughtful. 'The Vilnius place was only low volume, high spec manufacturing. We could always take that work to Seoul presumably... What about the South Koreans? Could they handle it if we switched everything there? Will that work?'

'They could handle it; but as for profitability, it depends what figure we agree with the Chinese.' Gryllock sounded anxious. 'That's why I want you here to meet them... On Monday if possible, Old Son.'

'You've got to be bloody joking!' Jamie did not sound best pleased.

'There are three of them, and they're due to land in London on an early bird flight from Bonn on Monday. They're talking of upping our costs by twenty-five to thirty percent. That's still lower than the South Koreans, but it will cut badly into our profits. You're much better at this sort of thing than I am... And one of them is a woman, by the way.'

'Is she sexy?' Jamie asked, pretty much as a matter of course.

'She's very sexy, yes... In an oriental sort of way', answered the man who best knew his friend's tastes in most things – cars, wine and, of course, women, admittedly also slightly ashamed that he had not yet actually set eyes on Laetitia Chou, the Chinese lady concerned. 'I think you'll love her... More to the point, you handsome bugger, I think she'll love you. That's why we need you here, to charm the knockers off her.'

Hooked, as his pal intended, Jamie made a quick decision. There seemed no better alternative. 'The golf finishes tomorrow evening', he announced, 'And I'm staying for the celebrations – although it looks as if Europe might go down to the Yanks this time. Either way, I'll get a flight Monday evening and be at Heathrow early on Tuesday. Keep them happy on Monday. You can take them to Felicia's if you like. Use my regular table. There shouldn't be any problem if you phone ahead. Then set up a meeting with me at the office for Tuesday midday. I'll see you then.'

'Thanks James', said Patrick, back in London. 'I knew I could count on you.' But Royle had already cut the connection, striding down the passageway to get Catherine out of bed to start making new arrangements. He was angry, fuming with a kind of slow-burn of energy that, if he were honest, he rather enjoyed. He was angry with the Chinese for going back on what had previously been a cast-iron deal; but he was also angry with himself, and he wasn't exactly sure why. It wasn't connected to business.

When Peter Harding first contacted him about the body on the golf course at Graffham, Royle assumed he was not directly concerned and refused to listen to details. However, the day before, he had received another text from the Colonel. This one mentioned the red chairs on the fairway. It also said that the police were increasingly keen to speak to him. Normally oozing with confidence, he suddenly felt a wave of alarm. 'Oh, no... Shit!' he thought. 'I could do without that.' But when Gary, close beside him, asked, 'What's up?' Jamie, switched the phone off, gave him a sheepish look, shrugged, and simply said, 'Nothing', then put the thing out of his mind.

About an hour after speaking to his business partner, Jamie was calmer and very focused. He and Gary were driving to the Medinah clubhouse in one of the two golf buggies that came with the rented house. 'Look', he was saying, 'Catherine and I will return to London. You and Louise go on to Portland as planned, fly down to Bandon and enjoy yourselves for a couple of days. You've both got company credit cards, so just have fun. You can still use my tee times. I'm hoping to rejoin you by Friday; maybe even Thursday. That still lets me play Bandon Dunes, the main course, and Pacific Dunes too with luck before we leave again for Hong Kong and Bangkok. It's supposed to be a fabulous resort Mike Keiser's built up there. That bit of Oregon coastline is just like Scottish links-land, apparently, and the courses are special.'

'Yes. I've seen their website', Gary agreed. 'The whole complex – four courses; three separate clubhouses; fabulous accommodation and several restaurants – it's a dream. You've cancelled our matches, I take it?'

'Sadly, yes', Jamie replied. I can't ask John Tonks to hang around for three or four days until I get there. He'll have to call off his ringer too, former tour pro Jonny Braggard, now back in the amateur ranks.'

'What a name!' said Gary.

'Braggard? Yes... It suits him too!' Jamie replied. 'Actually, that's his weak spot. He thinks he's so good, you only have to get slightly ahead and he's done for. His nerves kick in. That's why he had to give up the tour... Too temperamental... He and John came over for a game at The Berkshire last year. You remember I told you about it? I played with my friend Angus, down from Scotland. We beat them twice in two days on the red course and halved the decider on the blue on day three. I still wake up in horror at the five-foot putt I missed on the final green to let them off the hook. Even so, we cleaned up. Now John wants his revenge, but he's going to have to wait.'

The two men did not have to travel far to reach the course perimeter. From there, it was less than half a mile to the clubhouse, along cart paths that ran near the final fairway on Medinah's Course Number Two, skirting the practice area, then alongside Lake Kadijah, across the placid waters of which; on Course Number Three, the one being used for the Ryder Cup; players had to hit four times. Holes two, thirteen, fourteen and seventeen certainly made for exciting golf.

Earlier in the week, Jamie and Gary had played big money-matches on the other two courses against their host, Charles Flanagan, paired with the Medinah Club's leading amateur, plus-two handicapper, Rob Girt. It was honours even, the British pair having won the first game and lost the second. The third match was due to take place on Monday, the day after the Ryder Cup, on the championship course. This was another reason Jamie insisted on delaying his return to London.

Well-connected in the world of golf, he was a member of the Royal and Ancient club, based in the impressive grey building behind the first tee of the most famous links in the world, the Old Course at St Andrews. He was also a well-respected rules official, having acted in that capacity at two previous Ryder Cups and three Open Championships – 'The British Open', as the Americans insisted on calling it. So this time, although he was not officiating, he was being given full access to the Medinah clubhouse, practice area and all parts of the course. Chuck Flanagan, had seen to all that.

The two men had first met many years earlier at Sotogrande in Spain. They had been drawn as partners in a local tournament for low handicap amateurs, and had somehow managed to win. Luck was certainly with them. On one occasion, one of Chuck's worst shots fizzed low off the club, the ball bouncing twice on the surface of a lake before finding dry land on the other side. A 'Barnes-Wallis', Jamie called it.

Another time, Jamie mishit a short iron way off line to the right from a hundred and thirty-five yards, only to watch it bounce at forty-five degrees off a large eucalyptus tree, looping up over a bunker, hitting the sharp down-slope and rolling a full sixty feet in a graceful arc, right to the edge of the cup. Both men that day were deadly with the flat-stick, the putter, and their winning score was significantly under par. Shaking hands with the trophy between them, a lifelong friendship was born.

The Medinah clubhouse is a magnificent building, a temple of golf designed with Moorish features, created out of red brick with white edging picturesquely offset by a green tiling roof. There is a long, sweeping, curved cloister-like walkway on each side, lined by arched columns and flanked by two oversized, tall, square, cupola-topped minaret-like structures. In the centre foreground, framing the arrival area and entranceway, a rectangular portico, bordered by similarly high, narrower, hexagonal, cupola-topped towers, juts forward, its green roof pointing up towards a larger arch, framing windows that sit symmetrically below white plasterwork and a large, eye-catching, Byzantine-style green dome.

As Jamie and Gary arrived, Chuck was coming forward down the clubhouse steps to greet them. A short, stocky, powerful man, he was the same age as Jamie but looked considerably older, with thinning hair and a florid complexion, a busy restless man, always on the move. He was about to usher his guests inside when the sound of a flight of five or six small planes could be heard approaching. Looking up, the three men were astonished to see sky-writing appear against the blue above them. Jamie laughed as he read aloud, 'Anyone seen Tiger?' Tiger Woods and Steve Stricker had lost both their matches the previous day.

Another message was more sobering. 'Do it for Seve.' Other spectators nearby were looking skywards too, equally amazed. The messages were clearly aimed at boosting the morale of the

European team. As the men went inside, there was speculation as to who's idea it had been and, this being America, about who was paying for it. Chuck Flanagan thought it might have been his uber-rich friend and said so. Jamie, who knew nothing about the airborne encouragement until seeing it himself, simply smiled. There was no point scotching a rumour like that, casting him in such a favourable light. There was no point in doing that at all.

The golf duly got under way a little later, with frenzy on the first tee as Ian Poulter whipped up the enthusiasm of the European supporters, to the surprise of his opponent Bubba Watson, who had been doing the same for the American fans on the previous day. 'Anything you can do, we can do louder', they seemed to want to convey. The trick clearly worked, too, because Poulter and Justin Rose managed to beat Watson and Webb Simpson, if only by a single hole. Unfortunately, that morning, the three other European pairs were unsuccessful. By lunch, the US team led overall by 8 to 4, and Jamie Royle had a headache.

He and Gary were back at the clubhouse, having walked a few holes around the course following the action for most of the morning. They weren't hungry, having just picked up food from the hospitality area. Jamie was thinking of watching the start of the afternoon's play on television when he noticed something wrong with his eyesight. He was looking up at one of the big leader-boards and found he couldn't focus properly. Wherever he looked, the central part of his vision was blank. Shutting his eyes confirmed his fear. It was as if a nest of three or four jagged lines, alternating bright and dark, were moving slowly across inside his darkened eyelids. As he moved his eyes left and right, the flashing stripes followed. The headache had not arrived in full force yet, but he knew anyway that this was the start of a migraine. It happened two or three times a year, often when he was under stress and therefore when most inconvenient.

Turning to Gary, he immediately said, 'Go get the buggy and take me back to the house'. Taking one look at his employer's drawn, pale face, the golf pro did not hesitate and rushed off.

Catherine was sunning herself by the pool when they arrived, ensconced in a lounger and reading a book. Louise had gone to the local mall for provisions. Jamie, ignoring everyone, went straight inside. He swallowed down three pain-killers with a glass of water in the bathroom, walked into the bedroom, closed the curtains and flopped onto the bed, having taken out a handkerchief to cover his eyes. From experience, he knew this was the only way to deal with the situation. If he was lucky, the pharmaceuticals would soften the intensity, and maybe also shorten the duration of the one-sided headache. Silence and a darkened room were the only other things that might help. If Jamie had been more self-aware, he would know that it was compressed anger that usually brought on these attacks, anger bottled-up usually with an under-current of fear.

Gary, meanwhile, had whispered to Catherine what was happening, advising her to keep very quiet and stay out of the house, so she decided to go for a walk. Gary returned to Medinah, having left Louise a message about Jamie on the front door, for when she returned.

———

A little over two hours later, wrestling with a dream, Jamie half-woke, covered in sweat. He had been pulling a girl's arms over her head as she crouched down, bent over something. She was distraught, sobbing and shaking. He was in his father's dark study, and could sense the Judge's foreboding presence. Sitting up, he let the twilit memory of the dream fall away. Fully awake now, he realized that the headache had gone and his vision was back to normal, but he still felt fragile. Getting up, he turned on the Golf Channel and went for a shower, lingering for some minutes under its revitalizing stream. Loud cheers from the television eventually caught his attention, and he went back to the bedroom to dress. Louise returned at about the same moment, entering the house cautiously, happy to see Jamie up and about, having read Gary's note.

'How are you feeling?' she called through the open door.

Jamie simply grunted in reply. Looking fresh, he entered the living-room and turned on the big-screen set there. 'I'd be feeling a lot better if the Europeans would buck up a bit', he finally offered. 'They've already lost two of the afternoon matches. We're 10 – 4 down. It's dreadful... Rory and Poults are two holes adrift with six to go, and the other match is dicey too... I don't know if I want to watch this.'

Having stashed the groceries in the kitchen, Louise came and sat beside him. 'I'll watch with you', she said.

'Get me a beer, then,' said Jamie, all thoughts of his migraine having departed. 'That's better... McIlroy just sunk a monster putt to birdie the short thirteenth. Now they are only one-down.'

The next hour produced amongst the most riveting golf Jamie had ever seen. In the front match, Luke Donald and Sergio Garcia were one-up when they came to the seventeenth tee, facing Lake Kadijah for the final time, the flag front-left about 150 yards away. The US team fired first. Steve Stricker and Tiger Woods both put their balls on the green, Tiger's pretty close to the flag – a very makeable putt. Sergio went next and found the back of the green, not that close. Donald must have known how important his next shot would be. Despite the pressure, or maybe because of it, staying totally focused on the precision task required, he nailed the shot. The ball finished no more than three feet from the hole. Woods holed his putt for a birdie two. Donald followed him in for the team to remain one-up, setting up victory. They duly halved the final hole and thousands of European supporters breathed a sigh of relief.

At this stage, the team scores were USA 10, Team Europe 5. No team had recovered to win from worse than 10 − 6 at the beginning of the final day in all the years since 1927. The Americans had turned that exact score around just once, at The Country Club in Brookline, Massachusetts in 1999, on a remarkable day of golf that the European side much preferred to forget. A great deal was therefore riding on the final Day Two match. For this reason, Ian Poulter, in his trademark visor and shades, was beginning to look like the hero of the day.

Poulter had rolled in a remarkable putt on the fourteenth green for a birdie, and followed that with an even more remarkable three at the next, chipping his ball into the hole over a bunker from thirty yards. The crowd roar was deafening. He and McIlroy, having finally erased the deficit, were now level with their opponents. On sixteen, Poulter faced another opportunity. He was looking at a very tricky downhill twenty-foot putt that was going to break five or six feet from the left. Cool as ice, he stood over the ball and made a beautifully smooth, rhythmic swing with the putter, launching it tenderly on its way. Even the commentators were holding their breath as it rolled slowly, picking up speed down the slope, heading just off-centre for the cup. 'He hasn't done it again, has he?' comes the excited voice from the television. 'He has!' Applause almost drowned out his voice.

On they go to the seventeenth. This time, it is the American Zach Johnson who delights his partner, Jason Dufner, by landing his ball stiff, just three feet from the hole. Poulter's approach shot is good, but again leaves him a very missable twelve-foot putt that will swing, this time from right-to-left. Once again, the man from Woburn slots it square in the hole. He and McIlroy are, at last, one-up with only one hole to play. There is no way they can lose the match. A half is guaranteed, but both men still feel they absolutely must win.

The quiet American, Dufner, threatens to spoil the show on eighteen, this time with a terrific second shot inside four feet, from where he will surely be rolling in the final putt. With McIlroy out of it, the situation demands Poulter, once again, to come up with a superhuman display. He must sink his putt from fifteen feet for, unbelievably, his fifth birdie in a row. This alone will give the pair victory in the match.

The captain, Olazabal, the vice-captains, and all the European team players, are standing beside the green to watch... And Poulter does not disappoint. As if in slow-motion, the ball runs forward, takes the slight left-to-right borrow, and finally dives safely into the cup. Poulter, eyes bulging, immediately swivels, turning to his comrades, crying out 'Yessss' with the roar of a lion, fists pumping wildly. 'We can do it', he seems to be telling them, and in the playback later, you can see it in their tear-filled eyes. They believe him. 'Seve must be watching from heaven', says someone, to anyone who might listen. 'It's like having a thirteenth man on our side.'

Back at the house, Jamie was standing and cheering at the screen. This was terrific. He wished he had been there in person, instead of confined to bed for the afternoon, but at least he had witnessed the start of the fight-back and his next thought was to contact Chuck to double the bet they had on the match, preferably at favourable odds. For the visitors to win eight and a half points from a possible twelve on Sunday, as the home team had at Brookline, still seemed extremely unlikely, but this was exactly the kind of gamble that Jamie loved to take on.

Back in Sussex, it was late that Saturday evening. Holly was preparing for bed. She did not tune in to the golf and had no idea of the state of play. She had something else on her mind. She was sure that earlier she had actually heard the voice of the killer.

After leaving Rose Cottage, because it was on her way, she went first to the SRGC for a meeting with Peter Harding. In the event, there had not been anything new for him to report. He had not heard back from Jamie Royle. None of the staff or club members had mentioned anything helpful since the previous day. He gave Holly a list of the club's suppliers, mostly of food and drink, green-keeping requirements, their laundry service, the plumbers and electricians they used, and whatever else he could think of. He told her that he normally worked on Saturdays, when many club members came to play who were otherwise occupied during the week, and when quite a few club competitions took place. He added that he would also be there the following day as he only took alternate Sundays off, but Monday was his habitual rest day. Also, on Thursday afternoons with a regular group of friends, he regularly took time off to play a round of golf himself.

Holly had spotted Mark's car in the car park. He had not been in the clubhouse, so she guessed he was out on the course, playing. It could be a couple of hours before he returned, and she could think of no reason to linger. She thought about leaving him a note on his windscreen, but could not think of anything appropriate to write. She was a little annoyed that she had even thought about it. 'Get a grip, Girl!' she told herself, relieved that no-one could hear her. Then, whispering this time, with something like a sigh, she repeated, 'Do try and get a grip on yourself...'

It was only three minutes' drive from the club to 'Greenings' and the homicide incident suite. Two rooms on the ground floor had been set up, full of desks, telephones and people. As expected,

Holly found food and drinks in the kitchen. Someone with a sense of priority had brought in tea and coffee, bottled water, plenty of assorted rolls and sandwiches, soups and pizza slices, with both a kettle and a microwave oven to heat up whatever was necessary. There was also a bowl full of fruit. She helped herself to a cup of tea and a tuna roll before returning to the communications hub next door where the duty officer gave her a brief update.

'There's nothing much to report, Sergeant.' This was DC Sally Blackshaw, an eager recent recruit from the uniform branch. 'We've been trying to contact removal firms, but many of them, especially since noon, have just left their answering machines on, saying they open again on Monday. We've left messages saying how to contact us; and those we have got through to mostly say they need time to check their records and will get back to us next week. None of them report unusual or unauthorized use of a vehicle after dark on Wednesday.'

'We've also got detectives calling door-to-door in the neighbourhood, asking about any possibly suspicious goings on', she continued, 'But none have reported back yet.'

Holly asked her to spread the word about checking horse-transport vehicles as well… 'And another thing, Sally', she said apologetically. 'Can you please check psychiatric hospitals? We know poor Jane had severe anorexia. Could she have been treated, either locally or in a specialist eating disorders unit somewhere? '

It was going to be a lot of work, and would take time. 'Have any members of the public phoned in?' she asked finally.

'Only a few inquisitive people', the Constable replied. 'No-one with any useful info… Not so far, anyway.'

Holly finished her snack and was about to return to the kitchen for an apple or a tangerine when the phone beside her started to ring. The male voice, when she picked it up, sounded muffled or croaky.

'You're after the wrong people', it said. 'It's those golf club murderers you have to go after.' There was a click and that was it. Holly stood there, listening, trying to imprint the voice on her memory. All the calls were recorded, of course, and she later listened to that brief message a dozen or more times, but never again did it sound as chilling as on that first occasion.

By simply dialling 1471, Holly had the number. Quickly calling the duty officer with access to the reverse directory, she soon ascertained that the call had come from a public telephone in a pub called 'The Grapes' beside the River Rother just north of Midhurst. Holly called her boss and, getting the go-ahead, set off there at once. The journey took only twelve minutes.

Approaching the pub, Holly was realistically prepared to be disappointed. It would be too good to be true to find the man with the croaky voice quietly still sitting there supping away on a pint; but Holly was still fully alert. Once parked up, she quickly took photographs of all the vehicles in the car park and nearby, making sure to include their number-plates. Once inside the building, she identified the landlord and quickly showed him her warrant card. Muttering something about Sussex Police business, she drew him to one side, noticing at the same time that the place was buzzing, still busy with people finishing off their lunches.

She explained about the phone call, and her search for the caller. The landlord, a tall, genial heavily whiskered fellow called Dave, had no recall of serving a man with a distinctively gruff or husky voice that day. He said he would ask his staff. Sadly for Holly, he also told her that there was no CCTV in the pub or trained on the car park. She had already ascertained that there was none covering the roadway either. It was just too remote from the centre of town.

As for the phone, it turned out to be in a short passageway leading to the toilets and, as it happened, close to one of the exits. The caller could have entered from the car-park. If he had made the call and departed swiftly, without entering the bar or restaurant area, no-one need have seen him. Holly took pictures again. She noticed one man sitting alone, concentrating on a newspaper, the debris of a roast beef meal before him, a half-filled glass of red wine within reach. But this was not her man. In a clear voice, he said he was alone because his wife was in hospital, having had breast cancer surgery a few days earlier. His own cooking skills were rudimentary, he added, hence this visit to the pub.

On questioning, none of the bar staff, nor any of the waiters serving tables, remembered a man with a sinister, hoarse or gravelly voice. 'He might have been faking it', Holly told herself, 'When he spoke on the phone.' Climbing into bed, many hours later, she had the same thought once again. Either way, something macabre about that tone of voice persisted as she replayed the message over in her mind before finally falling asleep: *'You're after the wrong people. It's those golf club murderers you have to go after.'*

THE 11ᵀᴴ CHAPTER

Holly awoke the following morning to the muffled distant peal of Sunday's church bells. Putting on a T-shirt, shorts and socks, she then donned a track-suit and went to look for her trainers. Drinking tea in the kitchen, soon after, she gazed sleepily through the window into the mist for several minutes, then set off for a run.

It was cold as she made her way towards the Shoreham footbridge, but she soon warmed up as, taking the towpath westward along the river, she ran past the long row of beached houseboats, many drab and weather-beaten, but others painted gaily. There was one, in particular, that had been created in fantastical shapes and colours, cleverly assembled from copious junkyard material: the side of a small caravan, the front of a washing machine to make a porthole, a large section of a road-coach complete with front and back wheels; and, deliberately plunged into the mud beside it, great empty shell-casings and other warlike paraphernalia covered in slogans of peace.

Holly smiled at the incongruous scene then hurried on, shedding her top layer, wrapping the track-suit arms round her waist as she did so, crossing the main road when she reached it, heading for the tunnel under the railway that took her through into Shoreham Airport. Sticking close to the perimeter, running on grass beside the metalled road, she emerged minutes later on the north side, turned due east, crossed the picturesque wooden toll-bridge, then north on the towpath again, under the flyover and on beside the river until she reached the derelict cement works, at which point she turned, retracing her steps back past the toll-bridge into Shoreham Town and over the walking bridge home. She had covered just over eight miles, taking a few minutes over the hour, and would have been quicker had she not paused beside a riverside bench at one point to do body-stretches, standing briefly too in wonder at the majestic view of Lancing College's famous chapel building, rising splendidly out of the mist across the River Adur, its tall perpendicular gothic turrets reflecting back the sun's golden rays, seagulls circling, riding the air currents, swooping and rising again, a wonderfully uplifting vision.

As intended, the run had emptied Holly's mind of worldly concerns. Inside her kitchen again, she found herself singing. Having put crumbs out earlier, she could see a blackbird through the window foraging on her tiny back lawn. She found herself singing a barely remembered childhood hymn, popularised later by Cat Stevens: *"Morning has broken, like the first morning... Blackbird has spoken, like the first bird!"* Unable to bring any more words to mind, she continued humming anyway as she made more tea and toast. 'La La La-la-la... La La La-la-la', she sang, on and on. 'What has got into me?' she thought, eventually sitting down to eat. 'I suppose I must be happy.'

Police work was not always conducive to her happiness. Holly tended to be serious in mood much of the time, and was content most days to be more or less emotionally neutral. Maybe her current cheeriness was connected to having an excellent night's sleep; then she remembered another fleeting erotic dreamlet from the previous night, about a lover's nocturnal visit. 'Oh my goodness', she thought, connecting this pleasant but disturbing reverie instantly once more with Mark. 'What am I going to do about that man?'

At that same instant, spookily, her phone began bleeping. As if telepathically, the lover in her dreams had sent her a message: *'Golf lesson # 2? I'll be at the club later… 2.00 pm?'*

Irrationally feeling conspired against, Holly hesitated to reply. She decided to have a shower and get ready first.

There was, of course, still police work to be done. It may have been Sunday, with a reduced roster at Greenings and fewer people contactable by telephone but, on a case like this, Holly always felt she had to be doing something, especially at such an early stage when they had so little to go on. She would go to the incident suite, go through all the reports from the day before, then she would check on the group doing outside enquiries, mainly door-to-door calls on residents in the local area. Perhaps she would go to the golf club, if only to check in with the Colonel, but not before late in the afternoon. That, at least, was her plan.

In the event, when she reached it shortly after one o'clock, Greenings was closed. DI Garbutt had sent everyone home for the day, so Holly faced a dilemma. What to do?

After phoning her father and leaving a message to say she would be over to share an evening meal later, Holly decided to make her way back to The Grapes, where she sat for the best part of an hour over a soft drink, a tuna baguette and a packet of crisps, watching and waiting, admittedly with little real hope or expectation, in case her croaky-voiced murder-suspect should return. The man with the newspaper was there again too, seated at the same corner table. 'I'm making the most of it', he called across to Holly at one point. 'My wife's coming home tomorrow, and I won't be getting as good a feed as this for a while.'

Holly smiled back. 'What must it be like to have your life-partner diagnosed with cancer?' she was thinking. 'Maybe better not to have a partner...?' But when she had finished her snack and did not want another drink, she knew she was wasting her time. She also realized she was deliberately keeping Mark waiting, yet it did not feel right to go enjoying herself while there was still a killer at large.

When she left the inn, she got into the Nissan and looked at her map of the region, plotting a circuitous route backwards and forwards along unmarked country roads to get a better feel for the area, and possibly even spot something unusual that might be connected with the case. It was Holly's way of letting her intuition run free. Once during her perambulations she was stuck for a few minutes behind a tractor pulling a mucky trailer. This, she realized, like many other farm and equestrian transports, would have been too dirty to have allowed the red leather chairs to remain so clean when left in the open that night. Hay, straw, various seeds, horse-feed and manure would have contaminated them, or would at least have left traces. Even a regular removal lorry would have left telltale traces of dust in crevices or underneath the chairs, despite the rain's attempt to obliterate them. 'What would the forensic report reveal?'

These were her thoughts as she drove finally into the car park at the golf club, well after three o'clock. Mark, from the practice putting green, spotted her immediately. 'Here you are', he said simply, by way of greeting. 'I knew you'd come.' Holly was forced to admit to herself that she had known it all along too.

Less than six miles distant from The Grapes Inn, along a turning northwards from the road to Petworth, in run-down buildings that had once been a traditional farm dwelling with outhouses, the man with the husky voice was lying on a dusty sofa in a chaotically untidy room, in front of a grate containing the remnants of burnt ash logs and cold ashes from the previous night's fire. He was feeling unwell, short of breath, coughing intermittently, pale, sweaty, and his heart was racing. He was getting used to attacks like this since the diagnosis a month earlier. Tomorrow, he would be starting his final week of radiotherapy, but already had the feeling that it was not doing any good. He was angry about that, about the injustice of getting lung cancer not long after turning fifty when he had never smoked in his life; but there was also something deeper that he had been angry about for a very long time, and now, when he had finally tried to get justice, to do something about bringing shame and retribution on those who deserved it, everything seemed to be going wrong. His chances of making them pay were diminishing as his life ebbed away. The perpetrators of sheer evil, in his eyes, were getting away with it, and that made him angrier than ever.

That morning, pressure-cleaning his vehicle one more time in the shed across the yard, he had heard the announcer on a local radio station say the police were still trying to identify the woman whose body had been found on the golf course, and that the land-owner and President of the club, Mr James Royle, was away overseas on business and unavailable for comment. Coughing up a small gobbet of blood-flecked mucus and spitting it on the ground, the angry man knew his plan had backfired. His ambition, that Royle and Gryllock would be forced to admit their depravity in public, wasn't going to work, but he did not want to risk revealing his own identity, not yet anyway, if it could be helped. 'Something else… I'm going to have to do something else', he muttered to himself. 'If only I felt a bit stronger.'

A wave of nausea suddenly gripped him, so that he was forced to retrace his steps across the yard to go and lie down. He could not help thinking in his befuddled way that it might have been best to have buried his dead sister, Fran, but that was not how it seemed at the time.

Over in Chicago – while his cancer-ridden, would-be nemesis, exhausted from his latest efforts to remove all tell-tale signs of his vehicle's macabre night-cargo of a few of days earlier, was regaining strength – Jamie Royle was already at the Medinah clubhouse, eating pancakes and maple syrup and drinking coffee with Gary and Louise as Chuck Flanagan came by to join their small group. Catherine had stayed behind to finalize travel arrangements for Monday and monitor incoming messages and calls.

The first Ryder Cup match of the day was not due to tee off until shortly after eleven, which gave the breakfasting spectators plenty of time. They were discussing how best to catch the action, an impossible task with twelve vital and exciting matches about to take place. Television coverage would show everything, or as much as possible, but there was nothing like being out there, on the ground, in the moment, when things were actually happening. Chuck was officiating in Match Four, the match between Justin Rose and the accomplished left-handed American player, Phil Mickelson. Jamie would be able to ride in a golf cart close up behind that group, inside the spectator ropes. He had seen Rose beat Mickelson in a previous Ryder Cup, at the infamous Valhalla Club in Kentucky in 2008, when the hapless Nick Faldo's European team had gone down to Paul Azinger's Americans by eleven-and-a-half points to sixteen-and-a-half. Rose was obviously this very day going to have to beat 'Lefty' again.

Jamie and Chuck had already spoken to consolidate their bet. Chuck was giving two-to-one odds against a European victory, and Jamie was staking twenty-five thousand US dollars. 'What if there's a tie?' he asked. 'Then we're even', Chuck quickly replied, 'And the bet carries over to our match on Monday, if you like.'

'No', Jamie decided. 'If money changes hands today, we'll play double-or-quits on Monday… How's that?'

Flanagan agreed. 'Okay', he said. 'So, no money on a tie for today, even if Europe manage to retain the cup… There has to be a clear win.'

'Right', said Jamie. 'That's fair enough!'

The evening before, after watching the action reach its gripping conclusion, headache forgotten, Jamie had taken the second buggy to the clubhouse where, bold as brass, picking up a magnum of champagne and a fistful of glasses from the bar, he had gone straight into the European players locker-room to shake hands and congratulate everyone. By chance, the first person he encountered, coming out of the showers wearing nothing but a large towel wrapped around his middle, was Ian Poulter.

'That was so good, Ian', Jamie said, offering to pour him a glass.

'Actually', said the golfer, waving him away, turning towards his locker, 'I think I'd rather just have a beer.'

Another player's caddy, standing nearby, also took the opportunity to congratulate Poulter. When asked how he had managed to pull off such a stunning victory, the hero of the hour turned to look him calmly in the face. 'Well Mick', he said, as if the answer was obvious 'It just had to be done.'

Jamie enjoyed recounting that one later when he caught up with Gary and Chuck, mimicking Poulter's intensity, his icy look and matter-of-fact tone of voice… *'Well, my man, it simply had to be done!'* Intoxicated by the moment, completely ignoring that Poulter had simply dismissed him, Jamie could not help the embellishment. 'How cool was that?' he asked his companions unnecessarily. 'How brilliantly 'king cool was that! The man's a marvel.' His admiration was excessive. 'We are definitely going to win tomorrow', he added. 'Definitely…'

But now, with a new day facing the two teams, many European supporters were seeing a more realistic picture and preparing themselves for likely defeat. 'At least it won't be a walkover', Gary heard a man with a Union Jack hat say to his companion, a woman with the yellow on blue, twelve-star, European logo face-painted on either cheek. 'What do you mean?' she replied. 'I believe in them. I'm sure we can still fight back and win.'

Louise clapped her on the back. 'Good for you', she said. 'I agree! We're not going to stand for defeatist talk. Are we?'

She and Gary headed off in the direction of the first tee with their new friends, who were from Staffordshire, to try and secure a place in the stands. Meanwhile, Chuck and Jamie made their way to the practice range where players were going through their warm-up drills. Luke Donald left for the putting green soon after they arrived. He and his opponent, Bubba Watson, were out first, followed by Poulter and Webb Simpson. For the moment, Rose was the only European there hitting balls before Paul Lawrie and Nicholas Colsaerts appeared… But where was Rory? McIlroy's tee-time – 11.35 am – was before Rose's, and he had not yet appeared at the course.

Astonishingly, McIlroy had misunderstood which time zone he was in, and was still in his hotel room some distance from the course, thinking he had an hour and a half until his match was due to start. It was in fact thirty minutes. Someone soon got through to him and put him right, but there was serious traffic, and had he arrived even one minute late for his game, he would have been disqualified. Keegan Bradley would have been awarded the match.

Somehow Rory avoided panicking. Down in the hotel lobby, he spotted a US policeman who obligingly agreed to take him across to the course in his car. Using the siren made their journey quicker, and Rory was changing his shoes in the locker-room, picking up 'breakfast' – a single energy bar – with a full ten minutes to go. He made it to the tee box five minutes later, greeting his startled opponent, ready to play without so much as a single warm-up shot or practice putt. Nevertheless, as it turned out, he was confident and in excellent form. Not much more than three hours later, he had beaten Bradley by two holes up with one to play, an exemplary 'two-and-one' victory, by which time Luke Donald had triumphed convincingly, also 2 & 1, and Paul Lawrie even more so, the Scotsman's victory score a massive 5 & 3 against the luckless Brandt Snedeker, blitzed on this occasion by utterly superior play. Lawrie, an astonishing six under par for fifteen holes, said afterwards that competing in the Ryder Cup helped him play better than at any other time in his life.

Soon after Rory, Ian Poulter won his match too, as he had confidently predicted, although it had taken a miracle curling shot, a hundred and fifty yards around a stand of trees to the green on the final hole to do it. Astonishingly, the first four wins going to Europe, the match was now tied at ten-all… But it was a long way from over.

———————

Holly was ambivalent, both about the game of golf and equally about her budding friendship with Mark. Deep down she was afraid that things would go the same way they had with her husband, Tony, ending badly. Because it might encourage him past the point at which she felt comfortable, she was not at all sure she wanted another golf lesson, so she told Mark she had to see Peter Harding first. But, the Colonel having nothing new to say, she was left with nothing else to do but go outside again.

'Have a try at putting', Mark offered when she dawdled back over ten minutes later. 'It's pretty easy, and it is an important part of the game. Golfers know, "You drive for show and putt for dough!" That means sinking putts is how to win matches... Did you see Ian Poulter last night? His putting pretty much saved the day for Europe.'

Holly admitted missing the Saturday night Ryder Cup action. Mark shrugged. 'Well, I shall be glued to it later, but we've time before it starts again. The first singles match tees off just after five o'clock our time. Come on!'

The SRGC practice green, sheltered from the prevailing wind by a high beech hedge, was exemplary, covering over four hundred square yards of beautifully manicured greensward. The undulations were subtle, and the turf silky-smooth. Mark set up a row of golf balls six inches away from each other and about six feet away from one of the holes.

'This is how you do it', he said. 'The important thing is to keep the face of the putter lined up square, perpendicular to the hole as you swing through the ball... Like this...'

He showed her what to do, swinging the putter-head gently and rhythmically, backwards and forwards like a pendulum. After stroking each shot, he moved his feet forward exactly six inches, making contact with each of the balls in turn. Four of them went into the hole, the other two missing the cup slightly to the left.

'Have a go!'

Holly accepted the invitation hesitantly. The putter seemed a bit long for her, and she gripped it awkwardly at first. Mark was setting the row of balls up again as she took a couple of tentative practice swings. She thought she knew what he meant by 'keeping the putter-face square through the ball', but it was not easy to accomplish.

'Let me show you', Mark said, approaching her, putting his right hand forward to cover hers, turning to plant his feet either side behind her back, wrapping his left arm around, reaching for the putter with his other hand.

'Just stand still', he instructed, his lips now only a few inches from her left ear once again. 'You're very tense', he continued. 'See if you can relax'.

Holly was tense. 'Is this golf or love-making, or both?' she was wondering. Part of her wanted to be able to relax, but a stronger part seemed intent on resistance. Undaunted, Mark pressed his knees forwards gently against the backs of hers, forcing Holly into a slight crouch. He also said to keep her back upright, while bending her head forward a little so that her leading eye, her left eye, was directly over the ball. Then, hands clasped firmly over hers, he moved them first an inch away from the hole, then a couple of inches forward. The putter head moved correspondingly further, about six inches back and a foot forward, the resulting thrust propelling the golf ball in the right direction, but not quite hard enough to reach the hole.

Mark shuffled them forward and tried again, moving their fused hands slightly further in each direction. Holly had no time to watch the ball disappear below ground before Mark shuffled them forward again to repeat the process. It was, she had to admit, a pleasantly cosy experience. By the time the sixth ball was on its way, she had relaxed sufficiently to be able to feel, in her own hands and body, what Mark was making happen through puppetry. When he let go of her, saying, 'Now it's your turn', she was ready to give it a proper try.

The novice's first three shots went off-line, two to the left and one to the right. The first was also hit way too softly, and the others too hard. 'This is difficult', she said.

Mark, saying nothing, continued retrieving the balls, replacing them, extending the original row. Holly then hit three in a row, straight towards the hole. The first went too quickly, hit the back of the cup and bounced out. The second stopped short, and the third, after Mark swiftly got the second one out of the way, fell neatly into the hole. Holly looked to Mark for congratulations, which were duly forthcoming. 'Keep going', he said, placing the next ball a little further away than the others. 'One swallow doesn't make a summer, you know.'

Holly persevered. By the time Mark was placing balls twelve or more feet away from the cup, she was missing most but feeling more competent, especially when he explained that golfers are expected to take two putts per hole. 'That's what the par of the course is based on', he reminded her. 'If you can lag putts from this distance and over to within 'tap-in' range, which is to say about the length of a gin bottle, or maybe just over, that's great! That's all you need.'

'And speaking of gin', he added, 'Why don't we stop now, and please let me buy you a drink?'

Mark took the putter to his car while Holly made her way into the clubhouse. She chose coffee, when he rejoined her, rather than gin, and noticed that the golf matches were starting up again on the television. The crowd watching in the member's lounge was smaller than it had been on the first evening, but no less eager for European victory. As the excitement began building over the next hour, Holly decided not to stay and get involved. Mark was disappointed when she left, well before any of the matches were completed, but accepted her explanation that she was keen to reach her father's house before seven o'clock. She was already aware of the thrill surrounding the unfolding battle, though, and the tension had increased by the time she reached Oving. When she and her father sat for their meal in front of the television set, not very long afterwards, the first five matches were already over.

After the teams reached ten-all, there had been a setback for Europe. On Friday afternoon, the Belgian golfer Nicholas Colsaerts had managed an astonishing performance in his fourball match, partnering Lee Westwood to beat the redoubtable pairing of Woods and Stricker by the slenderest margin of one hole. In doing so, Colsaerts had scored an unbelievable nine birdies and an eagle, sinking a series of enormous-length putts. Sadly now, two days later, his putting skill had deserted him. He lost his match against Dustin Johnson by 'three-and-two'. Graeme McDowell for Europe also seemed to be struggling against Zach Johnson. Things were not looking good.

THE 12TH
CHAPTER

As well as whatever had happened since with work colleagues and such, Holly's hesitancy over Mark stemmed originally from the pain she had felt after the break-up with Tony. The couple had met when she was eighteen, during Holly's first term at Sussex University. She had quickly become infatuated, believing herself in love with her Greek god for a long time; but he turned out to be different from the person she thought she knew.

Her father had taken a close interest in her schoolwork and, responding to his encouragement, she had excelled, particularly at the sixth form college where she studied geography, English and maths. She was also in a cross-country running team and played badminton to a high standard. One of her teachers even suggested she apply to Cambridge, but Holly's ambitions were more modest. At that stage, she did not know where her talents might lie, and therefore what best to study. The only drive she experienced was to find out more about people, and about herself, perhaps something important about the meaning of life, so a degree in psychology held some appeal. It was a popular course, and there was competition, but she interviewed well and had no trouble obtaining a place.

Most first-year students took lodgings in town. Holly shared a large house not too far from the university campus with four other women, one of whom – Brenda – became a particular friend. Whereas Holly tended towards reserve, Brenda was outgoing and feisty, a social animal. They complemented each other, and it was Brenda who encouraged Holly to get involved during Fresher's Week and subsequently with the various activities on offer.

About half-way through the first term, her new friend told Holly she had started seeing someone, and Brenda's new boyfriend, it turned out, was a rugby player. The team were playing the following Saturday, so Brenda tried to make Holly come and watch the match. There would be a party after, she promised and eventually her persistence paid off. On the day though, Holly was standing on the touchline in a cool wind with rain threatening, wishing she was elsewhere, taking little interest in the game. Suddenly, she became aware of the ball hurtling towards her, chased by a motley mob of mud-spattered men. Out front was a short, lithe fast-running fellow with a halo of tightly curled black hair and a bushy drooping moustache, reminiscent of the young Che Guevara. Ignoring spectators, this figure barrelled right past Holly after the ball, retrieved it effortlessly, tossed it to an opponent and returned to his place, ready to catch the pass should his side happen to win the line-out. When the ball fell to earth, a wild mêlée formed quickly over it, many muscular legs mercurially intertwined such that the ebullient Sussex scrum-half had to work hard. Finally managing to scramble it free, he made a dummy pass to his right, jigged abruptly to the left, ran forward, stopped suddenly as an opposing player flew wide of him, then resumed his run for the try-line, putting on a terrific turn of speed, outpacing all in pursuit, finally running towards the centre of the pitch, deftly placing the ball on the ground directly beneath the goalposts before raising his arms triumphantly in the air.

Holly kept her eye on the try-scorer after that, transfixed by his alacrity and versatility, his sheer energy and inventiveness. It was, of course, Tony Angel, who scored another miraculous solo-effort try again towards the end of the match.

At the party in the evening, Brenda made a big deal of introducing them to each other. Holly felt awkward, but Tony was following his usual plan: to keep buying her drinks and keep talking. He told her he was a third-year student of economics, destined for a career in the City. His family were from Greece originally, from the island of Skiathos. His father and uncles were merchants. The family name had been changed from 'Angelis' to 'Angel' because this was better for business. He had two older sisters and three younger brothers. They all went to Greece every summer; parents, grand-parents, uncles, aunts, cousins and siblings, a large colourful tribe.

As Tony chatted on, feeling rather shy, Holly still held back. She was intrigued by this gifted, god-like individual, who seemed more self-assured than anyone she had ever met; but she was not going to let him knock her over on their first meeting. She wasn't just anyone's bimbo so, after stretching out a couple of weak gin and tonics, she said, 'No more, thanks. I've got to go. I've an essay to finish…' Tony, of course, did not believe her. No-one escaped his charm once he set his mind on seduction; but this time he seemed to have met his match. 'I'll give you my phone number, though', Holly relented. And that had been their first date.

Afterwards, when he phoned and asked her out, and asked her out again, she was unable to resist. They were sleeping partners within a month, but not before Holly extracted from him a kind of proposal. 'I will only go to bed with you if you promise to marry me one day', she said as they climbed the stairs to his room after a night out; but she knew it was already too late.

They became a couple. Holly took Tony to meet her father, who liked this sporty young chap right away but still urged caution and patience on his daughter. It was much longer, though, almost nine months, before Tony took her to meet his family, and then only for a fleeting visit to his parents in their big house near Richmond Park. Mr Angel senior, Alexis, was unfailingly cheerful and polite, an older, greyer, less agile version of his son. Tony's mother, Iphigenia, a large earthy person given to wearing black flowing garments concealing the mounds of her curvaceous, well-covered torso, also received Holly with courtesy, although her hardness of gaze suggested she would prefer her son to be spending his time with a Greek girl. By then though, her young heart fully committed, Holly told her self she did not care what the parents thought. Tony assured her his family would quickly come to accept her totally. Convinced too that she was the only one for him, he agreed to get married late in the following spring. By then, having graduated, he expected to be in work. The new rugby season would also by then be over.

They were happy together throughout the engagement. Tony was offered a good job in London with a firm of stockbrokers, commuting by train from Brighton every day. His father gave him a portion of his inheritance for a substantial down-payment on a new two-bedroom apartment in the fashionable Brighton Marina development, and they completed the purchase by getting a mortgage at a favourable rate.

Holly stayed on in her lodgings temporarily, but spent several nights each week at the flat with Tony. They planned a relatively low-key civil wedding, which went ahead in the May of Holly's second year, soon after her twentieth birthday. It was attended by Tony's parents and a big mob of his family, by Holly's dad, an uncle and aunt, by Brenda and some of the rugby team, including

Roger, the scrum forward who was still Brenda's boyfriend. Holly had not invited her mother, had not even told her about it. After the ceremony, there was a reception at Stanmer Park House, which went smoothly enough. Everyone, even the groom's mother, seemed joyful. The couple returned to the Marina for the night, and next day took a plane from Heathrow to Toronto, spending the first part of the honeymoon at Niagara Falls.

Entering the fourteenth-floor hotel room, Holly was instantly delighted at the superlative view through the floor to ceiling picture-window. There, immediately below, were the Horseshoe Falls, shimmering majestically in the sunshine. It was like magic, mesmerising. Both of them, drawn magnetically to it, just stood there and gawped. 'Amazing!' said one. 'Beautiful!' said the other. But they were both basically dumbstruck.

Later on that first afternoon, like any tourists, they walked along holding hands beside the great waterway at the top of the falls, then went into the tunnel underneath the cascade, unable to converse because deafened by the roar of countless tons of water flowing over the precipice every second only a few feet away. In the evening, they dined in the hotel restaurant from where they could see both the Horseshoe and the American falls, the whole scene fantastically lit in a kaleidoscopic display of shifting rainbow colours.

In the morning, as they looked out on the glorious vista once more, Holly pointed to a boat, crammed with people, heading straight up into the steaming vortex directly below the falls. It was one of the 'Maid of the Mist' fleet, passengers all in blue plastic capes against the drenching spray, the steamboat encircled by masses of wheeling seagulls flying hither and thither. 'Let's go on it, Tony!' she said. 'I want to go on that boat.' So, after breakfast, they did.

Still exhilarated, in the afternoon they took a ride across the bridge to the American side. However, quickly convinced that the Canadians had the better views, they soon returned. Still slightly jet-lagged, they went to their room to rest and do what honeymooners also do at such times, before going downtown to eat ribs in a traditional beer-house and grill. The next day, as planned, they flew on to New York.

When they checked into their hotel downtown, Holly had a question on her mind. 'Why is this city called the Big Apple?' she asked. The hotel was a massive edifice, once resplendent but now hanging grimly to only a fading residue of its former glory, catering for low-budget tourists, exchange-students, impoverished long-term residents and the like. 'I've no idea', Tony replied to her question, equally puzzled. 'I'll look it up.' Later he told her that, although the State of New York was indeed a big apple producing part of the country, this was incidental. New York City had first been called the Big Apple by a sportswriter in connection with horse-racing in the 1920's, and the nickname had been revived deliberately in 1970 for the purpose of promoting tourism. 'That's America for you', he added. 'It's all about capitalism, generating money... I love it!'

In the evenings, they went to a Broadway show, to a jazz club, to the movies and to try out different restaurants – Italian, Chinese, Mexican. During the day, they once took a boat ride around Manhattan Island, getting good views of the Statue of Liberty and many other landmarks. Another time, they went up to the observation level of one of the famous twin towers, the tallest buildings in the city. Here, Holly was surprised to find Tony upset by the sway. Although he tried to conceal it, she had not seen him anxious like this before. These monolithic structures were significantly affected by wind forces, and were moving noticeably back and forth in relation to each other. She knew it was perfectly safe, but Tony grew worried enough to want to cut their visit short.

'Let's get down, Holl', he said. 'I've got a bad feeling up here.' So they left. Holly often thought about that later, after the 9/11 terrorist attacks. 'Did Tony have some kind of premonition?' she wondered. The catastrophic outrages on both buildings the following year were going, in unforeseen ways, significantly to affect both their lives.

Their plan, the next afternoon, was to take a train from Grand Central Station to New Rochelle, to visit one of Tony's cousins and her husband. Before that, in the morning, Holly decided to take a brisk run in Central Park. Tony demurred, preferring to stay at the hotel and catch up with emails. It was a pleasantly cool spring day. They had enjoyed a stroll in the park a couple of days earlier, after visiting the famous Frick Collection of artworks. Familiar with the layout, Holly had a route to follow and soon got into her stride, jogging along at a good pace to the invigorating rhythm of the music emanating from the smartphone, strapped to her upper left arm.

Focused on the sounds in her earphones, almost in a trance, oblivious of her surroundings, coming across a trash can lying in the middle of the narrow path, she was suddenly forced to slow down. The trail at that point threaded through a small copse of trees. Ready to move the obstacle out of the way, Holly had stopped and was stooping to lift it when two young men appeared, menacingly forcing her into the shrubbery, pinning her up against the trunk of a tree. One of them held a short, sharp-looking knife to her throat. The other, with a longer blade, swiftly cut her phone free from its straps, carelessly lacerating her upper-arm as he did so. Then he slit and removed the small belt-bag she used to hold her credit card and small amount of cash. Holly was affronted, but she was also terrified, her eyes full of tears. Later, she could not with certainty recall what her hooded assailants had looked like, or even the colour of their skins. In fear, she automatically obeyed when one of them told her to take off her rings. Then, as quickly as they had appeared, the men vanished.

In the immediate aftermath, Holly sank to the ground, trembling, tears falling freely now. 'How could this happen?' She started thinking. 'It's daylight. There are people nearby... What shall I do?'

An older couple, walking a pair of ridiculously groomed white poodles, happened upon her soon after the attack, as she was stumbling back onto the pathway, blood trickling down her arm. Concerned, commiserating with her, they immediately took her in hand. 'Where are you staying?' they asked. 'We'll walk with you... How awful! We feel so sorry for you... This is no way for visitors to our country to be treated... It's drugs, you know. They'll take anything from anybody to get money to pay for drugs...'

On and on the couple, taking it in turns, kept up the one-sided conversation until they reached the hotel, handing her over to the concierge who called Tony down to the lobby to retrieve her like a damaged package.

Once up in the room, her husband was quick to show Holly his irritation. 'Did you report it?' he wanted to know. 'We'll have to report it, Holl! We won't be able to claim on the insurance without a police statement of some kind. I paid such a lot for that diamond ring too. It was expensive.'

This was what seemed to her to be troubling him most: not the trauma to her, but the financial consequences. Accordingly, while she had a shower and changed her clothes, he was on the phone to cancel the credit card, relieved to discover that it had not yet been used by the thieves. Next, he alerted the mobile phone company, so that the account was blocked. And even then he stayed tense.

'Come on, Holl', he urged her, when all she wanted was a reassuring hug. 'We have to go and report this right now...'

So, when she was dressed, Tony marched her back uptown towards the park and into the nearest police precinct house, where an overbearing desk sergeant instructed them to wait. Twenty minutes later, Holly was still shivering from shock when an unexpectedly kindly policewoman took her into a side-room and recorded the details. In a calm, unhurried, sympathetic way, she drew out from Holly as much as she could remember. She also filled the silences by echoing much of what the couple with the poodles had said.

'I'm real sorry', she said finally, when the formalities were over and Holly had the signed report she needed to satisfy Tony. 'We might catch those guys. They're sure to try it again, and they're usually pretty careless, but I very much doubt you'll get any of your property back. I apologize… I want to apologize on behalf of America. This truly, I know, isn't right.' Afterwards, Holly remembered her kindness.

Back at the hotel, Holly refused to leave. She wasn't hungry. She just wanted to lie in bed and rest, she told Tony. 'You're fine, Holl!' he pleaded. 'Everything's fine now… Jasmine and Steve are expecting us…'

But Holly could not be persuaded. 'You go', she said. And he did, naively unaware of what a turning point in their relationship this might be. On the train he kept telling himself, 'She'll be fine'. But when his cousin heard what had happened, she was quick to admonish him. 'You should not have left her alone, Tony. It's a big deal what happened to her. We love to see you, but we would have understood if you had called and said what happened. Have something to eat quickly and go back to her.'

But the damage had already been done. Something had closed off in Holly's heart. She no longer felt that she could trust Tony enough to look out for her, to care for her, to love her. He was young too, she realized on reflection later, young and out of his depth, especially as far as her powerfully stirred-up emotions were concerned in the aftermath of the mugging. He was probably scared, deep down, himself, feeling ashamed and helpless to comfort her, capable only of insisting on the one thing he was able to control – minimizing their losses. At the time, though, she simply felt betrayed. She was still his wife, she told herself, and she would do what she could to make the marriage work, but he had proved unreliable, and things were never going to be quite the same again.

Back in England, on the surface, their lives resumed as before. Tony went to London on weekdays. Holly went back to class. However, a change had occurred in her here too, regarding her studies. During the first year, Holly had been disappointed to have been taught more about Pavlov and his dogs, laboratory rats running around in artificial mazes and statistics, than she had about people and human psychology. At the start of the second year, these misgivings subsided but, when she returned from New York, her attitude altered again. She felt as if she was drifting along, with no real sense of purpose. What she was doing did not seem important enough. It did not seem relevant to real life. The feeling grew in her that she should be doing something different, something more practical. She spoke to one of her tutors about it, describing how her motivation had dwindled, but all he said was 'keep going'. She did persevere, but only until the end of the academic year. Soon after that, decided at last, she signed on as a police probationer.

It was in the first week of September 2001 that she started training. By then, Tony was spending all week in London, sleeping in a spare room at a work colleague's flat near Clapham Common. Holly wondered if he had found someone else to share his bed, but they were still okay together when he came home at weekends. He could still make her laugh. Perhaps their marriage might still have become a success. They might have had children and raised them, taking them for summer holidays to Skiathos with all their cousins, uncles and aunts; but the possibility was cut short when the terrorists struck. The twin towers in Manhattan went down. This was to affect them particularly because Tony's employers, the investment company, had a sister office in New York, located in the North Tower.

It was a quarter to nine on the East Coast and coming up to two o'clock in the City of London when the first plane hit. The North Tower fell only about an hour and forty minutes later. The Wall Street stock exchange does not open until 9.30 am, but there had been trading up to the minute in London. Alerted immediately, this one hundred minutes was precisely how long London office staff had to download an immense amount of live data from the Manhattan office's mainframe computer. It was done as a massive dump of encrypted information, which later needed very careful sorting. All the London staff were therefore asked to work around the clock, each one conscious meanwhile of the appalling fate being suffered by their counterparts, friends in many cases, in the stricken sky-scraper across the Atlantic. A kind of feverish numbness prevailed. Some of their transatlantic colleagues would escape – late arrivals at work that day mostly – but there would also be many deaths. The London people stayed, working in shifts round the clock, collecting and collating data for the next five days.

It was an opportunity for Tony. He worked hard to good effect, and this was noticed. Six weeks later, he was offered promotion and a big pay hike if he would agree to relocate for six months to New York, where the company had set up new temporary offices in Lower Manhattan. 'It's too good an opportunity to miss, Holly', he said, when he told her on the phone. She could tell his mind was made up. 'It's only going to be half a year.'

Intuitively Tony knew that, having recently embarked on a new career, and with a lasting aversion to the city that had brutalized her indelibly, his wife might not wish to accompany him there, but he decided to seize the opportunity and go anyway. Their separation, while in a sense accidental, was also partly a choice they each made. Telling themselves it was temporary made it easier. However, Tony did well in New York. The energy and creative versatility he showed at rugby shone through under the challenging circumstances he faced there too. His bosses liked what they saw, and naturally asked him to stay on after the six months was over. There would be another pay rise to help him make up his mind, and extra payments to cover regular transatlantic flights for himself and Holly, or relocation expenses if they wanted.

Holly knew that if she could make herself go across and visit him, perhaps for a weekend every couple of months, there was a still chance they could make the marriage work even now, but she simply could not face the prospect. She started having panicky dreams about men chasing her with knives, and about aircraft exploding in the sky. Tony visited her once. They went to the South of France for a few days; but when, more than a year after the twin tower attacks, Tony told her he had started seeing someone else – Amy, an American economist with a rival company – Holly was not surprised. She cried, but she knew the break-up was inevitable. They were divorced without fuss six months later.

THE 13TH
CHAPTER

You can gauge much of what is happening at a Ryder Cup by the noise. There is a permanent background hubbub, then every time a magnificent shot is played or a decent length putt goes in, whenever a hole is won or lost, a great cheer rings out across the course. From the moment Ian Poulter and Bubba Watson galvanized their respective supporters on the first tee, the clamour was always going to be a major factor in the excitement. The huge majority in the thousands strong crowd were American, but the equally vocal Europeans, despite being heavily outnumbered, could still be heard cheering on their players... And it made a difference. Rory McIlroy said later that hearing the US crowd shouting out comments throughout his final round on Sunday, mostly teasing him for his late arrival at the course, helped secure his determination to win. That's why he bowed to the partisan throng in defiant appreciation after winning his match.

Jamie Royle, conscious of his privileged position following close to the players in the Rose-Mickelson match, had to restrain himself at times to avoid disturbing the players by making a sudden noise. Rose had won the first two holes and looked comfortable with his game, striking his shots sweetly and stroking his putts confidently, but the experienced left-handed American had stayed with him, winning back the fourth and fifth, halving six. Rose went ahead again on the par-five seventh, only to lose the short eighth to a fine birdie two. Rose won the ninth; Mickelson the eleventh, and they were still all-square after thirteen. Then the American eagled the par-five fourteenth to win the hole and go one-up with four to play. As the putt dropped, the crowd went wild. Jamie, knowing – as Rose himself must have done – how crucial it would be for the Brit to get back to even and keep his hope of victory alive, had a brief moment of doubt. This was surely the key match right here.

Jamie's confidence was shaken again, though, as he followed the players up the par-four fifteenth. Having found the front greenside bunker, Rose then played a dreadful shot. Jamie thought he might be about to collapse. The ball just flopped forward. It not only failed to escape the trap, but dived vertically into the sand, half buried on the up-slope, plugged right under the lip. The next shot looked pretty unplayable to Jamie, who was near enough to see clearly, especially as the American's ball was only five feet from the cup; but the Englishman stayed cool. Taking an awkward stance, one foot higher than the other, he managed calmly to splash the ball out of its tomb in the sand, the club's momentum forcing it to rise up in the air, allowing it to land gently on the putting surface from where it dutifully rolled right up close to the hole. Now it was the European fans' turn to let out a cheer. Surprisingly, Mickelson then missed his five-footer and the hole was halved… But it was still one-up to USA in this match.

Unable to get close to the next tee, Jamie sped ahead alongside the fairway. From his forward vantage point, he watched both golfers hit good drives, and then follow each other with excellent approach shots. Near the green, minutes later, he watched Mickelson putt first from about ten feet, and cursed softly under his breath when the ball disappeared into the hole for birdie. The pressure on Justin was phenomenal, he was thinking, but the Englishman still seemed calm and highly focused, preparing to hit the remaining eight-footer. When his ball followed his opponent's into the bottom of the cup, unable to hold back, Jamie finally joined the masses and gave out a very loud cheer. Rose was still one-down with only two holes remaining, but Jamie was beginning to feel that something amazing could happen.

Medinah's seventeenth hole across Lake Kadijah had been lengthened from the previous day, now measuring a hundred and seventy yards. This brought the bunkers, left and right, dangerously into play, and there was a steep slope at the back of the green. To avoid any risk of going in the water, most players hit long. Jamie was not much surprised therefore to see Mickelson hit his ball over the green and onto short grass towards the top of the slope. The pin that day was placed towards the front-right of the green, so Phil was going to have to judge his pitch shot perfectly down the hill to avoid it running on towards the water. He was known for being a genius at that kind of thing, though, so Rose must have known he needed something special to happen if he was going to win the hole… And he knew that he *must* win the hole; the only option if he was going to succeed in the match.

Jamie knew this too. It was such a pressure tee shot, but to aim at the flag would surely be overly risky. It was too close to the lake and also pretty near the right hand bunker. In a way it was a relief when he saw the ball struck cleanly, flying to the heart of the green and rolling on towards the back. At least it was dry and out of trouble, but it was all of forty feet from the cup. Two putts from there – down the slick slope, curling significantly from left to right – would be good… But would it be good enough?

The crowd behind the green were massed tight. Jamie had to stand up in his golf-cart to see anything, and still had only a partial view of Mickelson, playing his shot. True to form, it was brilliant, almost perfect. Jamie's heart was in his mouth as the ball nearly dropped; but thankfully missed the hole on the left by a mere half an inch, coming to a stop a foot or so away from the hole … a tap-in, duly conceded.

The pressure back on Rose, he began eying up his putt, still outwardly nerveless. Jamie could only see the top of his head, motionless for the time it took to swing the putter rhythmically back and forward. The crowd were totally hushed as the ball appeared in Jamie's left view, tracking fast in a right-hand curve towards the hole, and then suddenly diving right into it like a rat up a drainpipe. It was an astonishing birdie two, and a win… Match all square! The noise was deafening. Rose did not give a fist-pump, but instead struck an intensely defiant pose, arms outstretched downwards, face stern. It seemed as if he could not let himself get excited yet. He still had to win the eighteenth.

Mickelson meanwhile, in a supremely sportsmanlike gesture, turned to give Rose a big grin and congratulatory thumbs-up. Jamie saw this and marvelled. 'I wouldn't be so happy in his shoes', he thought. 'Doesn't he realize what just happened? Europe could win.' But, on his way through to the final tee box, he caught sight of a leader-board and saw that Colsaerts had lost his match to Dustin Johnson at the sixteenth. The American team was ahead again: 11 – 10. 'Justin's got to win now', he thought, more conscious of his bet than worried about European glory. 'There can be no other way.'

In the end, it came down to a putt. Mickelson's ball was slightly over the eighteenth green in two shots. Rose was closer, about twelve feet from the hole, facing an uphill putt that was going to curl significantly from right to left, the opposite way to his putt on seventeen. Jamie, back down the fairway some distance, unable to get nearer, could see in the brilliant autumn sunlight, shadows lengthening, that the grandstands were completely filled. The green itself was now ringed by the players from both sides who had already concluded their matches, by the captains of the two teams, the vice-captains, the caddies and the players' wives... Everyone looked tense, and complete silence descended on the scene as Mickelson rolled his lengthy putt down the hill, finishing close enough to be confident of a par four.

So now it was Rose's turn again. Everything else was on hold. Time seemed to stand still. There was so much riding on this putt that the pause was agonizing, and again Jamie could only see the top of Justin's head. He was not aware of the exact moment he hit the putt, but he was instantly aware when it fell into the hole, because the European supporters went wild. Jamie saw Rose turn triumphantly, his fist briefly in the air this time. Then, like a gentleman, he was shaking Mickelson's hand. Against the odds, somehow, he had won. Right now the teams were level; the score: eleven-all.

For a moment, Jamie felt exhausted, the tension within him giving way. European players all around were smiling and hugging each other, celebrating Rose's win; but there were six matches still out on the course, and Europe needed to win at least three of them to tie and retain the Ryder Cup.

Jamie was also worried because only victory would be good enough to win his bet with Chuck, which meant getting three-and-a-half points from the six still out there. At that juncture, as it happened, Graeme McDowell was on the point of losing to Zach Johnson, and Swedish player, Peter Hanson, was down to Jason Dufner. Only Lee Westwood looked to be in control of his match.

Studying the leader board, adrenaline taking effect once more, Jamie was trying to decide where to go and which match to follow. The best thing, he thought, would probably be to stay near the green at eighteen, rather than charge back down the course. After handing over the blue official buggy he had been using to a tournament official, he made his way onto the mound at the back, close to where Mickelson had taken his final putt, which is where Chuck Flanagan found him soon after.

Having finished officiating, Chuck was now free to enjoy the finale too. He was still fully confident of a US victory, but Jamie correctly observed that a sea-change had come over the onlookers. After Rose's stunning triumph, the American supporters were more subdued, and the Europeans in the crowd were much more vocal. It was the kind of thing that could alter the whole momentum of a contest. In the next few minutes, McDowell lost, giving USA a brief lead again, then Westwood won, restoring parity: twelve-all.

The excitement automatically shifted to the Garcia – Furyk match. Sergio had won the second hole and lost the third. Jim Furyk had won the eighth and lost the tenth, won twelve and lost thirteen; then he won fourteen and they halved fifteen. With Sergio now one-down, the sixteenth was going to be crucial. Chuck and Jamie could see these events unfolding on the big screen in front of the clubhouse. After both golfers hit good drives, Furyk hit a magnificent shot up the hill with a fairway hybrid club to about eighteen feet, to the left and just past the flag. Garcia, in contrast, hit his four-iron second shot poorly, the ball finishing in the right hand front bunker. On the screen, Jamie could see that Luke Donald was down there, walking alongside Garcia, doubtless doing his best to help his friend stay focused and confident; and the extra support must have worked because Sergio's next shot, out of the bunker, was majestic, almost going in the hole, stopping at 'gimme' distance, less than a foot away.

Furyk duly conceded the putt, and now faced a birdie attempt to win the hole.

What happened next shows how exquisitely cruel the game of golf can be or, from the other player's perspective, how forgiving. Furyk made a lovely stroke. The ball seemed destined, for the whole of its path, to go into the hole. The crowd thought so, starting to cheer. Jim thought so, raising his arms getting ready to celebrate. Jamie thought so, with a sinking feeling in his belly. And Sergio probably thought so too... But the ball, slowing down, veered off line just enough within the last few inches to miss the centre of the cup, running into the left lip with sufficient sideways momentum to make it stay above ground. There were loud groans from some of the US spectators. It was another half, and Sergio remained just one-down.

The forty-two year old Furyk, normally the toughest of proven competitors, might have been slightly rattled by what had occurred, because he hit a poor shot across the lake on seventeen. His ball found the left-hand bunker, a long way from the hole. While Sergio went ahead and made a safe par, Jim could only get his bunker shot down to the front of the green, at least fifteen feet from the hole, from where he missed the putt, pushing it slightly wide, a couple of inches to the right. As a result, the two men were even.

Hitting first on eighteen, Garcia added to the pressure on Furyk by hitting a fine drive up this, the final fairway. His opponent followed by uncharacteristically again miss-hitting his tee shot, the ball finding another bunker, this one on the right side. Furyk's second shot then flew towards the back of the green, slightly past the end of the putting surface, close to where Mickelson's ball had been almost an hour earlier, almost at Jamie's feet. Unlike Phil, though, Furyk hit his putt a little too hard so that it ran eight feet past the hole on the slick putting surface. Sergio had played a safe second shot to the front of the green, from where he putted up to a few inches. Furyk conceded the four, and it was suddenly left to him to hole his eight-footer. This would halve the hole and tie the match. Just as on sixteen, though, the good-looking stroke veered a touch off line. The ball again hit the lip and stayed out.

By winning the last two holes, Sergio had turned the match around. The match score was now thirteen-twelve, his victory having put the Europeans ahead for the first time since the start of Day One. It was a momentary lead, however, because despite a valiant fight-back from the Swede, Dufner finished off Hanson soon after. The team scores were even again, and there were only two matches left. Not one of the four golfers still playing had won a point over the preceding two days. Which would hold their nerve and which crumble? The excitement was at fever pitch.

Back in Sussex, Holly and her father stayed up watching the contest, match by nail-biting match, riveted to the television. You did not need to be a golfer, Holly realized, to get caught up in this thrilling action. She had, for example, developed a soft spot for handsome Luke Donald, and was delighted when he won his singles contest against Bubba. It surprised her how much she now wanted Europe to win.

Her father had explained the emblem on their sleeves on that final day. It was an image of Seve Ballesteros, he told her, in the fist-pumping pose made famous after he sunk a tricky putt on the final green at St Andrew's in Scotland to win The Open for the second time in 1984, at the age of twenty-seven. He was invincible back then. Beneath the embroidery were his dates: 1957 – 2011. 'I've heard the Europeans say how much they want to win the Ryder Cup in Sevvy's memory', Sam added. 'Some think he is smiling right down on them from heaven, willing them on.'

'It does look as if something's helping them', Holly replied.

'Rose's putts on seventeen and eighteen... Furyk missing on sixteen, then bogeying the final two holes... Yes, I think I agree with you... But they still need Lady Luck on their side, don't they?'

Their conversation was cut short as a commercial break finished. The action from Medinah was resuming with German golfer, Martin Kaymer, about to play his shot from a bunker on the fourteenth. It wasn't special, but it became good enough when he went on to sink his eighteen-foot putt for a winning birdie and the lead in his match against one of the US Captain's picks, forty-five year old Steve Stricker. But the German spoiled it on the next green. A lapse in concentration resulted in him taking three putts and losing the hole.

Meanwhile the Italian, Francesco Molinari, a golfer of modest stature in terms of height, but a giant in terms of ability, was managing to hold his own against the colossus called Tiger Woods. He was even briefly in the lead at one point on the back nine, but was soon brought back level again. Sam explained that Molinari might halve his match, but might equally lose it. No-one was expecting the renowned and formidable Tiger to make it easy for him, so it was looking like everything was going to depend on Kaymer. He had to win his match for Europe to tie.

'That wouldn't be too bad', Sam explained. 'Because Europe won last time, they will retain possession of the cup... It's not as good as winning, but if you think where they were at the start of the day, it's still mighty impressive.'

But this was not what Jamie Royle was thinking, greenside at Medinah. He needed Kaymer to win and Molinari to at least halve with Tiger. A lot of money was at stake as, down by the sixteenth green, things were hotting up. Like Sergio before him,

Kaymer played his third shot to that hole from a bunker, but not as brilliantly as the Spaniard. After the German's ball finished well past the cup, Stricker made an excellent putt for his par four. Kaymer; absolutely having to sink his long effort; bravely then followed the American in for the half.

On seventeen, it was the American's turn to make a simple error. Stricker's chip to five feet was a good one, but he missed the putt, whereupon Kaymer managed to coax his four-footer into the hole for a winning par. It would have been disastrous to miss. Standing on the final tee, he was at last one ahead. Unless Stricker made birdie, all he would need was a par four, but his tee shot went right, into yet another of the course's treacherous bunkers, the same one Furyk had been in earlier on, with fatal results for the American.

At the same moment, taking it personally, Jamie was deeply incensed because Molinari was losing seventeen. With Chuck smiling now beside him, it felt like being robbed. His hands in his pockets were sweaty and tightly clenched. His eyes were wide, and his mouth dry. It seemed to be taking an age for the players on eighteen to walk up to their balls, decide on a shot and play.

Kaymer's shot from the bunker, though, was worth waiting for. His ball soared in the air, making a graceful left-to-right curve. It fell softly on the green side of the left bunker, from where the slope propelled it helpfully forward and sideways so that it came to a halt no more than twenty feet from the hole. Stricker, like Mickelson and Furyk before him, hit his shot to the green slightly too long. His ball was on the putting surface, but he looked set to get no better than four.

Kaymer almost certainly needed only two putts to win his match. The European onlookers were confident, sure now that, against all the odds, they would be taking their precious Ryder Cup home… Then things began to go wrong again.

Martin Kaymer had played only one match before this, partnering Rose against Dustin Johnson and Matt Kuchar in the afternoon four-balls on the first day. They had lost. Despite gaining a Ryder Cup place, his year on the professional tour had not been particularly successful either, and he was hungry for glory. After it was all over, he said that he had wanted to sink the first putt and beat Stricker outright with a birdie, imagining the adulation this would bring. Did he really think his opponent might sink his enormous putt and make a three? No... But the German's thoughts were a little scrambled, understandably so in the circumstances. Later, he also admitted that he had lain awake much of the night thinking about this very possibility, that the entire result of three days' hard fought battle would come down to him on the last green, putting for victory. This grandiose vision began to unravel, though, and with it Jamie's hopes of winning his massive bet, as he stood over his downhill, side-sliding putt and failed to settle.

At that exact moment, thoughts awry, Kaymer began to worry, convinced that he needed to take more borrow, to aim further left, which was probably true. As a result of the uncertainty, Jamie noticed him starting to twiddle his hands on the putter-grip and re-set his wrists, but without moving his feet or properly re-aligning his shoulders. The result, when the putter head finally made contact, was for the ball to shoot off, both too fast and too far to the right. There were gasps from some of the onlookers as the ball ended up a full six or seven feet from the cup. Chuck heard Jamie groan while Jamie, in turn, caught sight of Ian Poulter who, elated and confident a moment before, suddenly looked similarly dismayed. Down the fairway, the European Captain, Olazabal, could be seen ripping off his hat, closing his eyes and pulling out his earphones in despair, unable to watch or listen to any more.

'Remember Bernhard Langer at Kiawah Island?' Chuck whispered to Jamie, referring to another German golfer who missed an even shorter putt than the one facing Kaymer. This had been against Hale Irwin on the final hole of the final match back in 1991. That time, in South Carolina, Langer's miss meant the Europeans lost the Ryder Cup by a single point. 'I do', replied Jamie, stony-faced. 'But this is not over yet!'

Stricker made his four, courageously sinking a treacherous curling twelve-footer to do so. Then it was up to Kaymer to make good. Everything depended on it. As he lined up the putt and took his stance, Captain Ollie was covering his face with his cap. Rory, crouched down on his haunches at the edge of the green, having raised his hands over his face, was peeping anxiously through latticed fingers. Garcia and Colsaerts were both standing there, literally chewing their lips.

For a moment, the crowd was completely hushed. The German stood motionless over his putt, then struck it firmly. Unerringly, seconds later, it found the bottom of the cup, and immediately, there was uproar, all the noise being made by elated – and relieved – Europeans. Kaymer let his putter drop so as to raise both fists in the air, shaking them in triumph. His dream coming magnificently true at that moment, he then ran full-tilt at his team-mates, leaping up into Sergio's outstretched arms, the two immediately enfolded in a bear hug from behind by Peter Hanson. Other players too were hugging each other and laughing.

It was almost too good, too amazing, to be true... But it wasn't yet over. The score was fourteen-thirteen. Captain Ollie – and, obviously, Jamie – were still both hoping for an outright win. When things calmed down, everyone's attention naturally turned towards the final fairway where Woods and Molinari stood waiting to play. Olazabal was down there as well, urging Francesco on, telling him he had to win the hole. Woods was one-up, and this would tie the match to sew up the unlikeliest of European victories. Somehow, though, with fourteen European points already achieved, the diminutive Italian felt considerably relieved of pressure. Much less tense than during the preceding few holes, he made a good swing, safely finding the green with his second shot. Woods, in contrast, missed to the right – but not by much.

After his next shot, Francesco's ball was close, just three-and-a-half feet below the hole in three; but this meant Woods needed only, to get 'up-and-down' in two shots, for victory. He was certain to chip his ball close. It was on the fringe, level with the hole, only about twenty feet away.

Under normal circumstances, it was an easy shot; but knowing that America could no longer hope to win the cup, no matter what he did, seemed to affect Tiger. Whatever the reason, he played the shot rather too firmly. The ball ran forward, actually hit the hole, and might have dropped in but was going too quickly. Spinning away downhill, it came to rest past Molinari's ball, leaving Tiger a putt of about five feet, which he then also missed. He was down in five shots.

Even so, at this crucial stage, Molinari still needed to sink his tricky putt for a four to win the hole, tie the match, and secure the Ryder Cup win for his team. Jamie was still worried, because the Italian was not known to be the most reliable putter, having missed a couple of short ones under pressure two years earlier at Celtic Manor. Nevertheless, with Woods about to make bogey, Jamie still felt he had been given an improbable lifeline. Meanwhile, beside him, Chuck Flanagan was yet hoping Francesco would miss. The fifty-thousand dollar bet between the two men had come down to this simple question: would Molinari sink the crucial putt?

On tenterhooks, they were both waiting for the answer when something remarkable and entirely unexpected happened. Tiger Woods picked up his ball. This simple act was an irreversible indication that he was conceding the hole without making his opponent putt out. With that inexplicably generous gesture on the part of the most famous and talented African-Asian-American golfer in the world, their match was halved. More importantly, by 14½ to 13½, Europe had gained full victory in the 2012 Ryder Cup.

It took a second or two for the win to sink in. Then, cheering, Jamie leapt right in the air, landed, turned and tried to give his friend Chuck a great bear-hug. The unhappy Flanagan, though, evaded his outstretched arms testily. Forced to admit to defeat, like many Americans at that same moment, he was feeling somewhat betrayed. Not entirely in control of his emotions, he began walking away in disgust, then turned and, with an almost demonic growl, called loudly back to Jamie, above the raucous noise of the crowd. Somehow, despite the din, the Englishman caught Chuck's every word: 'I shall get even with you tomorrow, Mister. Make no mistake about that.'

THE 14TH
CHAPTER

As Holly made her way from her father's place to Greenings the following morning, the rain was drizzling down. While taking due care at the wheel, she found herself thinking about the exciting finale on television the evening before. The stunned looks on the faces of the American players in defeat had made her feel genuinely sorry, both for them and their supporters. Mickelson, Furyk and Dufner, all three staring silently at the turf, formed a perfect picture of disbelief and despair in the brief moments after Tiger Woods gave Molinari the win. 'Stricker looks particularly stricken', her dad had said, trying to make a weak joke. Only team captain Davis Love on the American side appeared to retain sufficient composure to react with good grace. Father and daughter had watched him advance across the turf, magnanimously shaking a weary and emotional Olazabal by the hand in congratulation.

They could also see that Ollie's feelings were running high during those moments after the victory. After praising his team members, when interviewed on camera about their success, he suddenly burst into tears, looking to the heavens and crying out, 'This one's for you, Sevvy'. Then, facing the reporter again, he obviously wanted to explain his words, adding in the sincerest of tones, 'You know… This one is for my friend'.

Unable to share it in the flesh with his *amigo* and great golfing mentor, this remarkable triumph must have tasted bitter-sweet; but the same volatile Ollie, shortly afterwards, was joking with Rory McIlroy, laughingly presenting him with an enormous alarm clock, the idea being to prevent the risk of his being late on the first tee ever again. It was funny, but also a serious reminder that the Ulsterman's mix-up of time zones had jeopardized the whole team's success.

Rory could not stop giggling as he accepted the hilarious gift, and the general jubilation of the team was infectious. As subdued American fans wandered off, making their way quietly home, some at least paused to congratulate their opponents, while many of the European supporters lingered on, gathering near the clubhouse, joining in with impromptu celebrations. The victorious team and their caddies were soon up on the raised walkway, armed with several large jeroboams of champagne, vigorously spraying the throng below amid prolonged cheers in what was now something of a tradition.

Later, spot-lit in the dark, showered and changed, immaculate in their matching grey-checked suits, the European stars clustered for final photos, holding high aloft between them the golden Ryder Cup trophy, McDowell out front, briefly imitating Ollie's famous fandango dance-steps as a tribute to such a splendidly passionate captain. They seemed set to party right on through the night.

The victory was wonderful because unexpected. The British press started calling it 'The Miracle at Medinah'. 'I don't know if you can say Sevvy was helping us today or not', Garcia told a reporter at one point, 'But something was… And we needed it.'

'The turning point came late on Saturday', said Rose in turn, 'When Ian somehow managed to turn his match around.' 'You know', he added thoughtfully, 'There's a difference between thinking you can win and believing you can win… We all came here this morning really *believing* we could win. That's what did it for me.'

―――――――

It was raining hard by the time Holly pulled up outside Greenings. Waiting in the car for the force of the downpour to subside, her mind back on the task in hand, she suddenly realized something. 'There's a difference between thinking you can solve a crime and really *believing* you can solve it', she told herself. 'This one, I believe I can solve.'

As the rain eased momentarily, Holly jumped out and ran to the door with her shoulder bag over her head. Inside, colleagues were already busy at work. All the phones were in use. Calling a brief meeting, she discovered nothing much new. They were still focusing on possible means of transport for Jane X's body and the red chairs. Looking at the list of removals companies, livery stables and so on, Holly said she would take Barrow & Sons. Their maroon-coloured vans were a common sight around Sussex, and she got through to Bruce Barrow right away.

'What can I do you for, Detective?' he asked cheerily down the line, after she introduced herself. 'I'd like to ask you some questions, please', she replied. 'Come on over, then!' he said. Fewer than fifteen minutes later, she was there. Luckily, it had completely stopped raining.

Barrows & Sons Limited were based at a large enclosed site near Fittleworth. 'My father Percy started the business in Pulborough years ago', Bruce explained, after showing Holly through to his office. I bought my brother Keith out and moved us here when I took over from Dad, ten or twelve years ago now. I was building up the fleet, and we needed more secure space to park them up in at night. We also needed to build lock-up storage, as you'll see if you take a look out of the window across the yard. That building opposite is all storage.'

Holly told him about the chairs on the golf course, showing Barrow a photo of one of them, supplied to the team first thing that morning by the forensics people. 'How hard would it be to do that?' she asked, 'To move a couple of heavy armchairs like these and place them down again on grass without leaving much of a trace?'

'Very difficult, I would say', replied Barrow. 'Why would you?'

'That's what I want to find out', Holly replied. 'Can I have a look at one of your vans, please? Were any missing on Wednesday night last week, by the way?'

Bruce Barrow stood up. 'Come with me', he said, leading her back to the reception area next door. 'Let me introduce you to Jill', he continued, indicating a short dark-haired woman intent on her work, sitting behind a computer. 'Jill is my wife, and anything she doesn't know about what goes on around here isn't worth knowing… Jill, this is Sergeant Angel. Can you print off the manifest for Wednesday, Thursday and Friday last week, please?'

A minute later, they were back in his office, looking at the three spreadsheets. 'As I thought', began Bruce, 'All the vans were in for the night on Wednesday except one.'

Pointing to a large publicity photograph on the wall, showing his entire fleet, he continued, 'As you see in the picture, we have five medium-size vans, three big ones and a couple of smaller vehicles for running around in. Jill and I use the little ones for visiting people to assess their needs and give them quotes. Not here on either Wednesday or Thursday was the biggest truck in the fleet. It's in the yard now, as a matter of fact, waiting for Paul, my senior fitter, to check the fuel, oil, tyres, brakes and whatnot after a long run. One of the lads... I call them the Barrow Boys... will probably be giving it a clean soon, too. We'll go and take a look at it, shall we?'

As they walked out of the office building, Bruce started to explain why the massive van had been absent overnight. 'It was on the way to a town called Banchory, in Aberdeenshire, with two of my best men on board: Robert and William Purvis – 'Bob and Billy'. They're brothers, and they both worked for my dad before me. On long runs, they take it in turns with the driving. One of their lads will have gone as well; Billy's grandson Alan, I expect.'

'You like to keep everything in the family, then?' said Holly.

'It makes everything go smoothly, I find', Bruce responded, 'Like clockwork most of the time... On Wednesday morning at eight o'clock sharp, the van will have turned up at the clients' house in Pulborough to pack everything up and start loading. They were probably on the road north before midday. Knowing Bob, who always wants to press on, they will have had a couple of rest stops on the way up, but carried on going until it was getting dark.'

They were in the yard now, approaching the lorry in question. 'Look above the cab there.' Bruce was pointing for Holly to see. 'That's a little cabin... See the curtains on the windows?'

Holly could.

'Because they're both in their sixties now, I pay for Billy and Bob to stay in a motorway hotel these days when they're on a long-haul job; but someone has to stay in the van, especially when it's fully loaded with some client's furniture and belongings; so that's where the lad sleeps.'

'It looks cosy', said Holly.

'There's a little heater in there, so it should be', replied Barrow. 'On Thursday morning, they were probably all up and breakfasted by seven-thirty, and on their way again to get to their destination before nine. They unload everything, of course – carefully, mind; no rushing. Then they make their way back. It's about twelve hours' driving altogether, depending on the traffic. They won't have wanted to spend a second night on the road, if they could help it. Bob has the keys to the yard here, so they will have let themselves back in, probably just before midnight, I imagine. After a run like that, I give them a day off, so the van was here all day on Friday. Normally it would go out again today, but Paul had the flu last week. I've spoken to him already this morning, and he's a bit better. He says he'll come in to service the vehicle this afternoon. I hope so, anyway, because it's due out again tomorrow! Billy and Bob will be here early, ready for another long run. It won't be so bad for them, though… They're only going to Exeter this time.'

Holly was impressed by Barrow & Son's obvious efficiency, and their liberal policy regarding older staff. She did wonder, though, how much pressure Bruce Barrow had applied on the phone to his mechanic, Paul, to resume work. The last time she had flu, it had taken her more than a week to recover her strength and get back to the job.

While talking to her, Barrow had climbed into the van's cab, and was soon starting the engine so that he could move the vehicle forward a few feet, away from the building, allowing them access to the back.

'We always park them like that, if we can', he said, by way of explanation, 'Even when they're empty… It's just another precaution against anyone breaking in. You can't be too careful these days, especially with trips to the Continent. We've had no end of trouble with asylum seekers trying to get back across the Channel. I've got CCTV inside the back of this van now.'

They went to the rear. Barrow opened the doors wide. Then he let down the hydraulically operated ramp for Holly to see.

'It's quite steep, isn't it?' she said. 'Yes... You need muscles for this job', Barrow agreed. 'It would take Billy and Bob, both, to carry one of your chairs up or down that ramp. No-one could do it by himself, I don't think.'

'That's what I'm thinking too', agreed Holly.

———

Back at Greenings, there was a message from Valerie Parton. Holly's boss had phoned the golf club to make arrangements for a helicopter landing there at noon. She had also wanted a taxi booked to take her and another passenger to the operations unit. Holly phoned the Secretary's secretary to thank her for being so thoughtful, also to suggest cancelling the taxi. 'I'll come and get them myself', she said.

Thinking about having a cup of tea, Holly went into the kitchen area where she found a young man in a dark suit sitting quietly at the table. 'Oh!' she exclaimed, revealing her surprise as the stranger stood up.

'Baum!' he boomed out.

'I beg your pardon', said Holly, nonplussed at the somewhat unexpectedly loud, barely intelligible noise emanating from such an immensely tall person who was now towering above her, his large, round face topped with close-cropped, pale blond hair, his ears sticking out sideways like handles.

'Baum!' he repeated. 'Richard Baum.'

'Oh, yes!' Holly gathered herself. 'I'm Angel... Holly!' Then she held out her hand, to be enfolded completely in the new rookie detective's massive grip.

'Okay', she said. 'Wait there! Have a cup of tea or something. I've got a couple of phone calls to make.'

Richard Baum looked down at her blankly; then, to her relief, sat down again. 'As you wish', he said calmly before folding his hands in his lap and closing his eyes. As far as Holly could tell, he had instantly fallen asleep.

To find a quiet space, Holly made her way upstairs, to one of the house's former bedrooms, carrying a foldaway chair to sit on while she made her calls. The first was to the head office of Regal Enterprises in Holborn. As expected, the receptionist told her that Mr Royle was away overseas, adding that his PA, Ms Pokorny, was away with him too. She asked Holly to wait, put her on hold, then connected her through to Patrick Gryllock's office. A moment later, she was speaking to Gryllock's PA, Madeleine Smith, who turned out to be much less defensive than Holly had anticipated.

'If you ring back at about five this afternoon', she said in a sprightly voice, 'I'm expecting Mr Gryllock back by then. I'm sure he'll speak to you. He's gone to collect some Chinese clients from Heathrow this morning and he's taking them straight out to lunch.'

'What about Mr Royle?' Holly asked. 'When are you expecting him back?'

'Oh, he'll be in tomorrow. He and Patrick have a big meeting with the Chinese people here at noon.'

Holly was astonished, but delighted; especially when Mrs Smith added that Mr Royle was flying into Heathrow from Chicago early the following morning. 'That man has to know something', Holly was thinking, looking forward to arranging the interview.

Downstairs at Greenings again, she logged into the Sussex Police network. Once online, she looked up the British Airways website, feeling sure that the patriotic Jamie Royle would not use any other airline. There were two possible flights that Monday evening: BA0294, leaving at 17.10 hrs, arriving Tuesday morning at 06.45; and BA 0296, leaving at 20.45, arriving at 10.20. 'He'll have to catch the earlier one', she thought, 'If he's going to make a meeting in London by midday.'

Holly's next call was directly to the BA offices in London, to try and confirm her suspicions; but in this she was unsuccessful. British Airways staff are not allowed to disclose passenger details, including flight details, to unauthorized personnel. Holly tried to explain that, as a Police Officer, she *was* authorized, but it made no difference, so her next call was to Brian Thatcher, a friend from her days as a police probationer. Brian was now with the anti-terrorist squad in London.

'Hi Holly', he said when she got through. 'How are things?'

'Great!' replied Holly. 'And how is married life?' They had last seen each other at his wedding nine months earlier.

'Terrific, actually, Holl… You should try it', her friend continued, forgetting that she was divorced. 'We've one already on the way!'

'Oh… Congratulations!' Holly was genuinely pleased. 'That's wonderful, Brian. Do give Tessa my love. When is it due?'

'In March… But what are you phoning about?' Brian, clearly busy, suddenly sounded more serious. 'I'm sure it wasn't just to be sociable.'

Holly admitted that she had another reason for the call, asking if Brian had access to transatlantic passenger lists, as she suspected he might. 'Oh yes', he said. 'Give me the name and I'll call you back'.

She only had to wait twenty minutes when the reply came through as a text:

'Royle confirmed on BA 0294 tonight – travelling 1st class. Booking made by Catherine Pokorny on same flight – Economy. Brian xx.'

As it was already after half-past eleven, Holly went immediately in search of Richard Baum. He was still sitting, Buddha-like, in the kitchen.

'How tall are you', she asked the rookie without ceremony as she swept into the room. 'I think my car's too small to fit you in.'

'194.5 centimetres', he replied, opening his eyes.

'How tall is that in feet and inches? Roughly, anyway...' she asked again.

'Roughly?' Baum paused, apparently surprised and disappointed that she wanted less than precision. 'It is six feet, four-and-a-half inches to the nearest half-inch.'

'What car do you drive, then?' Holly asked a third time.

'It's a BMW', he responded,

'You must be wealthy, then', she challenged.

'It's a very old model', he countered, 'A diesel, with a hundred and twenty three thousand miles on the clock'.

'I take it back', she said, noticing now that his suit was ill-fitting and rather cheap looking. 'Come on... You're driving me to the golf club'.

In the car, Holly brought Baum up to speed with the case. They arrived in minutes, but then sat in the parked car while he asked a few pertinent questions. Going into the clubhouse eventually, Holly suggested that he visit the bar and lounge areas, introduce himself to staff and members, get a feel for the place while keeping his ears open. Disobeying her, however, he went straight back outside as she made her way up the stairs. As hoped, once in the Secretary's office, she found both Peter Harding and Valerie Parton.

'I've had John Tranter cordon off a space adjacent to the practice range for the landing', said the Colonel as she entered. 'We're expecting the helicopter any minute.'

From the window, Mrs Parton said she thought she could see it approaching, so they quickly went outside. Richard Baum was already standing there. 'I heard it coming as you were going up the stairs', he said.

Holly could just make out the machine coming towards them from the east, flying low, still a long way off, but she could not yet hear the sound of its motor.

'Thank you, Radar', she said, unable to keep the sarcasm totally out of her voice, 'Can you also see who is in it?'

Quite seriously, Baum replied, 'The pilot, of course; and there's DCI Holroyd and DI Garbutt.'

'How on earth do you know that?' Holly was growing faintly alarmed at these apparently supernatural powers.

'DI Garbutt told me they were coming when I saw her first thing this morning', Baum said.

'Ah!' breathed Holly quietly, smiling now to herself. 'Elementary, Sherlock... Of course!'

'Don't you mean Watson?' Big Ears Baum had been listening. 'It's usually, "Elementary my dear Watson", isn't it?'

'No', returned Holly, a little irritated. 'I'm Sherlock... You're Watson. Get it?'

The police chopper came down a few minutes later. When the rotor blades came to a halt, the senior officers alighted, Holroyd calling back to the pilot to thank him and tell him to wait for them, get something to eat and charge it to expenses. They would be back no more than two hours later, he was saying, probably sooner.

Holly made the introductions. The Colonel, leading them inside, took the party on a short tour of the clubhouse building, finishing up at his office. This was where Holly first had the chance to mention her news about Jamie Royle, and to say that he would be back in the country the following day. Her immediate boss was non-committal at the news, but Holroyd seemed very pleased. 'Well done indeed, Detective Angel', he said, 'Very well done indeed!' He then suggested that, with her boss, she arrange to interview Royle at the airport.

'Can we do that, Sir?' Holly wasn't sure.

'I don't see why not', Holroyd replied. 'This is a murder investigation, isn't it?'

Holly refrained from mentioning Dr Narayan's ongoing doubts about the split cartilage; or the fact that, due to being in Chicago surrounded by witnesses, Royle had a cast-iron alibi.

The senior officers soon went back down with the Colonel, who showed them the professional's shop and arranged for Kyle Scott to drive Laura Garbutt out to the fifth fairway in one of the golf buggies while he ferried Hugh Holroyd to the crime scene in another. Left alone, Holly sent Baum back down to the club's social areas, taking the opportunity to speak in private to Valerie Parton.

'I should have thought of this before', she said, 'But have you got a mobile number for Gary Brooker?'

'I'm afraid not', said the secretary. 'I could ring Mrs Brooker for you, though, and try to find out.'

'Why don't you just give me the Brookers' home number', Holly replied. 'I can take it from there.' Minutes later, she got through to Meredith Brooker on her landline at home.

'Merry here!' came a cheery, and unmistakeably Scottish, voice. 'Hellooo…!'

Holly introduced herself. Without wasting any time, she then enquired if Mrs Brooker had heard from her husband in Chicago recently.

'Oh, yes…' she said. 'We Skype almost every day. He's having a grand time at the Ryder Cup. Did you see it?'

Holly admitted that she had.

'Wasn't it marvellous? I dinna play the game, but I found it awfully intriguing… Are you a golfer yoursel', by any chance?' She pronounced the word 'goffer', taking Holly slightly by surprise. 'Listen! I'm not', she said quickly. 'But I need to confirm something, if that's alright… Is your husband coming home tomorrow?'

'No... I'm not expecting him back for a couple of weeks', came the reply, causing Holly's heart to sink a little. 'He's on to Oregon and the Pacific Coast tomorrow with Louise Broad. Jamie and Catherine are returning, though, just for two days. Gary says it's something to do with business. They'll be out there again – or at least Jamie will – by the end of the week.'

Breathing a sigh, Holly was relieved. 'What's he like, Jamie Royle?' she thought to ask.

'He's my man's employer, and a generous one', replied the canny Scots lady. 'What do you want me to say? Most people think he's delightful.'

'But you don't?' Holly had spotted a deliberate omission.

'I'm over fifty, Lassie!' she answered... 'With a couple of grown-up kiddies... And I've been around the block enough times not to fall for every charmer that comes along. He's been good to Gary, I'll say that again; but I hate to think what would happen if they started losing many of those big money matches they play. Gary'd be to blame in Jamie's eyes, no question, and it would be the sack for sure after that.'

'You've been very helpful, Mrs Brooker', Holly signed off. 'Thank you.'

Merry Brooker wondered though if, as usual, she might have said slightly too much.

Ever attentive, staff-member Liam had provided Richard Baum with some lunch – delicious spicy Thai fishcakes – by the time Holly rejoined him. She accepted a prawn sandwich herself, as they sat in the bar to wait for the senior officers, but had to have her food wrapped up in tinfoil 'to go' as Holroyd and her boss re-appeared quite quickly.

There was silence in the car while Baum drove the short distance to the incident suite, Holroyd beside him, the two women awkward with each other in the rear. Back at Greenings, one of the forensic officers had arrived and a briefing was about to take place. The red chairs had been examined thoroughly, and a couple of relevant findings had emerged.

Starting with the least startling of these, close-up photographs, taken in deliberately oblique lighting conditions to show up shadows, and therefore indentations, had revealed a pattern of possible strap-marks.

'This is how we think they were moved', said the officer, 'With leather or strong canvas webbing... The visible marks are fewer on the chair without the body; that's the one on the right if you were standing behind them, facing away from the fifth green where we found them. We think two sets of straps were placed under the base, because they seemed to be cutting in at the sides, higher up, where the sides begin to bulge out at arm-height.'

The officer put up on the screen a close-up of the arms of the chair, showing two sets of very faint marks that really needed the eye of faith, Holly thought, to discern.

'The other one, the left, is a little clearer', the man continued. 'This one seems to have been upended and suspended upside-down.' He put up new pictures, then took out a laser-pointer, indicating what he meant on another close-up. This time, there were again two sets of indentations, but deeper, and right across the surface of the chair's two arms. 'You couldn't have seen this in daylight', he added. 'I think it means you're looking for a transport vehicle with a hoist.'

The next photo showed the underside of one of the chairs. It was the right-hand one again. This time, in high magnification a close-up revealed, as the red laser-spot hovered over it, an irregular stain, smaller in diameter than a 10p coin, overlapping the leather chair-covering where it was stapled securely to the base and the wood of the underside itself. Barely showing, reddish-brown against the red leather, it would have been easy to miss without the tiny splash on the lighter-coloured timber as well.

'It's blood', said the man, as one or two less seasoned among the audience gasped. 'Great!' thought Holly.

'But it is not human blood.' This was an unwelcome surprise. Holly was already imagining DNA evidence pinning down the perpetrator. 'No', said the voice from the other side of the darkened room. 'This is the blood of a horse.'

THE 15TH CHAPTER

There was a stunned silence in the room for a moment. 'Are you quite sure about that?' DCI Holroyd asked eventually. Ignoring the challenge to his expertise, the forensic man continued, telling the assembled team that although fingerprints and DNA samples had been obtained from the body of Jane X, she remained unidentified. Dental records were still being checked.

Holly suggested looking into psychiatric records too, because Jane was anorexic. Someone then asked if they needed to continue looking into removals companies and their vans. Holroyd said they could stop, and to concentrate on anyone – private owner or commercial organization – with horse boxes or trailers. Richard Baum then came up with the suggestion to include veterinary surgeons, an idea which the Chief Inspector duly commended.

Holly then asked about the possibility, as they seemed to be hiding something, of hacking into Jamie Royle's and Patrick Gryllock's phones. Holroyd seemed reluctant. 'Tabloid newspaper tactics', he called it, reminding Holly that they would need warrants. 'I'll get those', intervened DI Garbutt, to everyone's surprise. 'I'll speak to a magistrate this afternoon.'

After the meeting, Holly decided to return with Baum and the superior officers to the helicopter parked at the SRGC. This was perhaps out of courtesy, but she was also thinking she and her new protégé had started off on the wrong foot. This might give her the opportunity to clear the air and retrieve the situation a little.

They stood side by side and watched the chopper take off, circle and begin flying back up towards the Downs, then walked back to the BMW. Once inside, before Baum had the chance to turn on the ignition and start the motor, putting her hand on his outstretched arm, Holly asked him to wait.

'Tell me about yourself, Richard', she said trying to be nice, turning towards him in her seat. 'We are going to be working together, so it would be good to get to know you better.'

Richard Baum undid his seat belt again, the easier to face and look his new mentor in the eye. 'What do you want to know?' he said obligingly.

'Anything', Holly replied. 'Someone said you were in Kent before, and came here because of your parents.'

'Yes… That's correct', said the rookie, seeming surprisingly vulnerable at that moment, and younger than his twenty-three years. 'I grew up near Ashford. I have an older sister, Natalie. My father was a 'horologist'; that's a person who buys, sells, repairs and maintains old clocks. He's from Holland originally… Came to London as a young man, met my mum, who is English, and decided to stay. Once I was at school, my mother worked as well, helping dad in the shop sometimes, but she also became a teaching assistant in a nearby primary school.'

'Go on', said Holly, encouragingly. 'What else?'

'Well, my sister is a solicitor, and she's gay. She's in a civil partnership with an older woman, a corporate lawyer, called

Gayle. They have a baby now – my nephew, I suppose. He's called Luke… That's why my parents moved here, to be close to the grandson. They have a house in a place called Small Dole. Natalie and Gayle live in Hove, you see.'

Holly thought she detected more than a trace of resignation in his voice. 'Your sister was the favoured one?' She was guessing. 'The one who got all the attention?'

'My father dotes on her, always has', Baum said, confirming her hunch. 'I don't think mother takes sides, but dad's the force in our family. He's always very intense, very serious; and when he makes up his mind about something, that's it! There's no arguing with him.'

Holly opened the passenger window an inch. It was warming up in the car.

'When Nat shifted to Sussex, to move in with Gayle a few years ago', Baum continued, 'Dad immediately sold the shop and made plans to follow. It's less than two hours by car, but he just couldn't bear to be parted from her, even by a few miles. That, of course, meant my mum had to stop working at the school, which she loved. I also had to move out of the house. It was one of the things that helped me decide to join the force. Accommodation was available. I could live in as a probationer.'

'It was a good move, then', said Holly.

'Yes', Baum agreed, pausing to take a deep breath. 'By then, you see, Dad had a profitable sideline. He's a real expert on antique long-case clocks, what people call "grandfather" clocks. Say your name was Chandler and my father met you, maybe at an auction house, which he used to frequent deliberately. You'd get chatting, and my dad might tell you that he knew of a clock made by Timothy Chandler in 1820, and that it might be for sale. Then he'd locate such a clock, or maybe did already know of one. He would offer to buy it, let's say for three thousand pounds. Mr Chandler would then be offered it at dad's 'bargain price' of five thousand, and he would pocket the difference. In fact, he's still doing that caper now. It helps boost his pension, he says.'

'It isn't a crime', Holly advised.

'No... But it's not that admirable, is it?' Baum seemed more sad than disgusted. 'What my sister is doing is not so great, either', he added, after another pause.

'What do you mean?' enquired Holly.

'Having a baby by artificial insemination... Picking the father from a catalogue! Two women bringing up a boy without a father-figure in his life! It simply doesn't seem right to me.'

'Maybe that's where you come in...' Holly suggested. She didn't see anything wrong with the arrangement. 'You can be his role model. Is that why you followed your parents?'

'I came here mostly because of Mum', Baum replied. 'She's unhappy... My father doesn't seem to understand how much he made her give up when they left Ashford. It wasn't just the school. All her friends were there... And me, I suppose. I just wanted to be a bit nearer for her.'

'Okay, thanks', said Holly, reflecting that her psychology training might have been of some use after all. Closing the window again, she repeated, 'Thank you for telling me about all that, Richard. I do appreciate it... Now, let's go back to Greenings! I don't promise, but maybe I'll tell you all my troubles one day.'

'And remember', she said finally, 'Every silver lining has a cloud.' She laughed. 'That's what my Dad always says, anyway... Maybe this saga about your family has brought you here for a reason, to help solve this crime... Maybe it's all meant to be!'

Baum, much mollified by the conversation, refastened his seat belt and started up the car. Before releasing the brake, though, he paused. 'It's Rich, Detective Angel, by the way', he said. 'People call me "Rich", not Richard.'

'I see', replied Holly, jokingly. 'You're not wealthy, but you are Rich... That's perfectly okay with me... And, in return, I think you better start calling me Holly.'

––––––––––

The incident room was in a hubbub when they got back. Holly asked Rich to help out with calls to local stables and so on, while she phoned the only person she knew who had experience with horses. Monica Kidd's voice, at the other end, was as robotic as always. 'Please hold', it said. Moments later, Georgina Royle was on the line.

'I'm sorry to trouble you again', Holly began.

'It's no trouble at all.' Georgina sounded genuinely pleased to hear from her. 'How can I help?'

Holly got straight to the point. 'Do you know of any vehicles for transporting horses that come equipped with a hoist?'

'I've never seen one', was the disappointing reply. 'It wouldn't be very stable, would it?'

Holly could not help herself from remarking, 'It wouldn't be very stable in the stable, you're right.'

'I suppose there could be some kind of counter-weight system', she added to redeem the situation when her little joke seemed to fall flat. 'Would you have a think about it, and maybe ask around, please?'

Georgina said cheerily enough that she would speak to the folk from 'Riding for the Disabled' right away, and call back later if she discovered anything. Holly remembered then to thank her again for her hospitality at Rose Cottage, and for her gift of the 'Martsey Damsel', still giving off a beautiful fragrance from a small vase on her living room table. She had just put the phone down again when Rich Baum came up and said he'd like her permission to follow up his idea about contacting local vets.

'I was thinking about how horse blood got on the underside of that red chair', he said.

'Do you truthfully think a vet would be involved in this kind of thing?' Holly asked.

'Not really, I suppose', Baum responded, 'But farmer's vets might have the kind of vehicle we're looking for, don't you think? And someone else might have borrowed it from one of them.'

'Okay, then', said Holly. 'Off you go and phone a couple of vets. I'm going to try and get hold of Patrick Gryllock. He should be back in his office by now.'

Lunch with the Chinese had been tricky. Gryllock had found himself having to defend Queen Elizabeth and the institution of the monarchy, which his guests – as politely and inscrutably as possible – had suggested was inequitable, outmoded and therefore ridiculous. He had always been a staunch royalist. Through his charity work, he had been fortunate enough to meet Her Majesty on two occasions, both at Buckingham Palace garden parties. The second time, learning the name of his company, Her Majesty had charmed him by remarking wittily that she, too, was the head of some regal enterprises. 'I hope you won't bid for a takeover', teasingly, she had warned him. 'We still hang people for treason, you know.' Now, loyal subject to the core, he was growing increasingly irritated with his Asian guests..

Although he suspected that all three visitors spoke, or at least understood, English well, fortunately, he was using an interpreter, and she – Miss Welsh – had proved a valuable ally. Tempers were kept rather than frayed, mainly through her entirely unruffled demeanour and her frequent calming interventions. She was very good at downplaying the acidity of everyone's remarks around the table, so that by the time the Chinese finished their expensive *haute cuisine* meal and were setting off back to their luxury South Kensington hotel, Gryllock was much less flustered than he had been an hour earlier.

He was terribly grateful afterwards to the unflappable Miss Welsh, who told him her first name was Grace, and wondered briefly about his chances of seducing her that afternoon. In the end, though, he decided against pushing his luck. Regal Enterprises was going to need her again, the very next day, in fact. His mood had undoubtedly improved by the time he was alighting from the taxi in Holborn. The last thing he would have chosen next, however, would have been a phone call from the police.

Holly could sense his impatience down the line. Fortunately, Madeleine Smith had warned that her boss was not in the most tranquil frame of mind. She decided to try and humour him by, on this occasion, avoiding too much directness.

'Thank you so much for agreeing to speak to me', she said after introducing herself. 'I've met your sister, Georgina; and she has been so very helpful... Such an admirable person!'

Gryllock, although saying nothing, made a sudden grunting noise, which Holly found hard to interpret.

'Have you heard anything – from her, or from any other source – about the recent events at the Sussex Royale Golf Club?' she enquired as innocently as possible.

'No... Nothing', was the accurate response. 'Royle takes care of all that... My brother-in-law.'

'Yes. I know', Holly replied, 'But he's away at present, and I also know that you and he have been friends for many years.'

She explained about the two red chairs, and then about the body of Jane X, before asking if he could think of anyone who bore a grudge, or any other reason why anyone would want to make what seemed like such a truly vengeful statement in this way.

At the mention of the chairs, Patrick Gryllock had blanched, and an icy cold feeling had suddenly gripped his most private of parts. Thankfully, he noticed that his office door was shut, and the interior blinds closed, so that no-one could see him. Making an effort to sound normal, he repeated that he knew nothing about any of it.

'You'll have to wait and speak to Mr Royle', he told Holly. 'He'll be back in a couple of weeks.'

Ending the call, Holly's antennae for wrongdoing were fully on the alert. She was certain that Gryllock had been lying deliberately to protect his friend and business partner, unaware that she already knew Royle was due back the following day. His trickery made her angry, and even more determined to get to the bottom of what was still a very deep and dark mystery.

Putting the phone down, Gryllock made straight for the drinks cabinet across the room, helping himself to a good sized dram of the 1996 Distillers Edition *Lagavulin* he kept for special occasions. The first gulp of the fiery golden Scottish "Usquebaugh", the "water of life", burned his throat, almost painfully, without improving his mood, but he knew to give it time to work its habitual magic. Sitting back down, raising the tumbler once more to his lips, the troubled man closed his eyes and felt the welcome alcoholic glow travelling down through his trunk and limbs. A minute later, even his fingertips tingled; but he knew he wouldn't feel fully safe again until his protector was home. 'Jamie, Jamie, Jamie', he thought, 'What on earth have we done?'

———

Holly was still musing about the businessman's perfidy when Rich Baum returned from the other room where he had been working. Normally a somewhat lugubrious fellow, he seemed rather more animated than usual.

'What is it?' said Holly, as he appeared. 'Sit down... You make me nervous, standing there like a beanpole.'

The eager young rookie sat awkwardly down. 'I've just spoken to a vet', he began. 'He says we need to look for a knackerman.'

'A knackerman', repeated Holly. 'What's that exactly?'

'Someone who collects dead, dying and injured farm animals', said Baum. 'I remember now, there used to be a knacker's yard in Ashford. I never went there, but my father told me about it; somewhere to keep away from.' He gave a theatrical shudder to illustrate the point.

'Anyway', he added quickly, 'I've just looked it all up on the net. It's a trade that began almost two hundred years ago. In the early days, of course, they used horse-drawn carts; but now, it says, they have specialized vehicles with sealed floors and electric winches. A 35 hundred-weight lorry can carry up to three cows... or horses, I suppose.'

'Or a couple of red leather armchairs and a corpse', added Holly. 'Well done, Rich... Let's see if we've got any near here.'

'Since the dreadful 2001 foot and mouth disease outbreak', continued Baum, 'All dead farm animals have to be incinerated. This means knackers have to be approved by local authorities and the government department, DEFRA. They would keep records, but it might be quicker to check with the Licensed Animal Slaughterers and Salvage Association. LASSA is the trade association representing knackers in the UK, and I'm sure they'll keep an up to date list.'

Holly was delighted. 'See what you can find out', she said.

As Baum turned to go, almost immediately, Holly's phone came abruptly to life. It was Georgina Royle calling back.

'Hello Holly', she said sweetly. 'I think I might be able to help now... When one of the ponies died, a couple of years back, Riding for the Disabled organized a kind of memorial cremation for her, so that some of their riders could attend and pay their respects. I didn't get to the service, unfortunately; but they told me all about it afterwards; and it turns out they used a firm from Lewes that specialize in that kind of thing. Apparently, they came and collected little Bagpuss's carcase from the RfD stable using a specially equipped lorry with a hoist of some kind. I can get you the details, if you like.'

Holly thanked her without letting on that she and Rich had already worked out the likely form of transportation they were now investigating. She said she would contact Mrs Royle again if she needed any more information.

Meanwhile, Rich was discovering several businesses in the Kent, Sussex, Surrey and Hampshire areas that were offering "compassionate animal disposal", or, "fallen stock, equine and pet cremation services", including the company at Ashford. There was one at Plumpton, near Lewes, presumably the one used by RfD. The other two closest to Graffham were in West Chiltington and Romsey. He made a note of the names, addresses and website details but, it now being just past five o'clock, he failed to get through to any of them by phone.

'Do it in the morning', Holly said when he told her, 'And follow up the calls with visits if anything promising turns up… Or anything suspicious! I'm going to be at Heathrow.'

At five o'clock in Sussex, it was eleven in the morning in the Chicago area, and Jamie Royle was out on the golf course with Chuck. He had stayed up late, joining in the Ryder Cup celebrations where, to his astonishment, he had even received a friendly hug and slap on the back from the man who had gestured him to back off in so cavalier a fashion a day earlier, Ian Poulter. It was all 'forgive and forget'. He had chatted, laughed, danced, sung karaoke songs, and drunk far too much champagne into the small hours, and had to be driven back to the house in the buggy by Gary Brooker, who was not in quite such an advanced state of inebriation.

Despite the revelry, by force of will power, Jamie was up for his Eggs Benedict breakfast at the Medinah clubhouse in good time for the grudge match. He and Chuck had agreed on "double-or-quits" for the bet, so now there would be one hundred thousand US dollars riding on it. Accordingly, this had become very personal. Jamie therefore suggested they should dispense with their playing partners and take on each other, man to man. Gary and Rob Girt could go out after them and play a friendly game, deciding for themselves whether to play for money, perhaps just a sensibly low stake, enough to make it interesting. Chuck, having instantly spotted Jamie's hangover, and having himself spent the previous evening sober, was quick to agree.

It would be just the two of them, out there, with their caddies. No-one else had permission to play; but it was going to be difficult concentrating because there were workmen everywhere, busily – and noisily – taking down the spectator stands and television towers all around the course. Partly for this reason, the two men also agreed to use the forward member's tees, rather than the championship gold tees. The Ryder Cup course measured over 7,600 yards. From the white tees they were using, it was almost 1,000 yards shorter, but still a stiff test for ageing golfers. Another option; the green tees, another five hundred yards shorter; they decided would be too easy, only for cissies.

Predictably, Jamie got off to a poor start. He was already two-down after two holes, but then rallied slightly. One-down at the turn, he played the 550 yard par-five tenth particularly well, drilling his third shot to the heart of the well-defended green while Chuck found one of its thick necklace of bunkers. They were level, and the match stayed that way for the next hour or so as the two men went hammer and tongs at each other, with neither prepared to give way.

———————

When he got to the airport with Catherine, they found that the flight to London was delayed, but even that was not sufficient to dampen Jamie Royle's spirits. It was not so much winning the money that pleased him as the simple fact of beating Chuck, and the sublime manner in which he had done so. Waiting in the first-class lounge at O'Hare, reliving the round in his imagination, he was still feeling exceptionally satisfied about it that evening, particularly the finish.

The drama had been almost as exciting as at the Ryder Cup itself, a day earlier. Who was going to win, Europe or America? Standing on the final tee, he and Chuck were still level. He had experienced bad luck on the previous hole, fouled by a freak gust of wind that forced his well-struck tee-shot down into the lake. Fortunately Chuck had then mishit a low ball, which bounced on the water, but had no hope of rising above the five-foot retaining wall in front of the green. They both had to reload and play from the drop zone.

After escaping with a half there, Jamie recalled feeling surprisingly calm teeing off on eighteen. His shot had flown straight, carrying a good distance, before coming to rest on the final fairway about 170 yards short of the target, leaving a long, testing uphill shot to the green. Chuck hit well too, his ball just short of Jamie's, a little to the right of it.

They both wanted to win outright, of course, so what would they do in the event of a tie? Jamie asked the question. Brooking no argument, Chuck tersely replied, 'We carry on… Sudden death'.

'Okay', Jamie was thinking. 'I'd better try and finish you off right here then.'

Chuck's shot made the distance, but drifted slightly right, and then rolled to an unenviable spot, close to the front bunker, leaving a tricky steep shot up and over it. It was Jamie's turn. Normally, he made his own decisions about club selection and reading the putts, but this time he turned to his caddy, Dave. 'Rescue club or four-iron?' he asked. Displaying complete confidence, his man soundlessly handed him the hybrid. Jamie had been hitting that club brilliantly from the fairway on the longer holes all day. Now, he did it again.

'Terrific!' said Dave, but there was slight disappointment when, hitting the up-slope firmly, the ball failed to progress. It finished on line with the cup, but only on the front fringe, thirty feet short of the hole. As they walked forward, Jamie was still thinking he had the advantage. The hole being where it was on the previous day, Chuck would have little room to manoeuvre. Even Phil Mickelson would do well to get up and down from that lie.

'More likely', Jamie thought, 'He'll either duff the ball into the bunker, or thin it right over the green into the bunker across on the other side.' So it was a real shock when Chuck's ball, looping high over the sand-trap, came lightly to earth and rolled right into the cup. Even he seemed amazed at the feat.

'You've broken my heart, Chuck', said Jamie coolly, confidence coming from somewhere... 'Now I'm going to have to break yours'.

On reflection, he had no explanation whatsoever for this bold claim. 'The words just came into my mouth', he said later. It seemed genuinely unlikely that he could save the situation. Nevertheless, putter in hand, he strolled nonchalantly over to his ball, took aim and calmly rolled it up the incline, a little from the left, into the back of the hole.

'Just like Kaymer yesterday', said his caddy, Dave, impressed. 'Only longer...'

'But now I need to stay cool like Rose did on seventeen', thought Jamie. Despite Chuck's astonishing shot, and his remarkable putt, the match was still all square. There was still work to be done.

Down the first they went again. Both hit good drives, and both found the green with their seconds. Chuck putted first, from twenty feet, running the ball three feet by. It was missable, but Jamie wasn't counting on it. His putt from a similar distance ran true.

'Oh! You made it!' Chuck's voice sounded surprised. His caddy was already walking towards the second tee and had to turn around. 'Congratulations!'

Two threes in a row at par fours had been good enough for Jamie to win, a fantastic result. Dave was beaming. Chuck, too, eventually gave a half-smile.

'There's no arguing with golf like that', he said, golf cap off, shaking Jamie by the hand. 'I don't think I'm going to play you for money again.'

'You will', replied his friend, with assurance. 'I can't imagine you turning down the chance to get even some day.'

'Okay... You're right!' Chuck responded. 'But I'm going to take steroids next time...'

'It won't do you any good', Jamie continued teasing. 'Face it... I'm just too good a player.'

'Too damn lucky, anyway. I'll say that.' Making their way back to the clubhouse, it was Chuck who had the last word.

———

'Maybe I am lucky', Jamie was thinking, still at O'Hare, shortly before the call for boarding came through. Later, on the flight, before closing his eyes and settling down, he remembered what the great South African golfer, Gary Player, had said. The multiple major-winner had just played a marvellous bunker shot on the second hole at Wentworth in some big tournament. His ball went into the hole and a spectator called out, 'That was lucky, Gary'. Clearly irritated, Player turned quickly on the hapless fellow, responding sarcastically, 'And you know what, Mister? The more I practice, the luckier I get!'

'The more I practice, the luckier I get', thought Jamie, 'But then, I don't practice golf very much... Maybe I was just born lucky.'

Jamie Royle was not thinking of himself as lucky, however, by any means the following morning, when he arrived at Heathrow.

THE 16TH CHAPTER

At five-thirty the following morning, Holly was driving northwards along the Horsham by-pass. The sun was bright. There was little traffic. As her mind emptied, she suddenly remembered having another strangely intense dream during the night in which she seemed to be watching a beach scene from a distance of about two hundred yards. She had the impression that she had been standing on a raised roadside bank as the sun was going down, looking out towards a sandy promontory jutting out into a sea inlet. It was a beautiful sight. There was no wind. To the right, she was aware of a low brick building with prominent, white painted corner blocks. Nearby, in the centre foreground, four people wearing Parka jackets with the hoods up and their backs turned − a family, possibly, with parents, a son and a daughter − were looking seawards as a speedboat ploughed briskly backwards and forwards. A man and a woman could be seen in the boat, which Holly was viewing from above the heads of the family. It seemed to her that this was Jane X and her killer, and yet the man in the dream, with his arm around his female companion, seemed peculiarly protective towards her.

Then, although the scene did not change, Holly's vantage point seemed to. It was now like watching it on television, as part of a news broadcast that she had recorded. Also, she knew somehow that the newsreader had earlier mentioned the names of the two people in the boat, but that she had missed this vital piece of information. She felt the strongest impulse to pick up the remote and wind back the recording but, just then, she had woken up.

'What could it mean? Is there a hidden clue here?' The questions remained with her as she drove up, past Dorking, towards the M25.

———

Jamie Royle's plane, assisted by a strong trans-Atlantic tailwind, had made up some time, but was still forty minutes late on landing that Tuesday. The delay had given Holly and her boss plenty of time liaising with immigration and customs officials to set up the highly anticipated interview. There had also been time for Holly to take a call from Wesley Westland, the team's technical and communications expert.

'Hi, Holly... I've got something for you.' Wes's voice came over clearly. 'Gryllock telephoned Royle last night, soon after midnight our time.'

'That would have been while he was waiting for his plane in Chicago', Holly replied. 'What have you got?'

'It's not too long... Less than a minute', said the technician. 'I'll send you a transcript, but I can play it for you now, if you like.'

'Thanks Wes... That's great! Go ahead', she answered.

Listening, Holly thought Patrick Gryllock sounded tipsy. His first words were, 'Jamie? We need to talk... The police have been onto me.'

'Get a hold of yourself, Paddy', Royle sounded irritated. 'Have you been drinking?'

'They know about the chairs, Jamie... Your father's chairs!' Gryllock was almost sobbing.

'Get off the phone, Paddy', came the terse response. 'We can talk about this tomorrow... Go to sleep.'

'I can't sleep', Gryllock replied. 'Every time I close my eyes, I see those damnable chairs.'

'Forget about it... Take a pill... I'll be there in the morning.' Then the line went dead.

Holly showed the transcript to DI Garbutt, who then phoned Westland and got him to play her the recording. 'Well done, Westcliff', she said, possibly the first time Holly had heard her congratulate anyone, even if she did get his name wrong. 'Now, Angel', she added, turning to her efficient subordinate. 'What happens next?'

Holly was pleased. When they came to interview Royle, her boss was evidently going to let her be in charge. 'This way, Ma'am', she said, leading the way.

Having left his golf clubs and the bulk of his luggage with Louise to forward to Bandon Dunes, Royle was travelling light. Having only a carry-on leather hold-all, he was able to by-pass baggage reclaim at Terminal Five and proceed directly to Immigration, passport ready in hand. Expecting to breeze through, as usual, he stood slightly impatiently as he was made to wait at the desk, a short queue gradually building behind him. There was still time to go home to his apartment overlooking the Thames in Pimlico, shower, change, and get to the midday meeting with Gryllock and the Chinese, but he never liked feeling rushed. Having taken his passport, the officer looked closely at it and then excused himself. 'Wait here, Sir, please!' he said, marching off. It was over five minutes before he returned, and with him were two colleagues. One of them took over his place at the desk and started beckoning people forward; the other was someone from Customs, who asked Jamie to hand over his bag.

Jamie gave up his hold-all and followed the first official who led him towards a corridor to the left side of the hall, and then along it to an unmarked door. Once inside the plainly furnished room, Jamie was asked to empty his pockets on the table and sit down. When he had done this, the Customs man gathered his possessions into a medium-sized plastic box he had taken from a shelf against the wall, then walked out of the room with the box under his arm.

Jamie realized that the Immigration official also still had his passport. He was about to complain vociferously when the door opened again and Holly led in DI Garbutt. The two detectives sat down opposite Jamie as the immigration man in turn took his leave. Holly then made the introductions.

'We apologize for detaining you here briefly, Mr Royle', she said sweetly, 'But we are investigating a murder on Royle Enterprises property, and you are a material witness.'

'Well, I can't be a suspect, can I?' Royle replied dismissively, almost sneering. 'As you probably know, I was out of the country all last week.'

'So you know when the body was found', said Holly without missing a beat. 'But, no… At this stage, we simply want to ask a few questions. You are not a suspect.'

Royle decided it might be best to change tack. 'Please ask away', he replied, turning on the charm. 'I assure you I've nothing to hide.'

Holly brought out a pocket recording device and switched it on, giving it the date, time and location, and listing those present. Then, for Royle's benefit as well as the tape, she ran through a summary of events so far, from the moment the body was found. Observing closely, she noticed the self-possessed figure across the table looking bored. Neither did the expression on his face alter when she showed him the doctored photographs of Jane X that made her look relatively healthy, a close-up of her in her final emaciated state, then pictures of the two red leather chairs.

'None of these mean anything to me', he lied. 'Can I go now?'

Holly hesitated, feeling rather like Peter Falk, the one-eyed actor in the television series who played Lieutenant Columbo, with incriminating information up his sleeve waiting to pounce. 'Not yet', she said after a lengthy pause, enjoying the moment. 'We intercepted a phone call to you last night from your business partner.'

Holly let this information hang in the air between them, gratified to see some colour appearing in Royle's face, debunking completely his previous air of innocence.

'Why did Mr Gryllock refer to these as photographs of "your father's damnable chairs"? That's what we'd like to know', she eventually said, a clear degree of accusation in her voice.

'He was drunk', was all the angrily blushing Royle would say. They pressed him, but he held firm. DI Garbutt thought about arresting him, as he clearly knew something and was therefore 'obstructing the police in carrying out their enquiries', but she knew his lawyers would soon have him at liberty once again. She advised him against leaving the country for the time being. She knew that neither she nor the Immigration officers could legally retain his passport or prevent him travelling, but she let him understand that, in a murder case such as this, any failure to co-operate would be treated as highly suspicious. Reminding him of how interested the media were likely to be in those implicated in the situation, she played on his obvious wish to avoid unflattering publicity.

He doubted whether she would inform the press of his involvement. It would be highly unethical; and, after all, they already knew of him as the owner of the golf club involved. Nevertheless, he felt trapped, and his first response to her threatening stance was unprintable. He said he would be instructing his lawyers to sue the police if his name was falsely accused in any way, and he gave no undertaking to postpone or cancel his planned return to continue his travels to the Pacific coast and onward to South Asia. Remembering the icy, withering look Royle received in reply from her boss, Holly could not help smiling about it afterwards. No-one could stare a man down and make him feel small like she could. DI Garbutt was, she thought, quite likely a genuine witch.

———

Rich Baum was happy. He had been given something to do, following what might turn out to be an important line of investigation, enquiring into 'animal disposal' services. Phoning from his room in the police hostel, he contacted the businesses in Plumpton and Romsey that advertised on the internet. Neither had any vehicles go missing recently. When he called the third company, the one in West Chiltington, expecting the same result, things took a different turn.

'Halstead and Makepeace… Priscilla speaking. How may I help?' Something about this voice seemed genuinely interested in whoever was calling, and he found it attractive. Rich told the young lady he was conducting a police enquiry and, on impulse, asked if it would be convenient for him to visit later in the morning.

'Who am I speaking to, by the way?' he added.

'Priscilla Halstead', said the voice. 'I'm helping my dad out. He's only gone to fill the truck with diesel… Should be back soon.'

'I'll come over, then', the rookie told her.'About ten o'clock?'

'Fine', she said.

'Okay', he confirmed.

It looked like an ordinary farm. Turning off the main road, Baum drove past a dusty field full of pigpens, pigs and piglets. On raised ground in the distance were sheep, and in a big shed across the yard from the office were some cattle. Priscilla Halstead turned out to be a tall, dark-haired person of about twenty with a winning smile.

'I spoke to dad', she said. 'He's met some of his mates in the village and they've gone for a coffee, but he'll be back soon. How can I help?'

Baum was not sure where to begin. 'What happened to Makepeace?' he asked awkwardly, to kick off the conversation.

'Oh, he's dead', said Priscilla. 'Years ago... He and my grandfather bought the business in the early fifties and gave it their names, but Mr Makepeace never married and had no heirs. I think my grandfather bought his share eventually. The story goes that he sold it to him for a pound.'

'What a bargain!' said Rich, a little tongue-tied, wanting to prolong the conversation but unsure what to say.

'His name was Isaiah', Priscilla filled in the developing silence for him. 'Nobody gets called that these days, do they?'

'I suppose not', Rich replied. 'Priscilla is not very common, either; is it?'

'No', she agreed. 'We've all got unusual names. My grandfather was Eustace, and my father's name is Augustus... Although everybody just calls him Gus'.

'Don't tell me', Rich was smiling, 'You've also got an Uncle Julius'.

'Oh no', Priscilla laughed. 'My uncle's name is Claude... It's short for Claudius'.

'And you've an aunt Octavia, or something like that?'

'No aunts... But I do have a cousin called Flavia!' She was

enjoying the banter with this tall, shy copper. 'What's your name, by the way?' she added.

Rich told her, just as Gus Halstead drove up; a big man, taller by several inches than his daughter, dressed in boots, jeans, a crumpled blue shirt and a sleeveless brown leather jerkin.

'What's all this about?' he asked, striding into the office.

Rich explained. This time he went into more detail about the red chairs, but without mentioning the deceased Jane X. Then he asked about a possible missing vehicle.

'I don't think it could be one of ours', Gus Halstead told him, when he had finished. 'Come and see!'

He led Rich outside, Priscilla following. The flat-bed truck standing there was not particularly large. The aluminium sides only reached about halfway up the height of the cab window. The winch, mounted on the back of the cab, was only three or four feet above the height of the deck. Halstead unfastened and lowered the tailgate, which then became a ramp, and explained how he would use the machinery to haul animal carcases, one by one, up onto the deck.

'The winch only works in one direction, of course', he explained. 'But the truck is a tipper, see!' he added, 'So, when we want to empty it out, I just upend it slowly. I don't think it would work too well for moving those chairs of yours around the place, do you? They'd just tumble awkwardly onto the ground.'

Rich, disappointed, was forced to agree. He smiled, thanked them both and, reluctantly, took his leave. Later he phoned Holly who updated him about the interview with Jamie Royle. 'It goes like this', she told him encouragingly. 'You get setbacks, but you just have to persist. Something will give...'

They agreed to meet up back at Greenings later in the day.

Had Holly been able to interpret the message in her strange dream of the night before, she would have been astonished at what it revealed concerning a name. When he went to the Sussex Cancer Centre for radiotherapy that same Tuesday morning, the man with the husky voice was obliged to reveal his identity to the grey-haired person on duty at the reception desk. 'Pennycuik', he said softly. 'Daniel Pennycuik'.

The Pennycuiks had been a family of four. Daniel's sister was called Francesca. As children, they were inseparable; and, although younger, Dan did indeed feel protective of Fran. In Holly's dream, the family were wearing Parka jackets, and 'Parker' is a well-known brand of fountain pen, giving the first clue to the name: PEN. The white blocks on the corner of the brick building form the second part of that clue. These are 'quoins', a word sounding like 'coins'; the coin in question here being a penny – so, not PEN but PENNY. The final clue is found in the image of a speedboat, travelling briskly, conjuring up the word 'quick', which sounds like CUIK. Put them together and that's PENNYCUIK... But how was she to make the connection? Holly was far too sensible to expect help from the supernatural.

'You're very early for your appointment', said the reception woman to Dan in a kindly voice. 'Why don't you go into the canteen and have a hot drink. I'll call when it's your turn'.

Patients receiving treatment had special parking privileges, but Dan had been forced to wait up to twenty minutes even so on previous occasions. In addition, it was hard to gauge the traffic in the morning, so he preferred to set off in good time and wait if necessary, rather than risk being late for his treatment.

The canteen was busy that morning, and he could only find a place to sit and drink his coffee at a table already occupied by a smart looking woman in her fifties who reminded him of one of the television newsreaders. She said 'Hello', and he nodded in return. They sat silently, with people moving backwards and forwards all around them, chairs and tables scraping the linoleum floor, until suddenly there was a lull.

'I'm Linda', said the woman in the unexpected silence. 'Breast cancer… I had a mastectomy and a course of chemo. Now I've started three weeks of this too'. She waved her hand towards the door, indicating the extensive, modern radiotherapy suite. 'What about you?'

Dan was reluctant to speak about himself, but the atmosphere in this building was not like in other places. He felt alright about confiding a little in people, in strangers who he would not get to know properly and who, in turn, would not truly get to know him.

'Daniel', he said. 'That's my name… I'm called Dan', continuing after a pause, 'I've got lung cancer… That's why my voice is funny', he explained. 'The tumour has grown into one of the nerves to my voice-box, you see. One of my vocal cords is partially paralysed.'

'Oh, dear!' said Linda.

'It's not too bad', replied Dan. 'I don't get any pain; just a bit breathless sometimes… and a cough.'

The loudspeaker on the wall above them came suddenly to life. 'Linda Bingham to radiotherapy, please', said a voice. 'That's me', Linda announced. 'I'd better go… It's been nice meeting you, Dan. And good luck!'

He said goodbye. 'If it wasn't for bad luck', he was thinking, echoing the words of a blues song he remembered, 'I wouldn't have no luck at all!'

Going home later, he realized that he was still incredibly angry. That night, he went to sleep exhausted, but woke again after only a couple of hours, rage coursing like fire through his veins. After tossing for a bit, he got up, went to the bathroom, had a drink of water and went to lie down again. After lying awake in the unkempt bed-sheets for another forty minutes or so, he decided he had to go and do something. Pulling on some clothes, soon afterwards, he went out into the night.

———————

Arriving at the golf club shortly before eight o'clock the following morning, Wednesday, Peter Harding was greeted by a very animated and unhappy John Tranter. 'Come and look at this', was all he could say, leading the Colonel around the clubhouse to the practice putting green where the words EVIL BASTARDS could be read, inscribed in two-foot high letters.

'I reckon it's a mixture of weed-killer and old engine oil has done that', the head green-keeper said, sounding disgusted. 'Who would do such a thing?'

'The same one who left us a corpse and a couple of chairs, John, don't you reckon?' the Secretary replied. 'I'll get onto the police right away. Don't do anything yet, of course; but do you think you can fix it?'

'We'll have to lift all the affected turf, fill in and re-seed it', was the answer. 'It's the beginning of October now… Not the best time; but it might be alright if it stays reasonably warm and the seed takes. The members will just have to go around it for now.'

Just under two hours later, Valerie Parton, Holly and Rich were seated in the darkened Secretary's office, ready to view the CCTV images captured the night before. Other members of the police team were outside examining the hostile message on the ground. Peter Harding explained that the cameras had motion-sensors fitted, as did the car-park and clubhouse floodlights, switching on whenever movement was detected. 'We've had some wonderful wild-life shots', he added, digressing unnecessarily. 'Deer, badgers, foxes, pheasants and squirrels mostly'. As a result of the advanced technology, they did not have to wait long after he pressed the start button before something of interest appeared.

'You can see the beam of his headlights', the Colonel was pointing at the screen, 'But, clever fellow, he's parked outside the range of the cameras.'

'It might be a she, a woman not a man', Holly mentioned.

'I think you'll see it's a man in a minute', Harding replied. 'I've already had a quick look at these. We can't see him yet because he's hugging the hedge, underneath the lights and cameras, but his movement has triggered the devices. You just get a glimpse of him as he leaves the car park, coming round to the front of the building… There! You see?'

He played and replayed that three-second section of tape several times for them, then switched over to another view.

'Here he is now, walking along in front of the building, disappearing round the side', the Secretary's commentary continued. Holly made a note of the crouched, probably male, figure skulking slowly along, carrying what seemed to be a heavy container − like a petrol can − in one hand, and a large plastic bucket in the other. The images were rather fuzzy, and were in black and white, but it was still possible to make out that he was wearing loose dark overalls and a fully zipped track-suit top with the hood up over a baseball cap. The man's face could not be seen.

The next view covered the putting green, and the small group watched carefully as the interloper made his way to the middle of it, placing the two receptacles down on the grass, pouring a dark fluid from the can into the bucket and, fishing a long-handled brush from somewhere in among the folds of his overalls, begin writing his angry message. He did not seem to be in any hurry, but Holly was particularly interested when he seemed to take a long break from his exertions.

'What's he doing?' she asked. 'Can you play that bit again, please, Colonel?'

The figure, his back to the camera, had straightened up, dumped his brush in the bucket, turned his head to the side, and suddenly bent down again, bobbing up and down a few times. 'I think he might be coughing', said Rich. 'Let's look at it again', said Holly.

In the end, they all agreed that this was the most likely explanation. The man had been convulsed for a few seconds by a paroxysm of coughing. Holly immediately went down to speak to the forensic men outside. 'Look for spots of phlegm', she advised them. 'He was writing the 'T' when it happened. Look at the middle of this area carefully please. We're looking for a sample of his DNA.'

After he completed the message, the video-watchers saw the man as he took his bucket, brush and can, retraced his steps, marched across the car park without taking the trouble this time to conceal himself, and drove away. They could see the sweep of the headlights making a circle across the empty car park, but the vehicle remained out of sight. Back outside soon afterwards, the forensic expert told Holly they had found and collected two small pieces of turf on which were samples of what might have been blood-flecked pulmonary secretions. 'We've got the rotter's spit, you mean? That's wonderful!' Holly, of course, was delighted.

In the late afternoon at Greenings, it was time to take stock. With her boss listening in via speaker-phone, Holly ran through an update of the situation.

'We still do not know the identity of Jane X', she began. 'We think she was left on the golf course, and possibly killed, by the man with the husky voice. He is probably also the man in the overalls who left another message on club property last night. We have not established a clear motive, but revenge of some kind seems likely. Having canvassed removals firms, neighbours, horse people, vets and even equine funeral services, we are no nearer to understanding how the red chairs and corpse were transported, despite the tell-tale evidence of horse blood on one of the chairs... Is that everything?'

'I did phone several psychiatric units, Holly', Sally Blackshaw piped up. 'I worked out that Jane X, probably born around 1975, could have been treated somewhere for anorexia from roughly 1990 onwards. Unfortunately, with only an approximate age and no name, none of them could help us out. All I could clarify was that people from this area – women mostly, but apparently men can also suffer from eating disorders... These people would have been sent to Graylingwell Hospital before it closed in 2001, anyway to local psychiatric services, and then referred on to the eating disorders unit at the Atkinson Morley Hospital in Wimbledon, part of the Psychiatry Department of St George's Hospital Medical School in Tooting.'

'Okay... Thanks, Sally, That's helpful', said Holly. 'Anything else, anyone?'

'Yes', came the unmistakeable, if slightly distorted, voice from the telephone speaker. 'We are sure that Messrs Royle and Gryllock know more than they are currently willing to tell.'

'Thank you, Ma'am', Holly replied. 'Where do you advise we go now?'

'We have fewer lines of enquiry to pursue now, and a number of other cases to work on', said the voice, 'So I'm going to scale back the investigation and reassign half of you'. There was a pause before the DI resumed with a tone of finality, 'DS Angel and I will discuss it in the morning and get back to you.'

As Laura Garbutt finished speaking, another phone started ringing. Rich Baum picked it up then passed it to Holly, who listened intently for a few moments, said 'Thank you' into the mouthpiece, and put the receiver down gently.

'Well', she said, turning back to the assembled company. 'That is a surprise! The forensic team have the DNA results from some phlegm they collected at the golf club this morning and they think they have a near match, but not one we expected... It turns out that the overalls man is closely related to the victim. They might be cousins, but they are probably brother and sister.'

Dan Pennycuik missed his treatment that Wednesday morning, sleeping late after his strength-sapping nocturnal activities. He took a phone call in the early afternoon from a cancer specialist nurse at the centre, concerned at his absence that day. 'I'll be there tomorrow', he reassured her. 'Don't worry.'

Feeling rested, he was early again for treatment the next day, and was sitting in the canteen when the woman, Linda, came and sat beside him, putting her tea on the table between them.

'I was looking out for you yesterday', she said. 'We cancer sufferers need to stick together, don't you think? Support each other?'

'I wasn't well', he replied defensively.

'I'm not trying to make you feel bad, Daniel… On the contrary', she said. 'I have my husband to care about and look after me. He's been wonderful about all this, especially when I went through chemotherapy, lost my hair and everything. But I sense that you don't have anyone… Am I right?'

'I had a sister', Dan replied. 'But she died.'

'I'm so sorry', the woman, Linda, responded, laying a comforting hand on his outstretched arm. 'What was she like?'

No-one had shown this kind of interest in him before, and Dan was cautious; but something made him want to unbutton himself to this strangely trustworthy person. To him, she gave off a real glow of compassion so, husky voice notwithstanding, he began to tell her about his life with his sister Fran.

'Our mother's name was Stella. She came from humble roots in Hampshire. Our grandparents, her parents, died before we were born. Our father, George Pennycuik, was a sea captain. I don't remember him very well because he was seldom at home, always travelling the globe. I think he came from Scotland originally, made his way to Portsmouth and joined the Merchant Navy. He was older than mother, and he died of yellow fever in Argentina when I was only four and Fran was nearly nine.'

Dan paused to take a sip of coffee before continuing. 'There was no pension, so mother had to find suitable work somewhere, a job that included accommodation for us all to live in. That's how she came to be a housekeeper. Her first position was with a family in Southsea, near where we had been living in lodgings while father was alive. Even though the three of us were sharing one bedroom, we liked it there. All the same, after a couple of years, when the children of the house went away to school, we had to move on. That's when we shifted to Fotheringay House, near Ewehurst. An important judge had lost his wife some years earlier. His latest house-keeper was due to retire and my mother had got to know her somehow. It was this woman who recommended my mother to the judge.'

'So you and your sister had a new home', Linda interjected. 'Did you like that one?'

'We did at first', replied Dan. 'The judge was retired, a strict sort; but he was elderly and kept much to himself. We had the run of the place. It was a big house and there were extensive gardens too. I really liked one of the gardeners, who seemed to take a shine to me. I think I saw him as a kind of substitute for my father. But, I see now, he was probably just being nice to me as a way of getting close to my mother. He was a married man, though. She kept brushing him off, and because of it he seemed to become much less friendly to me. It was still okay. I mean, we weren't unhappy… But then everything changed when the judge's son came home for the school holidays. He was older than us and a real bully, so we tried to keep out of his way. When the judge became ill and finally died, of course, it all changed completely again.'

He found it surprisingly easy to speak about these matters after so long a time. Indeed, he wanted to go on confiding in Linda, but the loudspeaker cut into the narrative. It was his turn, this time, to go for treatment.

'I'll see you tomorrow, then', Linda called after him, waving, but that wasn't to be.

THE 17TH
CHAPTER

It was bad news for Holly that there were no matches for the sibling DNA on police computers anywhere. The identity of the man in the overalls was still a mystery. There was plenty of discussion in the room after the revelation from forensics, but no new ideas about what to do next. After a while, Rich Baum asked if he could leave a little early. It was his mother's birthday and he wanted to visit her with a gift before his father was taking her out for an evening meal at The Fountain, their favourite pub in Ashurst, a meal to which a manifestly disappointed Rich had not been invited.

The young man was distracted as he drove up to Halfway Bridge and turned right towards Petworth. He was listening with half an ear to radio, from which emerged the unmistakeable guitar sound of Hank Marvin, lead guitarist of The Shadows, Cliff Richard's backing group from a long time ago. Ahead was a brief stretch of dual carriageway. Coming towards him at speed, overtaking a slower vehicle where the road started narrowing, was motorcycle, a broad-beamed affair, like a Harley. Rich hardly saw this speeding bullet. It was on him like a shot, forcing him to swerve left and brake at the same time. The BMW turned sideways, rear tyres skidding along the tarmac, the nearside one lifting some inches off the ground. To Rich it seemed as if the car hung for several seconds in the air before mercifully falling back to earth. Traction regained, it shot forwards, up onto the muddy verge and on, until the front wheels fell into space and stopped, overhanging a ditch. He tried to back out again, but the wheels just spun. Nothing had happened with the air-bags, so he sat for a moment, the world strangely calm and quiet after he switched off the engine.

Fortunately, there was a signal, but not much life left in the battery of his mobile. The recovery vehicle, he discovered, would take an hour to reach him. He started explaining to his mother what was happening, to apologise and wish her well, but then the phone packed up. There were no houses in sight, but there was a lane nearby. Later, borrowing the recovery driver's Android to make the call, he explained things to Holly who was still at Greenings.

After briefly recounting his adventures, explaining why he had gone exploring, he said, 'It was called Dean Lane... I could see a roof in the distance, and I thought I might find someone at home. As I set off, I also noticed an old signboard. It had fallen over by the hedge and was covered by overgrown grass and weeds. The lettering was faded, but I could just make out part of the first word, "Pony"... "Pony-something". Then there was another word, but I couldn't make that one out. Anyway, I had this great hunch, so I decided to take a look up the track. I knew I had plenty of time'.

'Go on', said Holly. She liked her staff to be thorough, but still wished he'd get to the point.

'Okay', said Rich. 'I went about a hundred and fifty metres where I came across this almost derelict farm. All the buildings were locked up. There was no sign of life, although there were some fairly fresh-looking tyre tracks on the muddy ground in front of the main gateway to the yard. I knocked on doors and windows, but there was no response. The bell did not seem to be working.'

'Were there any more signs?' Holly asked.

'Oh, yes… I should have mentioned it,' Rich replied. 'There's a big one near the entrance, also very faded and obviously out of date… It says, "Ponyrest Place… *Cremations with dignity for your beloved pet*". There's a phone number, but I've tried ringing and it's no longer operational, must have been disconnected.'

'Okay… Thanks Rich', Holly answered. 'Let's look into it together in the morning. Well done!' Then she went to find a computer.

————

After his radiotherapy, Daniel had gone straight home, feeling weak. He managed to heat up and drink a can of soup, eating some dry bread with it, then went to lie down. An hour or two after that, while mercifully asleep, he had what was later diagnosed as a stroke. He was unconscious the following morning, but still breathing, when Holly and Rich arrived and found him at Ponyrest Place.

They had met up earlier at Greenings, where several people were already packing up at their desks, having received re-assignment emails from DI Garbutt, acting independently. Despite assurances, she had not discussed anything with her subordinate. Those remaining gathered round as Holly related what she had discovered from her computer search the evening before.

'Ponyrest Place was being run for about twenty years from the mid-1980's by someone called Anderson… First name Sybil', she began. 'Like Halstead and Makepeace, and the others we have looked into so far, this was an operation offering special collection, storage and cremation services for farm animals, licensed by the LMSSA until 2004, when it presumably closed for business. It was a small concern which, as the name implies, seems to have focused especially on disposing of children's pet ponies.'

'How sweet!' someone said at the back of the room, clearly impressed.

'You had a pony, then, Sally, did you?' Holly smiled.

'I didn't have my own exactly', Sally Blackshaw responded, 'But I did ride them, yes. I loved it.'

'Okay', Holly was brusque now. 'We're off to have another look at it... Come on Rich! We'll take your car again, shall we?'

It was lighter when they got there than it had been the evening before, and they could see more through the ground-floor windows. Holly was on the phone for the Fire Service and an ambulance straightaway. They had spotted Pennycuik's body, looking lifeless on the couch.

The men from the Fire Brigade soon forced the main gate open, and then the door into the house. Once inside, the ambulance team took control, ascertained that, although unrousable, the patient was alive, transferred him to a stretcher, put an oxygen mask over his face and put up a saline drip.

Holly, meanwhile, was looking around in the next room, which seemed to be some kind of office. There was, she noticed, a faded calendar from 2004 on the wall above the desk, which was strewn with documents, letters – some opened, others not – an old phone book, tattered farming magazines and various other forms of literature. Some of the correspondence was addressed, she saw, to Mrs Anderson, but the name on the rest was D Pennycuik. For some reason, the name seemed slightly familiar.

Meanwhile, Rich was searching the yard and other buildings. A rusting old brown Subaru estate occupied the former, the keys still in the ignition. Peering inside, he could see with satisfaction a plastic bucket wedged in the passenger foot-well behind the driver's seat. It still contained the brush and petrol can that he felt sure he had seen on CCTV at the golf club a day earlier. Then, in the barn opposite, he found a full-sized horse transport vehicle, also ancient but still, apparently, roadworthy. He made a note of both number plates and put in a request to headquarters for an immediate check to be made.

'It doesn't look safe… You should have borrowed one of our hard hats to go in there', one of the firemen teased Rich, when he finally emerged from the dusty and dilapidated barn after inspecting the horsebox, but the young detective shrugged and ignored him, having other things on his mind. A text message from headquarters had revealed that the horse box was still registered to Sybil Anderson. The Subaru belonged to Daniel Pennycuik.

Holly was following the stretcher into the yard as it was being wheeled towards the ambulance when Rich caught up with her and told her what he had found.

'It must be the vehicle we're looking for', he said. 'In the back it's all clean, spotless. The floor is sealed, like the ones the knackers people use, so it can be hosed down; but the real point of interest is the hoist. It's a very ingenious contraption; although I'm not sure how it works.'

Holly and Rich confirmed with each other the name of their suspect, now even more definite after the ambulance people had taken a wallet from his trouser pocket. Holly had also found and fished out his patient identity card from the Sussex Cancer Centre. As a result, the ambulance folk had called through to let the staff there know what had happened, and to get some more information about their patient. It was agreed that, although Chichester was nearer, he should be taken to Worthing Hospital. The stroke unit there was less busy, and he would be closer to Brighton for when the radiotherapy could start again.

The fire engine had left, making its way further up the farm lane on a long detour, as it had been impossible in the confined space to turn it around. The ambulance was set to go, too, when Holly remembered to ask about getting a DNA sample. The crew said it would be easier at the hospital, so Holly called Sally Blackshaw, sending her to Worthing to make sure the necessary evidence was collected.

'And liaise with Worthing Police, will you?' she added. 'I want someone in uniform beside this Pennycuik round the clock, just in case he wakens and tries to wander off. They can arrest him, if necessary...'

'On what grounds?' Sally replied.

'Suspicion of murder, I reckon', replied Holly. 'I'm sure we'll pick up the evidence.'

After this, both detectives went to look around some more. In a smaller storage area, next to the big barn, Rich came across a good-sized horizontal freezer unit, and a larger refrigerated storage space. 'Do you think this is where he kept the body?' he said to Holly, who was already returning to tell him in turn about the small industrial furnace she had found in a brick building round the back.

'Could be', she answered cautiously. 'The furnace looks as if it hasn't been fired up in years, by the way. The chimney's either been destroyed deliberately or it's just fallen down with age. That's why we couldn't see it from out front.'

Later, with the help of a police mechanic, they were able to start the horsebox, drive it into the yard and inspect the hoist in operation. There were three sets of runners riveted along the ceiling inside holding strong steel rods. The two on either side came out first when the mechanism was activated, ideal for covering the spot where any stricken horse may have fallen. Each of these rods came in two parts, the second part – which needed to be attached and fastened – cleverly hinged to hang down, angled outwards. Broad steel feet, which they found in the cab, could then be clipped securely into place at the lower ends, before positioning them firmly on the ground, the whole structure thereby made stable. A cross-piece ran between these two outer rods, to which a third, reinforcing leg could be attached in the centre.

The mechanic showed Rich and Holly how this worked, then turned his attention to the central runner, which was similar to the outer rods, but had no second part for hinging to it. Instead, it could also be secured into the centre of the cross-piece, on the opposite side from the downward-facing middle leg. Hanging from it was a hook device, with a pulley mechanism running back through the rod to the winch, by which the hook could easily be raised and lowered. The entire, ungainly but functional-looking thing was additionally braced by the very sturdy outer frame of the horsebox and a concrete counter-weight sitting on the chassis near the front.

'I've never seen anything like it before in my life', said Holly, looking on in fascination.

'I have', said the wizened old mechanic. 'I've seen this one.'

'Really... Where?' Holly asked.

'It was at Brighton racetrack, maybe twenty years ago', he said. 'A horse had fallen badly at one of the fences and was going to be put down, but the owner wouldn't agree. It was his young daughter's favourite animal... Its pelvis was smashed, I think, so it couldn't even hobble on three legs... I heard later that he offered the vet a large amount of money to save the horse, even if it couldn't run again. There was a very long delay. Nothing seemed to be happening, and the punters were getting restless. Then this thing trundled up with some woman at the wheel and a young bloke to help her. After positioning it on the track over the poor creature, they had it working in no time. I saw them sling broad webbing straps underneath the horse, fix them to the hook and winch the poor creature upright. Then, after raising it off the ground, they worked the machine to pull the hook slowly back into the vehicle, and the animal with it, sedated by now, using the webbing like a cradle. I imagine they kept it upright like that all the way back to its stables.'

'I never did hear what the outcome was… Whether it survived or not', he added ruefully.

The next day, on her way to Worthing, Holly heard news on the radio of the previous day's Metropolitan Police announcement concerning an investigation into new and historical allegations of sexual abuse, mainly against children, by men, some well-known, others not, but including particularly a celebrity television presenter and charity fundraiser. Jimmy Savile, the well-known eccentric cigar-smoker had died, aged eighty-five, almost a year earlier. The news caught her by surprise as she remembered watching some of his programmes, when she was much younger.

Her experience as a policewoman told her that lots more people would soon be coming out of the woodwork with accusations. However, she was not expecting to hear one herself that Friday. Sally Blackshaw had called the previous evening to report that Pennycuik had regained consciousness, but that the hospital consultant was not letting anyone interview him before the morning. A police guard had been posted, so Holly was not surprised to see a WPC sitting outside the side-room on the third-floor medical ward as she approached at around midday, having checked with the doctor that it would now be okay to make her visit.

'He's been lucky, in a way', the physician had said. 'It was a mild cerebral event caused by an embolism to the right side of the brain. He has a left hemiplegia, but he can still speak.'

'You mean, he's lucky to survive the stroke so now he can

die of lung cancer', Holly thought of protesting, but managed to restrain herself. 'What's the prognosis?' is what she actually said.

'We'll know presently, in a few days', she was told by the friendly, but rather old-school type of doctor, 'He could recover completely from this episode. However, bronchial carcinomas are known to increase a person's risk of haemostasis, so it could easily happen again.'

Fortunately, Holly could translate most medical-speak. She quickly realised this meant, 'lung cancer sometimes causes blood clots'. Entering the side-room, taking in the big picture-window and the view over the car-park towards the sea, approaching the rather pathetic, pallid-looking figure propped up on a stack of pillows, she decided a sympathetic approach would be best.

Quietly taking a seat on his right side, she reached out to touch the good hand of the dozing invalid, who reacted sleepily, only after several seconds lazily opening his eyes one at a time. Holly showed him her official badge and told him her name. She then mentioned that it had been she and a colleague who found him and called an ambulance. There was no reply, and no immediate change in the sick man's expression, so she continued, telling him they had been investigating what had happened to a woman, presumably his sister.

'Fran', he said simply, by way of confirmation.

'Fran... Yes... Was that her name?' Holly asked.

'Francesca.' Holly shivered, hearing that soft husky voice at close quarters for the first time. 'We called her Fran,' it said.

'What can you tell me about her, Daniel?' Holly continued.

'Dan, please... I don't like Daniel', he said. 'And thanks', he added, 'For the ambulance.'

Holly stayed with him for almost an hour, recording on her device – with his knowledge and permission – what he had to say, beginning at the same place and recounting much the same story he had told Linda Bingham, the lady at the Cancer Centre, two days earlier. This time, though, after speaking about the death of his seafaring father, and his mother's need to take a job as a housekeeper, he mentioned the Judge's son by name. As Holly expected, this was Jamie Royle.

'What did he do to you?' She asked.

'He called us names to start with', Dan said. 'He used to call us "Penny-slow" instead of Pennycuik, or just "Slow"; and I was always "Spaniel", not Daniel. It was appropriate, I suppose, as he treated me like a dog... And he used to pinch. He used to give me a pinch on the arms or the legs whenever he saw me. He made us play games too, like hide-and-seek, then he would pounce on us, one at a time. He used to tickle Fran without mercy, always pretending she liked it when truthfully she hated it. She'd start giggling and he wouldn't stop until she was unable to catch her breath, usually crying tears of frustration... There were other things too... He used to hide our things, our toys and sometimes our schoolwork, so we'd get into trouble. It was always such a relief when he went off to that posh college every term.'

'There's more, though, isn't there?' Holly asked.

'Yes', replied Dan. 'When he got older, he started bossing my mother around, treating her as if she was his private skivvy. It used to upset her, but she wouldn't complain about it to the Judge. She always worried that she would lose the job and not be able to find another like it.'

He was getting a little breathless, and his mouth seemed very dry, so Holly suggested a pause, handing him a half-filled plastic beaker from on top of the bedside cabinet for Dan to take a sip of water. Handing it back, he shut his eyes briefly, then continued.

'Eventually, Royle went away to the university, visiting home less often', he said. 'He spent a lot of his vacation time with his new friends from Oxford after that... But the following year his father became ill. It was something to do with his kidneys and his blood pressure, so he had to have dialysis and spent quite a bit of time in the hospital. This was the summer Fran turned fifteen. I was ten.

There was a pause. When Holly looked up, she saw he was weeping silently, looking just like a small boy. 'It's alright, Dan', she said softly, putting her hand on his arm for a second time. 'You don't have to go on with this now… I can come back.' Taking some tissues from a box nearby, she handed them to him.

'No', he said eventually. 'I want to go on. I want people to know what they did…'

'They?' Holly enquired.

'Yes… Him and his friend Gryllock.' There was poison now in Dan's gruff voice, slowly recounting events that had taken place over forty years earlier, pausing now and again to catch his breath or dab his eyes with the tissues. What had happened seemed vividly fresh in his mind.

'I suppose because the Judge wasn't there, Royle knew he could enjoy himself at Fotheringay House, and get up to all his nasty little tricks without anyone interfering. What's more, he obviously had that measly coward Gryllock wrapped around his little finger to do his bidding. They visited the house together, lording it over mother and the rest of the staff, throwing degenerate parties, terrorizing the locals when they got the chance… Royle always carried a shotgun wherever he went, and was not afraid of firing it off and endangering the public just to get a reaction… And he still used to pinch me or give me a Chinese burn on the forearm. I tried kicking him back for it once, but it didn't do any good. He just turned round and punched me very hard in the face. It gave me a terrible black eye.'

'But what happened to your sister?' said Holly, feeling slightly impatient. 'What happened to Fran?'

'That's what I'm coming to', said Dan. 'That's what all this is about…'

For the next ten minutes, Holly sat back in silence, outraged at what she was hearing, trying hard to maintain a degree of professional detachment. One morning that summer, Dan told her, his mother took him to the shops in Guildford for new shoes. He was of an age when his feet were growing fast. They left Fran reading quietly in the kitchen where it was cool; but on their return after a couple of hours, there was no sign of her in the rooms downstairs, and no response when they called out her name.

It was Dan who eventually discovered his sister, in bed, under the covers, in the bedroom they were still sharing at the top of the house. The curtains were closed. Fran was shivering and sobbing. She wouldn't answer when he asked what was wrong. Fetching his mother, he stood by and watched as she gently peeled back the bedclothes, revealing his sibling's lilywhite legs. They were uncovered, but she was still wearing her little summer socks; also her knickers, which – to his horror – had been stained bright red with blood.

Only years later, not long before she died, did Fran ever tell him about the terrible ordeal that had befallen her that day. Royle and Gryllock, out late carousing the night before, had slept in. When they finally came down, still in their night attire, finding Fran in the kitchen, they ordered her to make them breakfast. Then, while she was making coffee and toast, scrambling eggs and so on, they started taunting her, humiliating her about being a young woman now, inviting her to tell them about her periods, and to show them her developing breasts. After putting food down in front of them, she tried to leave, but they wouldn't let her escape.

'Before this', Dan told Holly, 'Although I never did, Fran had actually begun to like Jamie Royle. He was tall, handsome and rich. I suppose it's natural that she began to daydream about him. He used to tease her when she was younger, but in a nice way. She loved chocolate, and he always brought her Twirls and things like that. Twirls were her favourite… I suppose all along, though, he was just grooming her. That morning, he was ready to spring the trap.'

According to Dan's story, when they had finished eating, the two Oxford students had gone into the Judge's study, taking Fran with them, gripping her by the wrists and pulling her along. There they sat her in one of the big red armchairs while they opened the drinks cupboard, topping up their alcohol levels by helping themselves liberally to the Judge's very best liquor.

'They must have been drunk to do what they did', Dan explained, pausing hesitantly at this point, as if on a precipice. Once he said another word, he knew it would all have to come out.

'They put music on and forced her to dance', he began again finally. 'Then they made her take her clothes off, one by one: shoes, socks, cardigan, blouse, skirt; and the rest, you know, her underwear… Then they raped her… Royle made Gryllock hold her down over the back of one of the chairs and, when he had finished, insisted they change places. She said Royle seemed to enjoy that part the most, pulling on her wrists while she screamed and struggled, with the other one forcing himself on her from behind.'

'So you decided to make sure the world knew what they'd done, even though so many years had passed', said Holly.

'I just felt so bloody mad at the thought they'd got away with it and nobody knew about it.' Dan looked up at her, then collapsed back onto the pillows, closing his eyes again with a mixture of relief, exhaustion and shame, his family's dishonour finally revealed.

———

It's not the whole story yet', Holly was telling DCI Holroyd, DI Garbutt and Rich Baum when they met at Sussex House a few hours later, 'But I'll get the rest out of him in due course, don't worry. I think he's dying to unburden himself now he's started.'

'He is dying' said Holly's boss, without a trace of humour. 'That's for sure... According to the medics, he probably hasn't got long.'

She had spoken to someone at the Cancer Centre. The radiotherapy was palliative, they said, meaning that it might reduce the pain and discomfort, perhaps also delay his inevitable demise, but it could not keep him alive indefinitely.

'Are we going to charge him?' said Holly.

It was Holroyd who spoke up this time, 'With what exactly? I think we'd better wait. It looks like he could have murdered his sister, perhaps to put her out of her misery, but we've no real evidence for that.'

'Do we have anything on Royle and Gryllock?' This was DI Garbutt again.

'I'm not sure that we have enough', Holroyd replied. 'I'll try and speak to someone at the Met working on this new 'Operation Yewtree'. It seems we can no longer ignore strong evidence of historic sex abuse cases.

It was only ten minutes from her home to Worthing Hospital, so Holly went back that evening, but her hoarse-voiced informant was sleeping, and she did not like to wake him. The following morning though, when she returned, he looked brighter.

'I won't run away, Miss', Dan said as she walked in. 'You don't need to keep an officer outside all the time. I'm far too weak... And where would I go, anyway?'

'Alright... Thanks', she responded. 'I'll see to it... But first, please continue with your story. What happened to Fran after she was assaulted by Royle and Gryllock?'

'Mother stayed with her all night', Dan resumed. 'She drank a little water, but she wouldn't eat anything. That's when she lost her appetite for good, I reckon… That's when she became anorexic. It was a complete change of personality. She was such a sweet, pretty, bubbly person before, but she became depressed after that, and seemed to develop an intense kind of self-loathing, especially for her body.'

'I was only young, but I felt it. She had always loved and protected me, but now the roles had to be reversed. There were so many times I sat with her, trying to get her to eat a morsel of food. Even a few lettuce leaves or a small piece of a carrot would have been a success. I often saw her take food from mother, then spit it out again when she thought no-one could see. Also, she used to hide food and later flush it down the toilet. Eventually, of course, she learned how to make herself vomit food back. That was about the worst thing.'

'It must have been awful', Holly muttered in sympathy. 'Why did your mother not call in the police?'

'Well, for the same reason, I suppose', Dan answered. 'She did not want to lose her job. I don't suppose she thought it would do any good, either. It would only have been poor Fran's word against those two.'

'What about taking her to the hospital?' Holly asked.

'We did', Dan replied, 'A number of times… But she would never stay there. They called a psychiatric nurse or a social worker to her once or twice, I remember; but we were told Fran wasn't ill enough for them to force her into hospital; and mother didn't want that anyway.'

'Didn't your mother go and speak to Royle and Gryllock after it happened, make some kind of protest, threaten them with exposure even?' Holly was again beginning to identify with Dan's sense of outrage.

'It was too late', he replied. 'They packed up and left pretty quickly after the incident… Back to Oxford, I imagine, to start setting up a strong alibi… You know Royle. He really was that dreadful. We never saw him again; but a few months later his father died, and within weeks he had his lawyers send us a letter to quit the property. He was going to sell it… We had to go… Just like that!'

'What did you do?' Holly asked.

"Mum was amazing', Dan said. 'She didn't make any fuss. She just went to the landlord of a local pub, The Cricketers, and asked for work. From then on, she pulled pints three evenings a week in the bar. During the day, she worked as a cleaning woman for various people around town. She took a small unfurnished apartment, and contacted the Royle family solicitors for permission to buy cheaply some of the furniture from Fotheringay House, or perhaps just take it; so that's how we came by those awful chairs. We covered them over with blankets because Fran hated them so; but mother said we had no money to spare for new ones, and it was true; for example, we never had any holidays.'

'So Fran developed anorexia, your mother was working very hard, and you were still at school, I suppose', Holly clarified.

'That's right', said Dan, 'But I left as soon as I turned sixteen. Fran wasn't going to school or college by then either… I went to be a stable boy on a stud farm nearby run by the Andersons, Vic and Andy.'

'Do you mean Sybil?'

'Sybil, yeah!' She hated that name. We always just called her "Andy" or "Mrs A".'

'Go on', said Holly.

'I was with them for years, and they both seemed to take a bit of a shine to me', Dan continued. 'They didn't have any kids of their own, you see… They gave me lodgings at the farm after a bit, and that's when I took those chairs off mother, to get them out of Fran's way, like. Then, in the mid-80's, Vic decided to take on something a bit smaller and easier to run. He was getting on a bit by then. Andy, his missus, was a good bit younger… So that's when they sold up and bought Ponyrest Place. It's what Andy really wanted to do, and it gave her a chance to have some contact with children. She liked that… And it's just as well they moved to Sussex when they did because, only about a year later, Vic died of a heart attack.'

'You were there?' Holly suggested.

'Oh yes', Dan answered. 'I was there. They took me with them to help run the place, and…' Holly noticed he was suddenly blushing. 'And I used to keep Andy company sometimes, if you know what I mean.'

'You were sleeping with her?'

'Well, if you put it like that… Yes', Dan admitted, his cheeks burning. 'I think Vic knew about it, but he never said anything. I loved that man. He was like a father to me, and I owe him so much… He was clever, too. It was him who designed that horse-hoist, for example. He told me he had seen something like it as a boy in his native New Zealand… He was an amazing man!'

'That's the horse-box you used to take Fran's body and those chairs to the golf course?' Holly offered.

'Yes', agreed Dan. 'I'm coming to that…'

But he was not to reach that part of the story just then, being racked by a lengthy fit of coughing. When Holly heard a strange gurgling sound, and then saw a large amount of blood appearing on the tissues, she went and called for a nurse. The interview was suddenly over.

THE 18ᵀᴴ CHAPTER

Holly left the hospital and drove to Sussex House. Several armoured police vans filled with uniformed officers were leaving as she arrived at the car park.

'What's going on?' she asked someone, on her way to the canteen. 'What's all that lot doing?'

'There's a pitched battle going on at the beach between some rival London gangs', she was told. 'The riot shield lads are going to try and break it up.'

'Which one were you, Sarge?' someone called from a room across the corridor. 'Mod or Rocker?'

'That was the sixties, you cheeky blighter!' said the burly Sergeant. 'How old do you think I am?'

'That's right, Sarge', said another voice from within. 'You tell him… We all know you were a Punk!'

Holly laughed, joining in the general banter that followed. It was another reason she liked being in the police force. No-one took anything too seriously… Except DI Garbutt, of course! Ten minutes later, having found a spare desk, she was typing her report into the police computer, including Dan Pennycuik's account of things, more or less word for word. It took her quite a long time.

Later, on her way home, she went to the supermarket, then for another run. After a shower, she heated up a frozen meal and ate it in front of the television. The gang warfare on Brighton Seafront was one of the major stories covered, but Holly felt distracted. She was worried about her man, Dan, reflecting that she still did not know how his sister had died, and whether in fact she was murdered.

She thought of phoning the hospital for an update on his condition; then she decided it would be better to go in person. Pennycuik had been moved to the Intensive Care Unit (the 'expensive care unit', as Jack always called it, she remembered), but she was not allowed in. The nurse in charge, after inspecting her warrant card carefully, told her that Dan had lost a lot of blood after the tumour in his chest must have eroded into a blood vessel, but that the bleeding had stopped and he was receiving a blood transfusion. For the time being, he was also sedated.

Back home, she telephoned her father, who had had a successful afternoon playing bowls with his mates and was in a cheerful mood. Although she knew he would be interested, she felt she could tell him nothing yet about the case she was working on, except vaguely perhaps that there had been something of a breakthrough.

'What's the matter, Love?' her father asked, sensing something amiss.

'I'm alright, Dad', she insisted. 'It's nothing… I'm probably tired, that's all.'

Later, she put on a coat and went out for a walk.

———

Up in London that evening, high up in his luxury penthouse apartment, Jamie Royle was fretting. His lawyers had tried persuading him against leaving the country again too soon, so his plans had gone wrong and he was fuming. He had already instructed Catherine to recall Gary Brooker and Louise from Oregon, and there was not much else he could do. Paddy Gryllock was being a pain, wanting to discuss matters that, as far as he was concerned, were dead and buried. 'Everybody commits a few peccadilloes when they're young, don't they?' he told Paddy, during one of their more heated discussions. 'Just forget about it.' The news about Operation Yewtree had gone right over his head. It never occurred to him that he might be called to account.

The unexpected highlight that week had been the meeting with the Chinese. Despite all the hassle at Heathrow, he had made it to his office soon after midday on the Tuesday. At first he was disconcerted by the fact that Laetitia Chou turned out to be positively plain in appearance and over forty. Her lack of pulchritude was one thing, but he was mostly upset that his partner had lied to him. Nevertheless, putting on his best business face, he had eventually negotiated a satisfactory new deal. The prices would go up, but not by twenty-five percent, only by ten; and the increases would be staggered over the next three years.

He was so pleased afterwards that he forgave Gryllock his mendacity. 'But don't you lie to me again, Paddy', he warned over a celebratory glass of the Lagavulin. 'I might not be so forgiving next time.'

And there had been a bonus. During a pause in the discussion, Jamie took a comfort break. Mr Chou, the chief Chinese negotiator, who was not related to his female colleague despite having the same name, followed him into the toilet. Until now, Chou had spoken only in his native language, using the expert offices of translator, Grace Welsh; but, approaching Jamie, standing at the wash-basin, looking him in the eye through his reflection in the mirror, he spoke to him in perfect, American-accented English. 'Quite a match, wasn't it?' he said. It took Jamie a moment to realize he was talking about the Ryder Cup.

'I saw the final day's play on the television in Bonn, Sunday night', the Chinaman added. Then, before Jamie could respond, he began telling him about golf course construction projects his cousin was involved with, not only near Guangzhou but in other provinces too. He was sounding Royle out about engaging Regal Enterprises to help with both course and clubhouse design. If they played their cards right, Jamie realized, this was a deal worth many millions. He had arranged to meet Mr Chou and his cousin again in Hong Kong the following week, but now that meeting was firmly scotched by his lawyers' instructions, and he was pacing his flat in a fury.

On Sunday morning, Holly went to the hospital again. Pennycuik was still very weak and more or less unconscious, however. He was still unfit to be interviewed. Back home, she changed bed-sheets and put washing on, then went running again. Later she cleaned her bathroom and vacuumed all over the house, cut the tiny lawn with a push mower, and thought about tidying up her small garden later. After a sandwich lunch, she sat down in an easy chair, feeling restless. She needed to think about the case, but could not get her thoughts into focus. She wondered what Mark Berger was doing, and whether to go to the golf club at Graffham in the hope of seeing him; but then she talked herself out of it, ringing Jack and Brian instead. Unfortunately, there was no reply on their home number, so she ended the call without leaving a message. 'You could call Jack's mobile', she thought, but then decided it wasn't worth bothering him. The gay couple were probably out enjoying themselves somewhere.

In the end, she went out again for a walk. The ever-changing cloudscape over the sea was looking wonderful. A container ship in the distance moved impossibly slowly left to right across her line of vision. On her return home, there was a message from her father inviting her over that evening for a meal. 'You have to come', he said. 'I want to beat you at Scrabble' Somehow, not having to spend more time alone, she felt mightily relieved.

On the Monday, they told her at the hospital that Pennycuik was improving slowly, and that he would soon be transferred to St Catherine's, a hospice near the seafront in Hove. It would be best if she waited until he was there before trying to interview him again.

That same afternoon, she and Rich were back with DI Garbutt in DCI Holroyd's office for another meeting, this time with the Coroner's Officer from Chichester and a senior member of the Crown Prosecution Service, to consider all possible options.

'The Yewtree people will interview Royle and Gryllock this week', Hugh Holroyd began, 'But they've said not to get our hopes up... With Francesca Pennycuik dead, there's only her brother's hearsay evidence to go on, so very little chance of a conviction unless one or other of them is prepared to confess.'

'Royle won't', offered Holly, 'But Gryllock might. He's set up a charity for helping people with disabilities, including mental health problems, and they mostly run hostels for young women. I suspect it's his guilty conscience motivating him, don't you?'

'That's possible', Holroyd replied, 'But don't forget he has a disabled sister, Georgina. Perhaps it's just because of her...'

'They are called "D-i-D" hostels', Rich interjected. 'It stands for "Damsels in Distress" I believe.'

'Thank you, Baum', said Holroyd.

'Now, let's suppose, Lester', he continued, addressing the man from the CPS, 'That Dan Pennycuik did kill his sister by throttling her. Should we arrest him and mount a case against him?'

'We need to know a bit more about her final days', Lester Crowther replied. 'And we need to know if he's going to survive... But this is a suspicious death, and first there will need to be a full inquest to determine how and when she died and who, if anyone was responsible; in other words whether an unlawful killing took place. If she died because someone else was responsible – someone still unsuspected and at large, and therefore someone who could conceivably continue to pose a risk to the public – that person needs to be identified and apprehended.'

'I doubt there is such a person', Laura Garbutt spoke up. 'I think we've got this case sown up, thanks to Detective Angel.'

'Well, possibly', Hugh Holroyd commented. 'But we can't close the books on it yet.'

———

As expected, when Jamie Royle and Patrick Gryllock were ordered to attend a police station in South London for separate interviews by Yewtree personnel, they were accompanied by their legal experts. Royle brazenly denied everything put to him, or otherwise offered no comment. Gryllock was more circumspect, and seemed to the officers conducting the questioning to be in a highly anxious state. He acted, they said later, as if he was feeling the heavy burden of guilt, but was not yet ready to let it go by telling the truth.

While Royle was back in his office within an hour, the officers kept his partner much longer, talking to him about Daniel and Francesca Pennycuik, Fotheringay House, and the summer of 1971, until his defences gave, just a little. Finally, despite being cautioned against it by his legal adviser, he admitted going to the Royle family home on one occasion, but said he could not remember which year. He denied meeting the brother and sister, and had only a vague recollection of the housekeeper, their mother. He did say, when pressed, that – more or less bullied into it by Royle – the two had once shared a sexual experience with a young woman, but insisted that it had been in a hotel room somewhere, that the person concerned was over the age of consent, and that she had agreed to, even invited, the activity. Having nothing to charge him with, they had eventually let him go too.

The atmosphere at St Catherine's was surprisingly positive when Holly eventually visited, towards the end of the week. She noticed bright colours, plenty of flowers, and a general air of calm cheerfulness when she entered the vestibule. Finding his room, she was glad to see for herself, too, that Dan appeared to be making something of a reasonable recovery. He was sitting in a high-backed chair next to the bed. He was fully-dressed, with his left arm outside the sling round his neck. The sturdy walking stick with a three-pronged foot beside him stood witness to the physio he was receiving to get him walking again.

'They've been really lovely to me in here', he said when she entered. 'I've never known such kindness, except from my Mum and Andy, of course.'

Holly could well believe it. 'You're looking better', she said.

'It wasn't as bad as it looked', Dan explained. 'They were giving me anti-coagulants to prevent me having more blood clots, and this meant the bleeding wouldn't stop when I had that coughing fit. They had to give me something else – "platelets", I think they said – to reverse it and get me clotting again. The actual damage to what must have been only a tiny blood vessel in the lungs was only slight.'

'I'm glad', said Holly, truthfully. 'But now we have a little more work to do, Dan, if you feel up to it... First, I want you to take a look at these, please.' She was fishing a sheaf of papers out of her bag.

'What are they?' Dan enquired.

'I've typed up what you told me the other day on official police Witness Statement notepaper', Holly replied. 'I'd like you to take your time, read them, and then sign at the end if you agree that it's accurate. You have to initial every page as well...'

'Give them here!' Dan interrupted. 'I don't need to read them. You recorded what I said, didn't you? I'll just go ahead and sign. I've got nothing to lose now, have I? And I want those bastards to know they haven't got away with what they did to my Fran.'

Holly helped him sign the forms, then took out her recorder again. 'I'm afraid I need you to tell me how your sister actually died, Dan', she said. 'It's important that we know.'

'Okay', he replied. 'I understand... It was in 2004. That was a very bad year.'

Holly had fetched another chair, and was sitting quite close beside him as he told her how, in January that fateful year, Andy Anderson had died. This was the first tragedy. She had been suffering from a benign form of leukaemia for several years, and it had become more aggressive. She knew she was dying, so she instructed a solicitor to draw up a Will leaving some money to an equine charity, some to a hospice for children, and the remainder, including the farm, to Dan.

'I couldn't have run the business, though', he said. 'I didn't have the brains or the education... So she had it wound up. There was still plenty for me to live on; and I could always get odd jobs after that – anything with horses, farm work, tractor-driving, anything mechanical... I am good with machines.'

'Fran had been living with mother all these years. They stayed together in the flat in Guildford, but then Mum became ill too. At first, it was just a cough that wouldn't go away. She had antibiotics. Then they did X-rays, ran all the checks, but found nothing. Mum was not the type to complain, so it was many months before she went back to the doctor because she had been getting breathless. I suppose he thought she was looking a bit pale this time, so he ran another blood test, which showed she was desperately anaemic. On investigation, they finally found she had bowel cancer and, by then of course, it had spread. After giving her transfusions, they operated, but she died in theatre, on the table. I don't exactly know why.'

'Oh dear!' Holly exclaimed. She was growing increasingly sorry for this man, as he revealed these long-held sad secrets.

'Fran had to come and live with me, after that', he continued, 'But I couldn't look after her properly. When mother died, she was inconsolable... And I was pretty much an emotional wreck as well... She wouldn't eat. I begged and begged her, but she wouldn't eat anything... Next to nothing at all!'

Holly noticed he was sobbing again. Finding the tissues and blowing his nose, eventually he went on.

'She pretended to eat, but she basically just starved herself to death in the end', he said. 'I called an ambulance once, but she only sent them away. To be honest, I was drinking quite a bit in those days. I didn't take proper care of her. I shall always blame myself for that...'

'But it wasn't your fault, was it, Dan?' Holly asked gently, trying to help him feel better. 'Not really?'

'Well, Miss', he said, genuinely filled with remorse. 'I was drunk the day of my mother's funeral, and I was drunk the day my sister died. What do you think of me now?'

'I think you are human like all of us, Dan', Holly said. 'And like all of us, you did the best you could at the time.'

'Well, my best wasn't very good, was it?' He was still crying.
'I was drunk when I found her. I didn't kill her, although many
was the time she begged me to finish her off. Once, I even got
a pillow and stood over her while she slept, but I couldn't do it.
I knew she was in such pain, but I was too much of a coward. I
couldn't finish her off, no matter how much she wanted me to...
Then, one morning, I just woke up and found her dead, all curled
up in her bed. She was cold... Must have been dead for hours...
And I just left her there and got drunk again. I didn't know what
to do... I didn't want to call the police and have to answer all
their questions. I didn't want anyone interfering so, later that day,
I lifted her up... she hardly weighed anything at all... and took
her across the yard to the freezer. I wasn't thinking... Did it by
instinct... I wanted to keep her nearby, I suppose.'

'And that's where she's been for eight years, Dan?' asked
Holly, 'Ever since you found her dead that morning?'

'I never wanted to lift the lid on that freezer again', he
explained, 'So... Yes... That's where she was until a couple of
weeks ago... But when I knew I had cancer, I started thinking
about those two scum, about what they did and how they were
going to get away with it. I just got so incredibly angry, and
the only thing I could think of to expose them was to bring
poor Fran's body and those chairs back out into the open. Her
nightie was torn badly. I think it had snagged on something
when I moved her the first time, but I was so drunk I either
didn't notice or didn't care. In the end I just put one of my old
dressing gowns on her, to give her a bit of decency... But even
that was a problem. She was so stiff, I could only get one arm
in, so I just had to wrap it around her, like. I wasn't thinking
properly.'

'So, that was it', Holly reported back to Holroyd and Garbutt the following afternoon. In the meantime, she had typed up the rest of her report, printed more Witness Statement forms for Dan to sign, and was now awaiting instructions.

'You've done well, Angel', Hugh Holroyd said. 'And you, too, Baum.'

Rich wasn't sure he deserved this praise, but accepted the plaudits cheerfully enough. 'Are we going to say anything to the press or the media, Sir?' he asked.

'Not yet, I fancy', was the cautious reply. 'It will all be made public anyway, at the Inquest in due course.'

And that is what occurred several months later at Chichester Crown Court. Holly had been back to St Catherine's just once, to have Dan Pennycuik sign his second and final Witness Statement. After she told him that he would not be arrested for concealing Fran's death from the authorities, or for anything else, but that there would be an inquest to which both Royle and Gryllock would be called to give evidence, he seemed more than relieved. She thought she detected a new degree of contentment in his face, and wondered if perhaps he was learning to forgive himself for what he called cowardice.

'I've seen a solicitor', he told her, 'And the undertaker's just left. I've got my Will sorted out, and there's enough in the bank to pay for two cremations – a cheap one for me and the best that money can buy for my dear Fran. Then, when I'm gone, the farm will be sold and the money given to charity, although I'm not sure which ones yet...'

'How about "Riding for the Disabled"? That would do, wouldn't it?' Holly found herself saying. She didn't think he would be inclined to support the "Damsel in Distress" homes, given the connection with Gryllock. Yet maybe, she hoped, his attitude would soften later towards those despicable perpetrators of the unspeakable crime against his poor sister. However, there had barely been time for such a forgiving change in his outlook. When she said goodbye, Holly promised to visit again. The next day, however, she took a call from the hospice superintendent telling her that Dan had died peacefully in his sleep during the night. The doctor thought there had been another heavy bleed in his chest. He would not have felt any pain.

At the inquest, Royle was called to the stand first. With a full gallery and a good number of journalists watching, he had persisted in his denial of all knowledge of the allegations in Dan's statements, which had been read out in full earlier; and he took the opportunity of threatening to sue anyone who repeated and spread what he said amounted to unfounded and malicious rumours.

There were few who would take on such an adversary in the libel courts, someone with almost limitless financial backing and access to the best libel lawyers in town. However, Patrick Gryllock's testimony, which followed, was more equivocal. He did not say enough to be convicted of anything, but he left many suspecting that privately he knew himself to be guilty – and by the same token that Royle was guilty too. A rift had clearly developed between the two men, and it was no surprise to Holly, reading about it later, that Gryllock had resigned from Regal Enterprises, the reason given that he wanted to spend more time with family and concentrate on his charity work. She suspected strongly, however, that Royle had simply and unceremoniously kicked him out.

The final verdict was 'Death due to Natural Causes', specifically 'Starvation due to Anorexia Nervosa'. Dr Narayan gave firm evidence, firmer than she knew him to believe, that the crack in the cartilage of the dead woman's larynx had appeared after death as a direct and natural result of being frozen and later defrosted. He assured the court that it was not therefore an indication of foul play.

The inquest was reported in the local and national news. A few days later, a woman of forty-six reported to the police that she too had been drugged and sexually molested against her will by Jamie Royle. The incident had occurred in London when she was a teenager. Later, someone else came forward with a similar complaint. The information was passed on, in both cases, to officers from Operation Yewtree.

———————

Holly was pleased, after the inquest proceedings, to bump into Peter Harding, also there to give his evidence as a "witness to fact". Standing in the lobby, with people going past on either side, the Colonel told her that the entire unsavoury affair and all the attendant rumours had left quite a mark on the Golf Club. Several members had left, to disassociate themselves from the club and its owner. The Colonel, too, was on the point of departure, bringing his retirement forward by a couple of years. Valerie Parton had decided to go also. Young Kyle Scott had, in turn, accepted the post of head professional at a well-established golf club in Kent. Gary Brooker, on the other hand, had decided to stay loyal to his benefactor.

'And what about Mark?' the Colonel asked, as they walked out into the sunlight, surprising Holly with the question.

'Mark?' she replied innocently.

'Yes… He left the club too, didn't he? How's he getting on?'

Holly was slightly flummoxed by this, albeit friendly, interrogation. She thought she and Mark Berger had managed to keep their budding friendship well hidden. Once the case of Fran Pennycuik had been solved, though, she had given in to a strong temptation to call him and renew their acquaintance. Now, she was meeting him regularly, for golf instruction at the new golf club he had joined, and for a good deal more. Apart from her father, and her friends Jack and Brian, she thought that no-one else knew.

Seeing her discomfort, Peter Harding said, 'I'm sorry to be the one to tell you your secret's out, but Valerie Parton chanced to meet Mark in the supermarket one day. On a whim, she asked him about you. As a gentleman, he was quite unable to lie to her face. Anyway, she'd guessed already that you were seeing one another.'

Holly wasn't sure whether to be upset or pleased. Mark was a gentle man, kind and considerate to her all the time, very unlike Tony Angel. He was also appealingly attractive and an excellent teacher. Perhaps it was time to admit to herself that she was 'emotionally involved', maybe even falling in love.

After this brief conversation on the courthouse steps, they said their goodbyes. The Colonel, walking away, turned round after a few paces to look back at Holly. Raising his voice slightly, to carry the intervening distance, he imparted a final message, delivering it with a broad grin on his face.

'Val told me she's sure the two of you will be married by Christmas', he called out, holding his open hands to his mouth. 'Should I tell her she's got it right?'

'You're a cheeky man', was all Holly would say, smiling back. 'Why don't we just wait and see?'

Catch up with Holly again as she investigates

'THE CASE OF THE DOUBLE DUTCHMAN'

Out Soon…

ACKNOWLEDGEMENTS

A number of people have helped me write this book. I would particularly like to thank retired Sussex Police Detective Phil Bottomer, golf commentator Ewen Murray, and horse trainer Keith Scott for their generous and helpful contributions.